HOLLY BLUES

HOLLY BLUES

SUSAN WITTIG ALBERT

BERKLEY PRIME CRIME, NEW YORK

A1b

THE BERKLEY PUBLISHING GROUP
Published by the Penguin Group
Penguin Group (USA) Inc.
375 Hudson Street, New York, New York 10014, USA
Penguin Group (Canada), 90 Eglinton Avenue East, Suite 700, Toronto, Ontario M4P 2Y3, Canada
(a division of Pearson Penguin Canada Inc.)
Penguin Books Ltd., 80 Strand, London WC2R 0RL, England
Penguin Group Ireland, 25 St. Stephen's Green, Dublin 2, Ireland (a division of Penguin Books Ltd.)
Penguin Group (Australia), 250 Camberwell Road, Camberwell, Victoria 3124, Australia
(a division of Pearson Australia Group Pty. Ltd.)
Penguin Books India Pvt. Ltd., 11 Community Centre, Panchsheel Park, New Delhi—110 017, India
Penguin Group (NZ), 67 Apollo Drive, Rosedale, North Shore 0632, New Zealand
(a division of Pearson New Zealand Ltd.)
Penguin Books (South Africa) (Pty.) Ltd., 24 Sturdee Avenue, Rosebank, Johannesburg 2196,
South Africa

Penguin Books Ltd., Registered Offices: 80 Strand, London WC2R 0RL, England

This book is an original publication of The Berkley Publishing Group.

This is a work of fiction. Names, characters, places, and incidents either are the product of the author's imagination or are used fictitiously, and any resemblance to actual persons, living or dead, business establishments, events, or locales is entirely coincidental. The publisher does not have any control over and does not assume any responsibility for author or third-party websites or their content.

PUBLISHER'S NOTE: The recipes contained in this book are to be followed exactly as written. The publisher is not responsible for your specific health or allergy needs that may require medical supervision. The publisher is not responsible for any adverse reactions to the recipes contained in this book.

FIRST EDITION: April 2010

Library of Congress Cataloging-in-Publication Data
Albert, Susan Wittig.
   Holly blues / Susan Wittig Albert. — 1st ed.
      p.   cm.
   ISBN 978-0-425-23260-6 (alk. paper)
   1. Bayles, China (Fictitious character)—Fiction.   2. Women detectives—Fiction.   3. Herbalists—
Fiction.   4. Texas—Fiction.   I. Title.
   PS3551.L2637H65   2010
   813'.54—dc22   2009050296

PRINTED IN THE UNITED STATES OF AMERICA

10   9   8   7   6   5   4   3   2   1

For Natalee Rosenstein
and the rest of the Berkley Prime Crime team—
the best support group an author could hope to have,
for more years than any author has a right to expect.
Thank you.

Author's Note

Like many other novelists, I enjoy working with settings. I go to great lengths to create a fictional world that seems as real to you as the streets, shops, and backyards of your own community—and I'm always pleased to learn that readers have set out across Texas in search of the locations that appear in this series. That's a compliment. Thank you.

But for those of you who don't already know this, I have to confess that Pecan Springs is not a real town. It is modeled after the little city of San Marcos, not as it is now, but as it was in the early 1970s, before it was irrevocably changed by commercial and residential growth and the morphing of Southwest Texas State (where I was once a professor/administrator) into Texas State University. The town of Lake City and the Little Blue River are also fictional, although the description of Lyndon Johnson's support of efforts to dam the Little Blue are typical of the fifties push to build dams on flood-prone Texas creeks and rivers—like the dam on the San Gabriel River that forms Lake Georgetown. For those of you who are familiar with the area, Lake City is located in the neighborhood of the village of Salado, on Salado Creek. In fact, it might even look quite a bit like Salado, which boasts more shops per capita (sixty shops for nine hundred residents, at latest count) than almost any other village in Texas. Sanders, Kansas, isn't real, either. But if you have a map handy, you might place it west of Troy, on Route 36.

These towns and villages are fictional, and so are their residents. But the plants that appear in this series are the real thing. China Bayles and I hope that you will seek appropriate, informed advice before you use any medicinal herbs. Plants are "natural," yes, but they can have potent effects, especially when used with other medicinal herbs and/or with over-the-counter and prescription drugs, and these combinations are often not fully understood. Do your own careful homework and use all medicines with attention. China and I would not like to lose any of our readers—especially *you*.

Susan Wittig Albert
Bertram, Texas

HOLLY BLUES

Prologue

Sally

The Greyhound bus rolled to a stop in front of the Pecan Springs bus depot. Sally clambered out of her seat, slung her leather purse over her shoulder, and climbed down to wait while the driver pulled the bags out of the luggage carrier. The trip had taken longer than scheduled. They'd been stuck in traffic on I-35 just north of Austin—an eighteen-wheeler carrying live chickens had jackknifed across two lanes of traffic, taking out an SUV and a pickup truck. The carnage hadn't been a pretty sight, and Sally, who was more than a little superstitious, had crossed her fingers, hoping that the spilled blood wasn't an omen. She already had enough problems. Big ones. Problems she couldn't see her way out of.

While she was waiting for her bag, she bent over and did a couple of ankle stretches, pulling the kinks out of her back. This was the first time she'd ridden on a bus since she was in college, and how long ago was that? Twenty years? The bus wasn't what she would have picked if she'd had her druthers, but she didn't, and that was that. Life had its kinks. She needed to get her act together and find a way out of this mess.

The battered canvas duffle bag—her sister Leslie's—landed at her feet with a thud, and she straightened, looking around. Pecan Springs hadn't changed much since she'd been here to visit her son Brian—how long ago was it? A couple of years? She'd lost track. But it was still the same small Texas town with the same cozy courthouse-on-the-square look, although the place was gussied up for Christmas, with green garlands, red and white candy canes, pots of poinsettias, and decorated trees in the shop windows. Like Lake City, where Leslie lived. Small-town Texas Christmas. Okay if you were cool with that sort of thing, which she wasn't, not so much. She and Juanita preferred city streets, skyscrapers, bright lights, and action. If you had to have Christmas trees, they ought to be silver ones, big, really big, and the ornaments ought to be all the same shape and color. Blue was nice. Blue, with white lights, the kind that blinked, and glittery blue garlands. And instead of "Hark the Herald Angels Sing" caroling out of the loudspeaker, she'd rather hear something upbeat. "Holly Jolly Christmas," maybe.

Except that Christmas might not be so holly-jolly under the circumstances, as Juanita would no doubt remind her if she were here. She would chuckle in that sour, cynical way she had and say, *What we need is a party, Sally Jean. Come on, girl, let's go shopping. Let's get lively!* But Juanita hadn't been around much recently, and Sally was glad. Juanita made messes— awkward, ugly, dangerous messes—that Sally had to clean up, which was not a very pleasant way to live.

She gave another wary look around. She was pretty sure she'd managed to sneak out of Lake City without being spotted. She hoped so, anyway. That was the idea behind taking the bus and putting her hair into a ponytail and wearing ragged jeans and a purple Central Texas State sweatshirt under Leslie's scruffy old denim jacket. She caught a glimpse of herself in the bus depot window. Not exactly *Elle*. The sight of her would make Juanita break out in a rash of hysterical giggles. But this wasn't your usual holiday getaway, and Sally wasn't out to impress anybody with the way she looked. This was serious business. She had to be careful. She shuddered. Very.

She picked up her duffle bag. Maybe Pecan Springs hadn't changed in the last few years, but she had. The last time she'd been here to see Brian, she'd thought she was set for life. She'd still had some of that nice pot of money she had gotten (finally!) from her parents' insurance, a great condo in San Antonio, a top-dollar job as a sales rep with a multinational, a fab fiancé—although, as Juanita pointed out, Artie may have been fab to look at, but down deep, he was a total jerk. He had cleaned out her bank account and left her on her own, to start over again

It wasn't the first time. Sally had been down before, way down: detox, divorce, and some really bad credit card debt, not to mention those quirky episodes with Juanita, who took enormous delight in showing up at the worst possible times. But Sally was a survivor, like those roly-poly dolls she and Leslie had when they were kids, the ones you couldn't knock down. After Artie left, she'd sold her condo and the fancy furniture, given away Juanita's stuff (her therapist's idea), and moved to Kansas City, not far from the little town where she'd grown up. She knew her way around the city, which was a definite plus. She'd found an apartment right away and a job selling advertising at the KC *Star*. She'd hoped to get a position as a reporter. She'd been a journalism major in college, even had a part-time job in Features at the *New Orleans Times-Picayune* some time back. But she had to pay rent, and the advertising salary had been okay, for starters. What's more, News and Editorial were on the same floor. She could make a few friends among the reporters and editors. And when the time was right, she could pitch a story idea that would win her a spot on the news staff.

But that—the story, her big idea for a really great, knock-your-socks-off true-crime story—was what had gotten her into this latest trouble. Deep trouble. Bad trouble. Worse than detox or divorce. Worse than any of Juanita's escapades, even. Which is why she was here in Pecan Springs. She was hiding out. She was looking for help. Help from Mike McQuaid, Brian's father. Her ex.

A couple of college girls had gotten off the bus. Sally shouldered her duffle and fell in behind them as they walked up the hill in the direction of the campus, chattering. A couple of blocks later, she took the first right, onto Crockett Street. She wasn't happy about what she was about to do, but she had run out of options. She didn't have much choice.

What was it somebody had said about home and family? When you have to go there, they have to take you in? Well, now was the time, and this was the place.

She had to go there. And they had to take her in.

They *had* to.

Chapter One

The Holly and the Ivy
When they are both full grown
Of all the trees that are in the wood
The holly bears the crown . . .

Traditional Christmas song

In ancient Rome, holly was gathered to celebrate the solstice feast known as the Saturnalia, in honor of the god Saturn, whose season this was. The Romans believed that the shiny, sharp-pointed leaves of evergreen holly protected their homes against lightning bolts, and that the red berries repelled the witches and other mischievous or evil spirits who might seek indoor hospitality during the coldest weeks of the year.

Holly sprigs were also exchanged as tokens of friendship, offering a sincere wish that the recipient might enjoy a season free of bothersome bolts from the blue.

China Bayles, "Hollies for Your Garden,"
Pecan Springs Enterprise

"Well, what do you think, China?" Ruby took another turn. She was wearing silky green skintight pants and a gauzy, butterfly-sleeve knee-length tunic in red and green, studded with tiny gold stars that twinkled as she twirled. "I found it at Margo's Second Verse when I went out to lunch yesterday. I didn't mean to buy anything, but I saw it in the window and couldn't resist."

"It's pure Ruby," I said, adding another package of handcrafted rosemary-mint soap to the tiered display I was building on the shelf in my shop. "Makes you look just like a Christmas tree." I reached over and turned down the volume on the CD player, which was treating us to an old-fashioned rendition of "White Christmas." I gave her outfit a critical glance. "You know, what you need is one of those battery-powered strings of fairy lights. You could wear them as a necklace. Or in your hair. You could even get the kind that blink on and off. Green and red would be nice. Seasonal."

Ruby frowned. "You can stop teasing now, China." She sounded put out.

I was instantly repentant. Ruby is my best friend and business partner. I like to tease her, but I'd never do anything to hurt her feelings.

"I apologize," I said, putting down the soap and giving her a hug. "I love your outfit, Ruby. It's gorgeous. Really and truly. You should wear it to the party on Saturday night. People won't be able to keep their eyes off you."

She smiled, mollified. "You think?" She looked down at her strappy green high heels. "These go, don't they?"

"Perfectly," I said. The heels boosted her to six foot three, at least. But when you're already six feet something in flats, another couple of inches don't much matter. Especially when the guy you're dating is right up there in the stratosphere with you. I stood back, holding her at arm's length, and looked her up and down. "It's terrific, twinkle stars and all. Hark will love you." Ruby has been seeing Hark Hibler, the editor of the *Pecan Springs Enterprise*. I have to admit that I'm rooting for Hark. He's one of the good guys, about as steady as they come, which is a relief to Ruby's friends, given the recent crashes in her love life.

Ruby pursed her lips. "Well—"

"Don't tell me," I groaned. "You haven't broken up with Hark again, have you?"

"I'm considering it. He's just . . . he's so . . . I mean—" She sank down on the stool beside the counter, her gauzy sleeves fluttering like the wings of a wounded red and green moth. "He's so *serious.*"

"That could be because he cares about you," I said drily. "Seriously. And anyway, what's wrong with serious? Serious is steady. You can depend on serious." Which is more than could be said for—

"I just wish he were more exciting, that's all," Ruby said petulantly. "Is that wrong? I mean, isn't it okay for a girl to like a little excitement?"

"Maybe you could do with a little less excitement in your life," I said. I love Ruby dearly, but it's my considered opinion that somebody who has her head in the clouds, the way she usually does, needs somebody with both feet on the ground, like Hark. He's devoted. He adores her.

Ruby's shoulders slumped and she sighed. "I just keep thinking of Colin and wishing—"

"I know," I said sympathetically. Colin had been one of those truly dangerous men, the kind you love, lose, and long for until your very last breath. "But Colin has been dead since April, Ruby. Christmas is only two weeks away. The old year is almost gone. It's time to look to the future, don't you think?"

While Ruby is pondering my question, let's take time out for introductions. Some of you already know me and have visited my shop a dozen times or more. Others—well, maybe this is your first visit, and you haven't a clue to who we are or what we're talking about.

So. My name is China Bayles. I am the proprietor of Thyme and Seasons Herbs here in Pecan Springs, just off I-35, halfway between Austin and San Antonio, at the eastern edge of the Texas Hill Country. I am a no-nonsense, wash-and-wear kind of person whose wardrobe is mostly made up of jeans, tees, and sneakers. I usually have garden dirt under my nails, and my hair is a nondescript brown, with a gray streak at my left temple. I am shortish and fairly stocky, although I can brag about losing a few extra pounds since I began keeping my bike at the shop and riding it to do errands around town, rather than driving the car—part of a personal effort to reduce the size of my carbon footprint.

In my former incarnation, before I bought the herb shop and began spending a lot of time in the garden, I was a criminal defense lawyer in Houston, employed by a big firm that mostly represented big bad guys, the ones with enough bucks to buy a free pass out of the justice system. It was a fast life, full of thrills and chills, and it paid well, but as Ruby might say, it did nothing to satisfy my soul. I have never regretted leaving. Now, I am happily married to Mike McQuaid, an independent private investigator and part-time faculty member in the Criminal Justice Department at Central Texas State University. McQuaid has a son, Brian, who is a high-school junior. And I have . . . *we* have legal custody of my brother's daughter, Caitlin, who is just eleven. But that's a long story, and very sad, and there's not time for it just now. We'll get back to it later.

The tall, slim gal dressed in her holiday finery is Ruby Wilcox, my business partner. Ruby is a hoot, that's all anybody can say—and we certainly say it often enough. Her tipped-up nose is liberally dusted with sandy freckles, and her mouth is as generous as Hot Lips Houlihan's. Her hair is finely frizzed, the color of fresh carrots, and her eyes are variously brown, blue, or green, depending on which contacts she's wearing. Admittedly something of a flake, Ruby is a free soul with a habit of leapfrogging to the creative solution while I am rationally and systematically plodding through a list of alternatives. She owns the Crystal Cave, Pecan Springs' only New Age shop, next door to Thyme and Seasons, where she offers books on astrology, tools for divination, and classes on getting in touch with your innermost self, channeling spirits, and using the Ouija board. If you have a question for the Universe, Ruby can help you find the answer.

Now, I'm a skeptic by nature, and communing with the Universe is not exactly my cup of tea. But Ruby has a strong sense of empathy and an intuitive streak that manifests itself every now and then, usually at the most unexpected moments. Like the time she received a horribly true message about a murder from a perfectly innocent Honda Civic, left in a parking lot in Indigo, Texas, with its lights on. A few minutes later, we found the owner's body in the basement of an abandoned school. Laugh if you will, but when Ruby pulls one of those psychic rabbits out of her hat, she can make a believer out of you. Out of me, anyway.

But there's another side to Ruby, the practical side. She is the co-owner of Thyme for Tea, our tea shop, which is conveniently located behind our shops, and my partner in Party Thyme, a catering service. And both of us are partnered with our good friend Cass Wilde in a personal chef business called the Thymely Gourmet.

Ah. You're wondering how in the world we manage to stay on top of this three-ring circus. Well, it's true that these enterprises keep us busy and that sometimes I have the feeling that I'm in a car with no brakes that's about to dive over a cliff. But Ruby, Cass, and I aren't in business just for the fun of it—although it *is* fun, since we enjoy working together. It's our theory that businesswomen who aren't busy are broke, especially when the economy is singing the blues, the way it is right now.

Across Pecan Springs, this holiday season hadn't been as profitable as previous years, and on top of our money worries, each of us is coping with her own personal challenges. Ruby has recently moved Doris, her mother, to a nearby senior care facility. From this vantage point, Doris (who has Alzheimer's) is slowly driving her daughter crazy. Cass took a tumble at the gym a week ago and is learning how much fun it is to cook with a broken right wrist. And I—in addition to dealing with the shop, the garden, and the holiday shop traffic (such as it is)—am getting on-the-job training as mom to my eleven-year-old niece, Caitlin.

So, yes. Ruby, Cass, and I are staying busy. And on this Tuesday morning in December, a little more than a week before Christmas, we are *not* singing the blues. We are staying optimistic. We love what we do, we're doing what we love, and we are confident that there are better times ahead. That's our story and we're sticking to it.

The bell tinkled and I turned to see a walking stack of cardboard wreath boxes pushing through the door. "Hello, hello," said a woman's voice behind the boxes. "Anybody here?"

I hurried to help with the door. "Good thing you got here, Donna. I sold your last wreath about an hour ago." I took half the boxes off the top of the stack. Donna Fletcher set the rest down with a thump.

"I was late getting away this morning," she said. "My help didn't show up and I had to pick the spinach by myself and drop off an order at Cavette's Market. But here are the wreaths I promised, along with your mistletoe. I've also brought the stuff for Cass. Spinach and bok choy. And a couple of pounds of fresh snow peas. Tell her that this is the last of the season. She's on her own until next spring."

Donna owns Mistletoe Creek Farm, on Comanche Road, south of Pecan Springs. She and her sister Terry used to operate the place as a flower farm, but Terry got into some trouble and hasn't been around for a while. Donna has recruited several local helpers and expanded into market gardening as a CSA—community supported agriculture. The climate in our part of Texas makes it possible to garden for a big part of the year, and cool-weather crops do well during our mild winters (even milder, now that global warming is here). Donna supplies Cass with fresh produce and eggs, and her holiday wreaths and packages of fresh mistletoe are always big sellers at Thyme and Seasons. Plus, she sells memberships in her farm. Her subscribers get a basket of fresh produce every week during the growing season, as well as fresh eggs from her chickens, and jams and jellies and breads from her kitchen—her state-inspected kitchen, of course.

"Cass is in the kitchen," I said. "Spinach salad is on today's menu, so I'm sure she'll be glad to see you."

"I'll get her order out of the truck," Donna said. She cocked an envious eye at Ruby. "Woo-hoo, Ruby. That outfit is really cool. I sure wish I could wear clothes like that." She sighed, looking down at her plaid shirt and denim overalls. "But if I tried, people would say I looked like a Christmas tree." She glanced up. "Not that you do," she added hastily. "You look great."

"It helps to be tall and thin," I put in. "Ruby can wear anything she likes and get away with it."

Ruby frowned down at herself. "I don't know. Maybe it's too Christmassy. Do you think?"

"Of course not," Donna and I exclaimed, in unison. "There's no such thing as being too Christmassy," I added heartily.

"All you need is a star on top of your head and some tinsel scattered here and there, and you'll be perfect," Donna said with a wicked grin. She turned to me. "Don't forget that I'm saving a Christmas tree for you, China. We're cutting tomorrow." Several years ago, when she bought some nearby acreage and expanded her operation, Donna planted twenty-some acres in several types of pine trees. They've just begun maturing. A few weeks ago, I went out to Mistletoe Creek Farm on an errand, spotted a tree that I thought would be perfect, and asked Donna to hold it for us.

"I haven't forgotten," I said. "McQuaid and I thought we'd bring the kids out tomorrow evening. Will that work?"

"That would be perfect," she said. "I've opened the Christmas shop, and we're planning a bonfire and a hayride for tomorrow night. There'll be caroling, too."

"Sounds great," I replied enthusiastically. "The kids will love the hayride—it'll be a first for Caitlin." I grinned at Ruby. "Maybe I can talk Ruby into coming with us."

"I'd love to," Ruby said promptly. "I'll get a tree, too."

"Fantastic." Donna grinned again. "Support your local tree farmer. Oh, and be sure to wear your Christmas outfit, Ruby. We'll put you in the shop. You can be Mrs. Claus." She headed for the door. "I'll get Cass' veggies and take them around to the kitchen."

When she had left, Ruby got off the stool. "I'm going to change before the tearoom opens for lunch," she said in a huffy tone. "I am tired of being mistaken for a Christmas tree."

I chuckled and gave her a quick hug. "We love you, Ruby."

"It's a darn good thing," Ruby muttered. "I'd hate to think what you might say about my clothes if you *didn't* love me. Keep an eye on the shop while I change, will you?" With that, she headed for the door that connects Thyme and Seasons and the Crystal Cave. We keep it open during business hours to encourage customers to shop in both places.

At the door, she turned. "Drat. I forgot. I have to go to Castle Oaks to take Mom some cookies. You'll be here all afternoon?"

"I'll be here," I promised. "Take all the time you need."

Ruby's mother's senior care facility is only a ten-minute drive from the shop, which makes things simpler for Ruby—although her relationship with her mother has never been simple. Doris is one of those mothers who always has to have the upper hand. When Ruby was nineteen, unwed and pregnant, Doris made her give up her newborn daughter for adoption. It was decades before Amy—the long-lost daughter—came back into Ruby's life, and both deeply regret all the time they wasted.

But now, instead of having the upper hand, Doris has lost her grip. It all started when she was living in a retirement community in Fredericksburg, about an hour's drive from Pecan Springs. She began mislaying her checkbook and car keys, forgetting appointments, and getting lost in familiar places. Then she bloomed into a full-fledged kleptomaniac with a deep-seated passion for pricey doodads—hand-painted silk scarves, jewelry, alligator bags. Apprehended by security guards on her way out the door, she claimed that she had forgotten to stop at the cash register, but Dillard's surveillance videos told a different tale. There was more stolen merchandise stashed under Doris' bed, too, which Ruby found and returned.

A month or so later, the diagnosis was inescapable: Doris was suffering from dementia. As the colorful colloquial expression has it, she was a few fries short of a Happy Meal. Or, variously put, a few carrots short of a casserole, or just back from surfing in Nebraska, or—

But of course, it's not funny. Ruby moved her mother to Castle Oaks, here in Pecan Springs, so she can have better supervision, closer to home. Which does not please Doris—but then nothing has ever pleased Doris, even when she had all her marbles.

Ruby appeared in the doorway once again. "I forgot," she said. "I ran into Alice Mitchell when I was at Margo's yesterday. She wants Party Thyme to cater her New Year's Eve party."

"Three cheers for Alice!" I said. We'd catered for the Mitchells before. Their parties were a lot of work—planning, cooking, hauling, serving—but a party brought us as much as we'd make in a day at the shops, especially in the slow couple of weeks after Christmas. "And for you, too, Ruby." Ruby is a go-getter when it comes to bringing in the clients.

"Thank you," Ruby said modestly and disappeared.

Still thinking happily about the prospect of a big-ticket catering job, I opened the top box on the stack Donna had brought. I took out a fragrant herbal wreath, added a price tag, and hung it on the wall behind the counter. Donna and most of my other suppliers work on consignment. When their products are sold, I write them a check, minus my consignment fee. Good for them (their wares are nicely displayed for sale) and good for me (I can return what doesn't sell). A fair deal all around.

Ten minutes later, I had hung the last wreath and was stepping back to admire the arrangement, when the bell over the shop door rang again and a pair of customers, both women, came in.

"Are we in time for lunch?" the one with the purple scarf asked brightly. "What time does your tearoom open?"

I smiled cordially. I love it when people arrive early for lunch. It gives them time to shop. "In about ten minutes. Please make yourself at home."

"Oh, look, Ruth!" the other one exclaimed. "There's some of that rosemary-mint soap I was telling you about. It's handcrafted, isn't it, China?"

"Yes," I said. "Sarah Paulson makes it. She lives in Wimberley."

"She makes it herself?" Ruth asked, impressed. "Isn't that awfully hard?"

"Sarah is a gifted soap maker," I said. "A good teacher, too. There are some of her cards by the cash register."

With a murmur, both of them moved toward the display I had just finished putting together. A few moments later, they had bought not only

Sarah's soap, but her matching toilet water and one of Donna's holiday wreaths, as well.

While the ladies were making their purchases, the UPS guy brought in the day's shipment, a box of books and another, smaller box, a new product—not new on the market, of course, but new to the shop. Pepper sprays, tiny canisters filled with pure capsaicin, extracted from chili peppers and pressurized to make it aerosol. The canisters are packaged to resemble lipsticks, key rings, even rings, and while they might look like toys, they're serious weapons of self-defense. I was carrying them for a serious reason, too. There had been several rapes in the campus area over the past six months, and some of the coeds had asked me to stock the sprays. They're not legal in all states, but the Texas penal code permits the carrying of "small chemical dispensers sold commercially for personal protection." That's what these are, and while they're purse- and pocket-sized, they pack a substantial punch. Hot peppers for potent personal protection—so combustible that they're over the top on the Scoville heat scale, which is used to measure the heat in hot peppers.

By the time I finished putting the pepper sprays on a shelf at the back of the shop, safely out of reach of small fingers, several other people had come into the shop, ready for lunch. I opened the door to the tearoom, announced that lunch was being served, and seated everyone. Laurel Riley, who helps out in the shops when one of us is gone, was handling the serving today. She lives a block away, so it's easy for her to come in for just a few hours at lunchtime—which is especially good, since Cass is temporarily one-handed.

We don't offer a large menu, but our lunches (soups, mini-croissant sandwiches, Cass' specialty quiches, imaginative salads, and fresh fruit) are a welcome alternative to the fast-food burgers and Tex-Mex cookery that is standard Pecan Springs lunch fare, and we've developed a group of loyal lunch patrons. The tearoom looks very nice, with hunter green wainscoting halfway up the old stone walls, green-painted tables and chairs, and floral chintz napkins and matching table runners. At Christmas, the tables are decorated with mistletoe, holly, ivy, and rosemary—herbs appropriate to the season—and fat red candles that give off a cinnamon-scented glow. Cass leaves her Thymely Gourmet card at every table, and Ruby is always glad to mention Party Thyme. It's our theory that each business helps to boost the others.

I was on duty in the shops, so when things quieted down a little in the tearoom, I fixed a lunch plate and perched on the stool behind the counter. I turned on my laptop, and settled myself to munch and work on a piece for my weekly garden page in the *Enterprise*. I've been doing these features for several years now, in return for free newspaper advertising. It's a good trade, especially in times when business is slow and I don't have many advertising dollars to spend.

I was holding my sandwich in one hand and bringing up the file with the other when the bell tinkled again and the door opened. "Hi," I said, without looking up from the screen. "We're serving lunch in the tearoom, if you'd like to step on through."

"I thought maybe you and I could have lunch together, China," a tentative voice said. "If you have time, that is."

"I'm afraid I don't, actually," I said. I glanced up and put on a friendly, half-rueful smile. The woman, in her late thirties, looked vaguely familiar, but I couldn't place her. Probably a customer who hadn't dropped in for a while. "Somebody's got to mind the shops," I added, "and it's my turn." I brandished my sandwich.

"That's too bad," the woman said. She dropped her canvas duffle bag and rubbed her shoulder as if it hurt. "I think both of us could use a little break. It's only been a couple of blocks, but it feels like I've been carrying this thing for miles."

"I'm sorry," I said slowly. "I'm afraid I don't—"

She tilted her head, with a little sidewise smile. "You don't recognize me, do you, China?"

I frowned. "Not exactly. I mean, you certainly look familiar, but—" I stared, disbelieving, as the light dawned. "Sally? Sally Strahorn? Is that *you*?"

"Yep, it's me." She grinned broadly. "Fooled you, did I?"

"You certainly did," I said, still staring. "Are you in disguise or something?"

It had to be a disguise. The woman wore jeans, a faded CTSU sweat-shirt, dirty sneakers, and a well-worn denim jacket. Her hair was pulled back in a ponytail. She wasn't wearing makeup, and her eyes looked naked. This was not the Sally Strahorn I knew—my husband's first wife, Brian's mother.

Sally has had her ups and downs. Lots of downs, unfortunately, but even when she was all the way down, she had always managed to look like she'd just come out on top. The last time I saw her, she had been wearing a chic, tight-fitting beige suit with a matching silk blouse, clunky gold jewelry, and beige stiletto heels. Her eyes were darkly lined, her lashes were heavy with mascara, and her honey-colored hair was worn in a classy chignon, wrapped in gold net. She looked and acted like a million dollars.

But what looked and acted like Sally, it turned out, wasn't always Sally. Sometimes she was a character named Juanita, Sally's other self. Juanita loved to party, dressed to kill, and spent Sally's money as if the sky was the credit-card limit. Juanita emerged, it seemed, whenever Sally was under a great deal of stress.

After we learned all this, McQuaid realized that he had met Juanita often during the few years that he and Sally were married, although the two of them were never formally introduced and he'd never known that this fragment of Sally's personality had her own name. After their divorce, Juanita began appearing with greater frequency—we saw her several times, although we still didn't know who she was. It wasn't until we found out that Sally had been diagnosed with dissociative identity disorder that we could begin to make sense out of some of the silly, senseless, and dangerous things that Sally—or was it Juanita?—had done in the past.

Ultimately, McQuaid learned that Sally was in treatment and that Juanita had finally (and permanently, it was hoped) gone away. We hadn't gotten that information from Sally, of course. She has always been very secretive about what was going on in her life. The news had come from her sister Leslie, who lives in a small town north of Austin and whom we see and hear from on a regular basis. Not so Sally. In the past year, Brian had received only a birthday card from his mother. It didn't have a return address, but it was postmarked in Kansas City, where—according to Leslie—her sister was working and living.

To tell the truth, Sally's prolonged silences aren't a problem for me, since I'm not anxious to have my husband's kinky ex-wife living in our laps. McQuaid doesn't find it a problem, either, for Sally is a raw reminder of a very bad time in his life. It's Brian who suffers. When he was younger, it was painful to watch his disappointment when his mother promised him something and failed to come through. Now he's a teen and "cool to the max," so he tries to pretend that he doesn't care whether she remembers his birthday or calls to congratulate him on his science project. But he does. He cares, and he worries about his mother, although he knows there's nothing he can do to change her. And when she finally does show up (usually without bothering to email or phone), he has to be even cooler. He has to keep from showing how much he cares—which probably makes her feel even less inclined to connect with him again. Funny how that works, isn't it?

McQuaid, bless him, tries to make a joke out of Sally's occasional reemergence, calling her Sally-the-Bad-Penny and saying that she only turns up when she's broke or in trouble. But it's no joking matter. For a long time, he took the blame for the meltdown of their marriage, believing that it was his work as a Houston homicide detective that made Sally come apart at the seams. It was years before he could disconnect from the marriage and from his feelings of responsibility—and he still isn't there, not yet, not quite.

Personally, I don't share his view. Being a policeman's wife isn't easy, I grant you. Plenty of law-enforcement marriages have wrecked on the reefs of raw nerves, frequent absences, and the constant threat of injury and death. But this was no excuse for Sally's dramatic and frequent misbehavior, in my opinion. We're all responsible for our moral choices, and it's wrong of us to push the blame off onto someone else. In his head, McQuaid knows this, although deep in his heart, it's a different story. He still feels at least partially responsible for what happened to Sally and believes that he has an obligation to help her get back on the right track. Get the picture? His heart wants to help and his head wants to tell her to help herself, which makes for some pretty powerful conflicts. And in this case, the conflicts produce anger, which is what he usually feels when they're together—anger at himself, anger at her. Unfortunately, there's not much I can do about this except to be as supportive as I can, even though the brutal truth is that I don't much like Sally, or Juanita, or whoever she is. She's made my husband unhappy, she's opted out of her son's life, and she causes trouble whenever she shows up.

I hope you don't think I'm not a compassionate person. I have as much sympathy for people in need as anyone else. But when it comes to Sally, I can't summon up a huge surge of goodwill. I mean, here it is, Christmas. And not just any Christmas, but one of the most difficult we've faced. Sales at the shop are down. McQuaid is teaching part-time to patch together enough income to keep his P.I. firm afloat. Caitlin—fragile, vulnerable Caitlin—has only been with us for a couple of months, and we're trying to help her recover from her many sad losses. And now, just in time to celebrate Christmas with us, here comes Sally-the-Bad-Penny.

Please. Give me a break, Sally. Give *us* a break. Tell me you're just passing through.

I swallowed my feelings and managed a smile. "Looks like you're on your way somewhere."

She gave a casual toss of her head. "Actually, I was thinking I might hang out here until after Christmas. In Pecan Springs, I mean. I'd like to spend some time with Brian."

"Oh, right," I said. "What's it been since you've seen him?" Pointedly, I added, "Two years, isn't it?"

She shifted her weight. "Something like that. Gosh, I'll bet he's grown."

"He has. Two years is a long time in a boy's life." I leaned forward. "A very long time."

A burst of laughter and the scrape of a chair came from the tearoom, and Sally glanced over her shoulder. "Listen, China," she said in a lower voice. "I wonder if we could talk."

Rats, I thought to myself. *Here it comes.* "What do you want to talk about?"

She cleared her throat. "Privately. Not here."

I shook my head. "Sorry, Sally. I'm a working girl, and today is a workday. In about ten minutes, customers will be coming through that tearoom door, and I'd love to see them buy a thing or two. In the meantime, I'm trying to finish an article for the newspaper. If you don't mind—"

"After work, then." Her voice thinned. "Look, China. I know how you feel about me. I know I haven't always been a good mom to Brian. I . . . I know I've caused you and Mike a lot of unnecessary unhappiness." She swallowed. "Please believe me. I wouldn't be here if it weren't important."

It's always important, I wanted to shout. *Important to you, that is. Brian isn't important, McQuaid isn't important, it's always* you, *Sally. Just* you. *Or Juanita, or whoever the hell you are today.*

But I didn't. Instead, I said, as evenly as I could manage, "Well, okay, then. I can probably take a break about three thirty or four o'clock. Want to come back then?"

Her face cleared, and she smiled. "Yes, sure. Oh, gosh, China, thank you!" She turned to go. "Three o'clock. I'll see you then."

"Don't forget your duffle," I said.

She bent over and picked it up. It was obviously heavy. I hesitated, and then relented. "If you want to leave it here until you come back, you can stick it behind the counter. I don't think anybody will bother it."

Her smile was broadly relieved. "Oh, thank you, China," she said again. "You're a lifesaver."

No, I'm not, I thought grimly. *I am definitely not a lifesaver. And whatever it is you've come for, Sally Jean Strahorn, you are not going to get it.*

I was wrong. On both counts.

Chapter Two

McQuaid: A New Case

Mike McQuaid leaned back in his office chair, clasped his hands behind his head, and frowned at the pile of exams on the desk in front of him.

Social Deviance. He liked the course. He had met more than his share of deviants in this world, and he liked being able to explain, at least to himself, what made them tick. But one of the older professors in the department had taught the class until he retired last year, and he'd always made it far too easy. Unfortunately, that reputation still lingered. Droves of frat rats signed up for it, expecting a takeaway B, even an A, especially when they found copies of the quizzes—mostly short answer or multiple choice—in the frat files. But McQuaid didn't teach the class that way, and after the frats had flunked the first test on illegal drugs, a dozen of them had dropped the course.

The drops weren't a problem, as far as McQuaid was concerned, since they meant fewer poorly written papers for him to read. The department chair (who kept urging the faculty to generate more semester credit hours, so he could defend the department's budget against the dean's red pencil) had not been too happy. But then, Lyle (Lyle Ellis, the chair) hadn't been too happy when McQuaid dropped back to part-time. He didn't like the idea that an associate professor with tenure would leave the academic fold, jump the academic fence, and go off on his own.

Which is what McQuaid had done when he left full-time teaching in the Criminology program at CTSU and opened his own private investigation agency. He liked the security of his faculty position—tenure was good, tenure was safe, the pay was fine. But paradoxically, it was the security that bothered him. McQuaid was a risk-taker. He liked going out on a limb, the thinner the better. He liked the challenge of digging into something new, something he'd never seen before, something with a lot of crazy pieces that didn't fit, patterns that kept shifting every time he looked. The more deviant, the riskier, the more puzzling, the better he liked it. Teaching had been a challenge, but after a while even that challenge had gotten old, even when he factored in the impossible task of motivating the frat rats to actually learn something.

McQuaid sighed, leaned forward in his chair, and picked up the exam on the top of the stack. He didn't take many *real* risks anymore, not the way he used to when he was with Houston Homicide, back in the days when he and Sally were unhappily married. Being a private eye was . . . well, he couldn't say it was dangerous. It was nothing like those wild and wooly P.I. novels, those old Philip Marlowe and Sam Spade books. And certainly nothing like the Spenser series, where the dead bodies, laid end to end, would stretch from here to Dallas. Most of McQuaid's cases were undeniably tame: corporate bad conduct, fraudulent insurance claims, missing persons, and the occasional marital shenanigans. Not much chance of getting shot or knifed, as long as he kept his head.

He read the first answer on the exam, gave it five points out of a possible fifteen, and went on to the next. He was trying to puzzle out a sentence—did this girl really mean to say that concealed weapons should not be "permeated"?—when the phone rang.

It was Charlie Lipman, a Pecan Springs attorney and friend who often threw work McQuaid's way. "Yo, McQuaid. I need to send somebody to Omaha to locate and interview an ex-employee on a business-to-business litigation case. Locating might be hard, but the interview shouldn't take long. Are you my man?"

McQuaid red-penciled a "3" in the margin of the girl's answer. "I'd like the work, sure. But the holidays are coming up. Can this wait until after the new year?"

"Sorry, ol' hoss," Charlie said regretfully. "Gotta get it done in the next few days. Depositions in the case are scheduled for January third. Reckon you kin do it?" Charlie grew up in the wealthy Highland Park area of Dallas and went to college in the east before entering UT Law. But in Pecan Springs, it pays to talk like a reg'lar Joe Six-pack, and Charlie (who was gearing up for a run at the state legislature) was as bi-dialectal as your average Texas politician. He spoke standard English before the bench and talked Texas the rest of the time.

McQuaid looked at his calendar and thought about the family checkbook, which—as China had pointed out the other night—was in serious need of a substantial cash infusion. Sales had been slow at the shop this holiday season, and his caseload had been light in the last few months. A couple of background checks, several asset searches, and the surveillance of an ex-husband who claimed he was broke and couldn't pay his court-ordered child support. (He could.) Part-time teaching helped to fill the gap, but not enough.

"Yeah, I guess I can do it," he said reluctantly. "As long as we're only talking a day or so."

"Two at the outside," Charlie said. "Tell China you'll be home in time to hang the tinsel." He chuckled. "Or tell her I'll come and hang it for you. You know, I've still kinda got a thing for your wife. Smart gal. Purty, too."

"I'll tell her." McQuaid returned the chuckle. Charlie talked a good game, but China had handled him adroitly for years. "Tell you what, Charlie. I'm through here at the university as soon as I finish marking exams and turn in my grades. How about if I stop by the office and pick up whatever you've got on the case? I'll head up to Omaha tomorrow, give it Thursday and Friday, and fly back on Friday night."

"You got a deal," Charlie said cordially. "Hell, I'll even throw in a little bonus, seein' as how you're doin' it on such short notice. Use it to buy China's Christmas present."

"Works for me," McQuaid said, putting down the phone, and going back to the exam. He was still scowling at the second answer, trying to make out what the writer meant, when the phone rang again.

"McQuaid," he said shortly.

"Hey, it's me," China said. "Are you busy?"

"Hey, you," McQuaid said and softened his tone. "No, I'm not busy. For my sins, I am reading exams, although if the rest aren't any better than the first one, I may put the whole damn lot through the shredder and call it a day. This student thinks that carrying a concealed weapon should not be 'permeated' by the law because—" He picked up the paper and read. "'Because it might go off accidental and shoot an innocent parson.' Innocent is spelled i-n-n-a-s-e-n-t."

China chuckled. "Innocent parsons better beware." She paused, and her voice changed. "Guess who just left the shop."

McQuaid grunted. "I give up." He hated guessing games, and China knew it. "Who just left the shop?"

"Our favorite bad penny."

"Bad penny?"

"Your ex-wife."

"Oh, jeez." He threw the red pencil on the desk. "You're kidding."

"I wish."

"Hell," he said disgustedly. "What's she doing here?"

"Your guess is as good as mine. She seems to be masquerading as a hippie."

"Sally?" McQuaid barked a laugh. "A *hippie*?"

"Well, she certainly doesn't look much like her former fashion-model self. Wasn't that Juanita? The one who liked to max out the plastic? Maybe there's another personality coming through. Destitute Dottie. Hard-luck Hannah." She sighed. "Sorry. I'm being tacky."

"Another one?" McQuaid muttered. "God help us."

He didn't even want to think of the possibility. He had learned to dread Juanita's appearances during the four years he and Sally were married. Sally had always said she wanted to be an actress, and at first he'd thought that maybe she was trying on some sort of role, complete with costume changes—expensive costumes, at that. Acting fit her. She was like a chameleon, taking on one persona after another. When he'd learned about the diagnosis—that multiple personality business—he'd been initially skeptical. But he had to admit it made a certain kind of sense. As far as he was concerned, one Sally was bad enough. Two were terrible. Three were unthinkable.

"I thought you ought to know that she's in town," China went on.

27

"She's coming back here to the shop for a chat about three thirty or four."

He sighed. "Do you want me to be a party to this . . . chat?"

"I'd love it," China replied wistfully. "But somebody has to pick up Caitlin. She's got soccer after school. And anyway, maybe it's better if it's just the two of us—Sally and me. You know. Girl talk."

"Yeah, right. Girl talk." McQuaid suppressed a sigh of relief. He was glad to be off the hook. "Did she say where she's staying?"

"No." China paused. "Her luggage isn't exactly conventional. She has a duffle. Looks pretty full. Looks like she's planning to stay awhile."

McQuaid slitted his eyes. Damn. "She's up to something."

"Undoubtedly."

"Has she been in jail?" If so, it wouldn't be the first time. There was that business a few years ago about a forged check. On another occasion, it had been a DWI.

"If she has, she didn't tell me. But she wouldn't. Tell me, that is. Looking at her, though, I'd say it's a possibility. A very distinct possibility."

"Tell her to go away."

"You have no pity, McQuaid."

"Damn straight. Tell her."

China sighed. "I would if I could, but I can't. She's Brian's mother. She has visitation rights."

"Which she only exercises when it's in her interest to do so."

"Of course. But that doesn't dilute the right."

"I hate it when you talk like a lawyer," McQuaid said testily. "I thought you were supposed to be on my side. And she could at least call before she shows up."

"I am on your side. Our side." China paused. "Anyway, I'll point that out—about calling, I mean, although it won't do a dime's worth of good. You know Sally."

McQuaid knew Sally, all right. Impulsive, unpredictable, unreliable Sally. Five-alarm-heartburn Sally. The one good thing she had done for him was to let him have the divorce without going after custody—and that was only because she was in such bad shape, psychologically, that her lawyer counseled her to forget it. The judge would never have let her have the boy.

But if she'd been responsible for Brian, maybe she would have stayed out of trouble. Maybe Juanita would have stayed away—motherhood was not exactly *her* career path.

Or maybe not. There was no way to know.

China was going on. "Oh, and when you get home, please stir the corn chowder I left in the slow cooker. That's what we're having for supper tonight." She paused. "I think there's enough extra for Sally. I'll get some bread out of the freezer, and we'll have coleslaw. Oh, and there are some of Cass' peppermint cupcakes left from today's lunch—I'll bring those."

"You're not inviting her to supper!" McQuaid exclaimed, alarmed.

"Yes, I'm inviting her to supper. She's Brian's mother."

"I wish you'd stop saying that. I'd like to forget."

China chuckled. "Just don't forget Caitlin. Soccer field, four o'clock."

"I'll remember," he replied huffily. Actually, he was looking forward to picking Caitlin up. He planned on asking the soccer coach if they needed a volunteer. He'd helped to coach Brian's team when the boy was in middle school. It would be a chance to encourage Caitlin, who spent too much time alone in her room. Reading was good, sure, but she needed to get more physical exercise. Not that he wanted to push her into competition, just get her moving more, get her out with other girls her age. She needed friends who could help her forget.

"Thanks, McQuaid," China said seriously. "I love you."

"Love you, too." As soon as he had put down the phone he remembered that he had forgotten to tell her about going to Omaha for Charlie. Not the best time for a trip, with the holiday coming up—even worse, with Sally-the-Bad-Penny on the scene. Or Sally and Juanita. Or Sally, Juanita, and some hippie chick with a duffle bag. He grinned ruefully. Destitute Dottie.

And then he thought, Well, maybe not. Maybe it was good timing. While he was in Omaha, Sally could rediscover her inner mother, spend a couple of days with Brian, maybe the weekend, and then be on her way wherever she was going.

But that was a cop-out. And anyway, it wouldn't be that easy. Nothing was ever that easy with Sally. He rubbed his forehead with his fingers, feeling the headache behind his eyes. She wouldn't show up just before Christmas unless she meant to hang around until after the holiday. And of course, she'd have to pick *this* year, when everything was sort of up in the air. China was worried about cash flow. He was trying to decide whether to take Lyle's offer of a second course for the spring semester or put more effort into marketing his agency. Caitlin was getting used to living with two grown-ups again plus a big brother. Brian was getting used to having a little sister.

And Sally? Well, as far as he was concerned, Sally at Christmastime was pure disaster. Brian would be on edge when his mother was around, wanting to please her, but deep inside, knowing she didn't really care. Sally, always the performer with a love for the dramatic, would hog all the attention, so Caitlin would slip back into the shadows. They might even be treated to a surprise visit from Juanita or from this new character, this hippy, whoever *she* was. And China . . .

He sighed. He loved China with all his heart—loved her quick mind, loved her firm, responsive body, loved the way she loved him. But it could not be said that patience was one of her virtues. Before long, Sally would begin bitching about something inconsequential. China would be annoyed. China would tell her where she could go and what she could do when she got there. And he would be caught in the middle.

His grading pencil had rolled onto the floor. He picked it up and went back to the exam with something like relief. All things considered, it was probably a good thing that he was grading papers tonight and going to Omaha tomorrow, before the war broke out.

He might be a coward, but at least he'd be out of the line of fire.

Chapter Three

There are hundreds of species of hollies, native to every continent except Australia and Antarctica. They come in all sizes and shapes, from tiny rounded shrubs only eight inches high to robust columnar trees seventy feet tall. Two of our Texas natives, yaupon holly and possumhaw holly (*I. vomitoria* and *I. decidua*), are suited to xeriscapes. The holly's great variety and attractiveness, ease of maintenance, and value as a wildlife food all make the family useful in landscapes and gardens in all parts of the world. Plant the smaller shrubs around your house instead of the usual thirsty landscaping, and the taller trees and shrubs around the perimeter of your yard. They will grow into a dense privacy hedge that will effectively screen unwanted views and keep out unwelcome trespassers.

China Bayles, "Hollies for Your Garden,"
Pecan Springs Enterprise

I finished talking to McQuaid and went back to working on my column until the lunch crowd, happy and no longer hungry, came into the shops to browse, buying enough to keep the cash register ringing at agreeable intervals. An hour later, Cass finished up in the kitchen and went off to deliver a batch of her gourmet meals to her regular customers: mostly singles who commute to jobs in Austin and don't have time to cook, but want to eat healthy, good-tasting meals. Working out of our kitchen, Cass gives them what they want at less than they'd pay for a restaurant meal. Less fat, salt, and sugar, too, with most vegetables locally grown.

Later in the afternoon, after Ruby got back from her visit to her mother at Castle Oaks, I took a basket and went out to the garden to harvest the last of the fall herbs. Our first frost is officially scheduled for mid-November, but autumn seems to be lengthening in the past few years (yes, Virginia, there really is such a thing as global warming). It's not unusual for us to wait until the winter solstice for our first hard freeze. And if we're extra lucky, December might even bring us a couple of inches of rain.

But today, like many of our Texas cool-season days, was bright with sunshine. The leaves had fallen from the cedar elms and hackberries, but the live oaks were still hanging on to their foliage and the yaupon hollies—one of our native holly species—were bright with berries. The yaupon bears the unappetizing name of *Ilex vomitoria*, and its leaves and twigs contain about as much caffeine as China tea. If you ever run out of tea or coffee, you know where to look. Natives of southeastern North America brewed the leaves into a tea they called *Asi*, known to the colonists as "the black drink." In some tribes, *Asi* is reported to have been used as a ritual emetic, meaning that the men (this was a guy thing, and women weren't allowed to participate) drank buckets of the stuff and then threw it up. There's some disagreement about this, however: a few anthropologists say that the men only threw up the tea if a woman happened on the scene and saw them drinking it. Seems extreme to me, but what do I know?

Later, settlers brewed yaupon leaves as a caffeinated hot or cold drink, sometimes flavored with other fruits. I've drunk it myself, and it's tasty, especially when you flavor it with a fruit. The red berries are said to be mildly toxic, but the birds, deer, raccoons, skunks, and armadillos don't seem to care. After the first couple of freezes soften the fruits and make them more palatable, wildlife will have a royal feast. Until then, our native hollies are a feast for the eyes.

Like neighboring New Braunfels, Pecan Springs was settled in the 1840s by German emigrants, which accounts for what's called the "German vernacular" architecture you see so much of here in town. The century-old two-story limestone building that houses Thyme and Seasons, the Crystal Cave, and Thyme for Tea was built by a German master mason who knew his business so well that every piece of square-cut stone still fits snug and true. There's a second floor, too, unfinished, that I've been thinking of renting out as retail space for crafters. In the meantime, I call it the "loft" and use it for drying herbs and storing supplies and out-of-season decorative items. The building sits about ten yards back from the street on an attractive, sunny lot. I bought it with the wad of cash that I took out of my retirement fund when I left the law firm, settled down to make the herb shop a paying proposition, and filled every inch of the lot with herb gardens, both for display and for harvesting.

And yes, you are welcome to gather your own herbs. (If you didn't happen to bring a basket and scissors, I'll provide them.) As you walk along the mulched, brick-bordered paths, you'll find a culinary garden planted with thyme, basil, dill, rosemary, sage, parsley—all the herbs you need to prepare dozens of delicious meals. The apothecary garden offers healing herbs: echinacea, comfrey, garlic, horehound, lavender, and roses, as well as more rosemary, dill, and thyme. (Many culinary herbs are also medicinal, and vice versa.)

There are other gardens, as well: a dye garden, a tea garden, a butterfly garden, a fragrance garden, and more. All this takes a heckuva lot of work, yes, but I have help from friends who trade a couple of hours' work in the gardens for credits they can spend in the shop—an idea I got from the gardens at Mount Zion, the Shaker village that I visited with

Martha Edmonds a few months ago. (If you're interested, there's always room for another helper at Thyme and Seasons.) And when I'm feeling anxious, a half hour of weeding or planting or harvesting seems soothing. Especially harvesting, which reminds me that the earth is abundant, even when I'm feeling the pinch of scarcity.

With Sally on the scene, I was definitely in need of soothing. I had a big basket, so I clipped plenty of sage, lavender, rosemary, oregano, and savory, planning to hang them to dry in the loft. Parsley is a biennial here, and since it stays green all winter, there's always fresh parsley for Cass' kitchen. I kept myself occupied for a half hour, letting the autumn sun warm me, the earthy fragrances wash through me, and the chipper song of a chickadee cheer me. I would like to say that I didn't once think of Sally, but that wouldn't be exactly true. I stayed pretty busy *not* thinking about her, though.

At the back of the lot, near the alley, is Thyme Cottage, where Ruby, Cass, and I teach classes and hold workshops. If you didn't know, you'd never guess that the building—also made of stone—was originally built as a stable, in the long-ago days when everybody in Pecan Springs had at least one horse. When live horsepower was replaced by the gasoline engine, the stable became a garage. It was eventually renovated by the architect who also refurbished the main building, where our shops are located. He lived there for a time, so the stable-cum-garage-cum-cottage has a fully equipped kitchen and spacious main room with a fireplace and plenty of comfortable seating. A couple of years ago, I redecorated the large, airy bedroom that opens out onto the deck, so I can rent the place as a bed-and-breakfast when it's not otherwise in use. It's listed in the *Pecan Springs B&B Guide* and online, so the rentals have been coming fairly regularly.

In fact, starting tomorrow and continuing until the day after New Year's, the cottage would be occupied by Mr. Cowan's middle-aged daughter, Hazel. Mr. Cowan lives with Miss Lula, a yappy Pekinese, in the house across the alley. Hazel feels the need to visit her father (one of the most crotchety old men you'd hope never to meet) a couple of times a year, but she draws the line at Miss Lula. I can't say I blame her, because this tiny dog has the loudest and sharpest bark in Pecan Springs. Miss Lula can outbark the Great Dane who lives on the corner and the mezzo sopranos of the Methodist Choral Union when they're winding up for the Hallelujah Chorus at the church down the street. Pound for pound, I'd even put her up against such operatic divas as Beverly Sills or Joan Sutherland, although I don't think she could manage the repertoire. She'd give it a try, though. What Miss Lula lacks in versatility, she more than makes up for in volume and intensity of expression.

Of course, when Hazel comes to visit, her father could board his dog at the Hill Country Kennel, where Ruby's daughter Amy works. He could—but he won't, because to do that, he'd have to acknowledge that Miss Lula is indeed a dog, a fact that seems to have escaped his attention. Miss Lula sleeps on the bed in Mr. Cowan's guest room and snaps whenever she's threatened with eviction. Hazel (who is betting that she will live longer than Miss Lula) refuses to argue with Miss Lula or her father, and stays where she has a bed to herself, in Thyme Cottage. It stands behind a tall holly hedge and has such thick walls that when you're lying in bed with the doors and windows closed, you can barely hear Miss Lula taunting the squirrels.

I parked my gathering basket on the deck and went to the kitchen to put the kettle on. I was ready for a cup of hot tea. Then I took a quick inspection tour through the cottage to make sure it was ready for Hazel. The bedroom looks very nice, I think. There's a four-poster maple bed made up with lavender-scented sheets and spread with an antique Texas Star quilt that my mother found at a yard sale. There's a scattering of red and blue quilted pillows on the bed; a mahogany dresser against one stone wall and a blue-painted rocking chair in the corner; a red and blue braided rug on the wood floor; wood shutters and curtains at the windows; and framed colored prints of herbs on the walls. A bookcase holds a couple dozen mysteries contributed by Ruby, who is a dues-paying member of Sisters in Crime. (Ruby grew up with Nancy Drew and prefers female detectives, like V. I. Warshawski, Annie Darling, and Stephanie Plum.) If mysteries don't appeal, there's a television, a DVD player, and a few DVD movies. (I'm telling you all this in case you or someone you know plans to be in the area and might be looking for a quiet, pleasant, affordable place to stay. Please spread the word.)

I put several branches of rosemary, some stalks of lavender, and some trailing oregano stems into a crystal vase, filled it with water, and set it on the bedroom dresser. I checked the bathroom for towels and soap and the bathtub (the old-fashioned kind, with clawed feet) for general cleanliness, remembering with a little shudder that Rosalind Kotner had died in this room some years ago. This isn't something I like to think about, but even though I have scrubbed away every trace of blood, the ugly memory comes back every now and then. Pecan Springs is an attractive, comfortable community, but life here is not always as cozy and crime-free as our diligent Chamber of Commerce likes to portray it. Sometimes people die before their time, helped to their end by someone else.

I was reflecting on this criminal truth as I went back to the kitchen, took down a box of yerba mate tea bags, put one in a cup, poured hot water over it, and added a spoonful of honey. When I heard the front door open, I took down another cup, poured in hot water, and added another bag and honey. That was probably Ruby with the cereal, juices, and drinks that we stock for our guests, and it was time we both took a break. Yerba mate is a nutrient-rich tea made from the leaves of a South

American holly, *Ilex paraguarensis*. The taste is similar to that of green tea, only stronger. It is traditionally drunk as a friendship tea, shared from a gourd that is passed from person to person. I didn't have a gourd handy. Mugs would do just as well.

I headed for the living room. But it wasn't Ruby I saw.

"I stopped in the shop and said I was looking for you," Sally explained cheerfully, dropping her purse onto a chair. "They told me where you were."

"Oh," I said, wishing "they" hadn't been quite so helpful. "Well, maybe we can just talk here. Would that be okay?"

"You betcha." She turned, casting an admiring glance around her. "Gosh, this is a great place, China. I've seen it from the outside, but I've never actually been in it. What do you use it for?"

"Classes and workshops, mostly. When we're not scheduled, I rent it out as a bed-and-breakfast. It's listed in the—"

"Bed-and-breakfast?" Her eyes widened. "Gosh. You mean, like, people actually sleep here?"

"I assume so," I replied drily. "I don't check the sheets, but—"

But she wasn't listening. Ponytail bobbing and without a by-your-leave, she was bouncing down the hall, poking her head into the bathroom, where I could hear her cooing admiringly over the claw-foot tub, and then into the bedroom, where she gave little squeals of pleasure. While she was gone, I went to the kitchen and fetched the yerba mate. A moment later, she was back, flopping into the chair by the fireplace.

"I love it," she announced, with an over-the-top enthusiasm. "The bathtub, the quilt, the rocking chair, everything. Even a TV! It's totally, absolutely fab, China. And it just so happens that I'm looking for a place to stay. This would be perfect. I could hole up here for weeks."

I suppressed a shudder and handed her a mug of tea. "It's as perfect as a lot of hard work can make it. But it just so happens that it's rented. Starting tomorrow, until after the new year." I didn't say *I'm sorry*, because I wasn't.

She deflated. "Boo-hoo. You're sure? I was really hoping—"

"There are plenty of motels along I-35," I interrupted. "How long are you staying?"

For weeks, she had said. Please, God, don't let it be true. Please!

"I don't know." She took a sip of her tea and her eyes popped open. "Yikes! What *is* this stuff?"

"You don't like it?" I asked evilly. "It's a South American tea, traditionally drunk only among friends. If you'd rather have a soda or something . . ."

"Among friends? Well, then, I'll try it." She sipped. "Actually, it's good. You just have to get used to it, I guess." She sipped again, then sighed and dropped what was left of her artificial gaiety. "I'm afraid a motel won't work for me, China. I don't have a car, and from I-35, it's too far to walk."

I stared at her blankly, trying to figure this out. "No car?"

"Well, I *had* a car. A really terrific Mini Cooper convertible, bright yellow." A drawn-out, dramatic sigh, a little wave of her hand. "But I couldn't make the payments. It was repo'd."

I asked the next reasonable question. "So how did you get here? To Pecan Springs, I mean. Did somebody bring you?"

"Nobody brought me." She sipped again. "I came on the bus."

The bus? I was nonplussed. Pecan Springs is pretty much like any other town. The things you have to do—work, shop, buy groceries, visit friends—are scattered all over, not clustered in a single neighborhood. You get in the car and you drive from one place to another, not as far as in a big city, maybe, and with a lot less traffic. But you do have to drive, which means you have to have a car. And if Sally didn't have a car, how did she plan to visit Brian? As she knows, we live about ten miles outside of town. Too far to bike, even if I loaned her my bicycle.

"Well, that's okay," I said, trying to come up with a work-around. "Darryl Perkins owns a used car lot here in town. I rented an old VW from him when I had car trouble last year. It wasn't spiffy, but it wasn't expensive, either. As I recall, it only cost—"

"Doesn't matter what it costs," she said flatly. "I can't rent a car."

"Oh." I paused. She'd been picked up for DUI and lost her license? "How come?"

She set the mug on the table next to her. "Because I don't have the money to rent a car." She looked up, her face sober, her brown eyes grave. "I only have enough money to get by on. And no credit cards," she added. "I cut them up." She made a scissoring motion with her fingers.

Oh, rats. If there's anything worse than Sally when she has a lot of money to burn (or rather, when Juanita is burning through Sally's money), it's Sally when she's broke and wants to borrow money. We've had it both ways.

"I see," I said. It was time for some straight talk. "Okay. Well, then, why exactly did you come to Pecan Springs?" I gave her a direct look. She could say she was here to see Brian. She could say she was here to borrow money, or get a new start, or . . . Whatever it was, I needed to know. I needed it spelled out.

She heaved a heavy sigh. "Well, to tell the truth, China, I've had some trouble."

"I'm sorry," I said, keeping my voice neutral. "Nothing very serious, I hope."

"I wish." She sighed again. "You heard about the flooding in the Kansas City area a month or so ago? I was renting a really cute little house not far from a creek, with trees and everything. A really nice neighborhood, you know? But there were these horrible storms, one after the other. They just wouldn't quit. The creek came up and the house got flooded. All my stuff . . . well, it was ruined. Clothes, TV, furniture, everything. I lost it all." Her eyes were filled with tears. She gulped back a sob and looked down at herself. "What you see is what I've got, China. I'm homeless."

It was impossible for me to stay neutral in this kind of situation. "Oh, gosh," I exclaimed impulsively, reaching out. "I'm so sorry, Sally. That is too bad. Really."

Now, my history with Sally is not a pleasant one. She has an amazing theatrical talent for self-dramatization that could have landed her on the stage, if she'd had the discipline to pursue an acting career. She has always seemed to me to have no secure, sustained interior life—she's all surface, and much of that surface is deceptive. With Sally, what you see is *not* what you get. I've learned to discount at least half of what she tells me and seriously question three-quarters of the rest. Or maybe (as she claimed in one instance) it was Juanita who was telling the lies. Who knew?

But all that history was swept away by a sudden and overwhelming surge of pity. McQuaid and I have too many friends who have gone through devastating hurricanes along the Gulf and the coastal bend of Texas and Louisiana. They lost everything, too—homes, neighborhoods, jobs, pets, even loved ones—and it's costing years of their lives to put the pieces back together and get to the point where they can go on. But their experience of disaster has made them vulnerable and fearful. Even after they've restored their lives to some measure of normalcy, most will never be the same. They've lost too much, and they're afraid of losing it all over again. Every time I hear from one of these friends or see images of those hurricane-ravaged cities, I share their pain, at some deep level. It's a potent reminder of how fragile our lives are and how easy it is to lose a home. That was what made me reach out to her. It was an impulse, and it was genuine. I meant it.

Sally took my hand, held it for a moment, then let it go. "Thank you," she said, making an obvious effort not to cry. "But that's not the worst of it, I'm afraid. I had a job selling advertising, but the newspaper where I was working—the *Star*—cut back on the payroll. I mean, I know I'm not the only person this happens to. Lots of people lose their jobs. That's what I keep telling myself, anyway." She straightened, tried to smile, and I saw a flash of the old, confident Sally. "It even happens to people who are good at what they do. Like me."

She had lost her job? This was even worse. And of course she was right: it happens all the time. Not to me (at least not yet, knock on wood), but to people I know. When it happens, it hurts—and must hurt a lot worse when you've just lost your home, as she had. I shivered, thinking how awful that would be and wondering how I would cope. Probably not very well.

Sally leaned forward, giving me a straight look. "Like I said, China, I don't have a place to live. I don't have a job. And I don't have much money. I'm here because I want to spend some time with my son. I've missed a lot, and I'd like to catch up. But I also need . . . well, I need some downtime. Time to get my act together. I know I'm not the best mom in the world, and I know you don't like me very much." Her lips trembled and she paused, pressing them together. "I've been a pain in the you-know-what for both you and Mike. I admit it, and I wouldn't blame you if you gave me the boot. But it's Christmas. Can you find it in your heart to—" Her eyes filled with tears. "To be a friend and take me in for the holiday? Please?"

Back when I worked in the tough, competitive world of cutthroat litigation, I developed a remarkably tough skin and an exceedingly hard heart. I learned how to see through liars as if they were transparent. I could stand up to anybody, look him straight in the eye, and deliver a powerful, pithy, and final *No. Hell, no,* when the occasion warranted, which it often did. Even today, when someone tries to lie to me, my antennae go up and I get a feeling across the back of my neck, unmistakable but hard to explain. I haven't lost my nay-saying habit, either. I say no when people ask me to take on more projects than I can manage or when I'm asked to give money to a cause I can't support or when somebody asks for something I don't have.

But in this case, I didn't hesitate. Whether it was Sally's homelessness, the loss of her job, or her honest admission that she had been a troublemaker—whatever it was, my heart was touched, and I heard myself saying something I never thought I'd say.

"We'd be glad to do what we can." I didn't ask myself who *we* was. I knew I couldn't speak for McQuaid, who was going to be very, very angry when he found out what I was about to offer. He hadn't even wanted me to invite her to dinner, for pete's sake.

"You will?" she breathed. "Really?"

"Sure," I said generously. "The guest room at our house is empty. You can come and stay with us. Brian will love it." Would he? I wasn't even sure he would want to see his mother again, after she skipped his last birthday.

"Oh, gosh," she said, clasping her hands. "That would be wonderful!"

"And if you need a car," I went on recklessly, "we can probably work something out. We might even be able to help you find a short-term job." Short-term. At last. I was exhibiting some sanity.

"A job? Really? Really, truly, China?" The tears shone in her eyes, but she was smiling. "I can't believe you would do all that for me, after all the pain and trouble I've caused you."

I couldn't believe it, either, but I wasn't going to admit it. I glanced at the clock on the wall and stood up. "It's getting late, and I need to take some herbs up to the loft to dry. We're closing at five. If you'll stick around, you can go home with me."

"I'll help you hang them," she offered eagerly. "It'll go faster with two of us."

"Sure," I said. "I'm always glad for a little help." Well, almost always. But I was stuck with her, so I might as well make the best of it.

Impulsively, Sally threw her arms around me. "Thank you!" she whispered. "Thank you, China, thank you! You're a true friend. I promise you won't be sorry for taking me in. I promise!"

As it turned out, it wasn't a promise that Sally could keep. I *was* sorry. Very sorry.

But that wasn't her fault. At least, not entirely.

Chapter Four

Christmas decorations are said to be derived from a custom observed by the Romans, of sending [holly] boughs, accompanied by other gifts, to their friends during the festival of the Saturnalia . . . The origin has also been traced to the Druids, who decorated their huts with evergreens during winter as an abode for the sylvan spirits . . .

An old legend declares that the Holly first sprang up under the footsteps of Christ, when He trod the earth, and its thorny leaves and scarlet berries, like drops of blood, have been thought symbolical of the Saviour's sufferings, for which reason the tree is called "Christ's Thorn" in the languages of the northern countries of Europe. It is, perhaps, in connexion with these legends that the tree was called the Holy Tree, as it is generally named by our older writers . . . Pliny tells us that Holly if planted near a house or farm, repelled poison, and defended it from lightning and witchcraft, that the flowers cause water to freeze, and that the wood, if thrown at any animal, even without touching it, had the property of compelling the animal to return and lie down by it.

Maud Grieve, *A Modern Herbal*, 1931

McQuaid, Brian, and I—and now Caitlin—live in a big white Victorian house just off Limekiln Road, about twelve miles outside of town. If you're looking for us, turn left when you see a wooden sign painted with bluebonnets and the words *Meadow Brook*—the whimsical but descriptive name given to the house by its previous owners, who were planning to turn it into a bed-and-breakfast. You'll be following a gravel lane between rocky pastures grazed by our neighbors' longhorns and spiked with prickly pear cactus, agarita (a holly look-alike), and twisted-leaf yucca—*Yucca rupicola*, meaning "a yucca that loves rock." Stay on the lane past Tom Banner's maroon mailbox, which is shaped like a Texas A&M football helmet and bears the words BANNERS FOR AGGIES! A quarter of a mile later, the lane ends in a circular gravel drive in front of our house, a big white two-story Victorian with a porch on three sides and a turret in the front corner. There's a wide lawn in the front and a garden in the back, the whole thing separated from a patch of thick woods by a low stone fence.

In summer, the lawn is green (at least until August, when the rains stop and the heat cranks up); the garden is rich with herbs and vegetables; and the stone wall is nearly obscured by blossoming wildflowers. But it's December now. The lawn is biscuit-brown and frostbitten, the garden debris needs to be cleared away, and the wildflowers are taking their usual midwinter snooze. But we love the place in all seasons, and for our own private reasons.

McQuaid covets the workshop in the back, heated in winter and air-conditioned in summer, where he can use his gunsmith's tools and lock up his gun collection.

Brian adores the creek that meanders between the garden and the woods, inhabited by all the frogs, lizards, and snakes a boy could ever hope to collect and house in cages in his bedroom, from which they occasionally escape and turn up in odd places, like the laundry hamper or the washing machine. (Don't laugh—it has happened.)

For me, the attraction is the sunny space behind the house, just right for a large garden, where I can grow plants that don't fit conveniently into the display beds at the shop, and (until it became Caitlin's) the round room at the top of the turret, which is the perfect place to read and dream.

With its five bedrooms and large downstairs, the house is too large for us. When we bought it, I liked the previous owners' idea of turning part of it into a bed-and-breakfast and filed it away as something to do when I had the time. This hasn't happened yet, and as long as both kids are with us, maybe it won't. I'm not sure it's a good idea to have strangers in the house. Unless we need the money, when it might be the lesser of two evils, one of which is not being able to pay the bills.

For now, the extra elbow room helps to keep the peace in a family where something always seems to be going on. It proved to be a very good thing when McQuaid requisitioned the big corner room downstairs, the one with the outside entrance, as the office of his private detective agency, M. McQuaid and Associates. "Associates" does not refer to me or Ruby, if that's what you're thinking, in spite of our occasional involvement in criminal mischief. McQuaid draws a strict line between business, family, and friends, and I promised him I would not intrude.

And now that Caitlin—Caitie, as McQuaid calls her—has come to live with us, I'm glad of the extra room. When she visited the house with her father last spring, she was entranced by the round room in the turret: the Magic Tower, she called it. When she disappeared from the family gathering, I found her there, asleep on the window seat, my tattered child's copy of *The Secret Garden* open on the floor beside her. The room belongs to her now. We painted it pink, like the room she had when her father and mother were alive, and she hung her drawings of fairies on the walls and filled the shelves with books and stuffed animals. She spends a lot of time here, reading and looking out the window. I'm hoping that her Magic Tower will be a magical place where she can heal.

* * *

WE'VE made it a rule that we all sit down to supper together, around a real table, with real food on it. We eat in the kitchen even when we have company, because the dining room table is usually taken over by our various projects (the kids' homework, McQuaid's paperwork, my crafts). Tonight, we had company. Sally was joining us. McQuaid—who was helping me fix the food—was irate.

"I can't believe you invited her," he growled. "For supper, yes. But the whole freakin' holiday? Damn it, China, you know what Sally is like. She'll do whatever it takes to make us miserable."

"Shh," I cautioned, ladling the corn chowder into the bowls—my favorite blue Fiestaware, which I save for company. "She's in the dining room. She's helping Brian with his calculus."

"Helping?" McQuaid snorted. "That woman has no clue when it comes to calculus. She's number-phobic." He finished shredding the cabbage and tossed it into the bowl with the shredded carrots and chopped pecans. "When we were married, we were constantly overdrawn at the bank. She'd write five or six checks and forget to enter them. Or maybe it was this other character—Juanita—who wrote them, and Sally who forgot to put them in the register." He slammed down the knife. "Whoever did it couldn't subtract worth a damn."

In his dog bed beside the kitchen range, Howard Cosell made a whining noise. Howard is McQuaid's elderly basset hound. It upsets him when we argue.

"Well, she won't have that problem now," I replied in a reasonable tone. I lined up the filled bowls and dropped a healthy dollop of sour cream into each. "She doesn't have any money, so she won't be bothering with checkbooks."

"So she says." McQuaid made a disgusted noise. "She got to you, huh?

You felt sorry for her. Poor Sally. Poor, mistreated Sal." His voice dripped sarcasm. "I thought you were too smart to fall for that woman's sob story, China."

Now it was my turn to be angry. I spun around to face him. "You bet I felt sorry for her, McQuaid. She lost her house and everything in it, and then she lost her job. She lost her car, too—a little yellow convertible she really loved." I could feel my temper flaring. "And she's not just 'that woman,' damn it. She's Brian's mother, she's homeless, and it's the holiday. The least we can do is give her a place to stay and extend some friendly—"

Howard Cosell clambered out of his bed and lumbered in our direction. He tries to get between us when we argue and generally ends up standing on both our feet. This usually serves to distract us, as it did now.

"Hey." McQuaid put his hands on my shoulders, then bent and kissed me. He is six feet tall and still has the slim hips and well-muscled shoulders of a football quarterback, which he was, once upon a time. When he kisses me, I know I've been kissed.

"I apologize," he muttered, stepping back and shoving the dark hair out of his eyes. "I admit it—I don't want Sally staying with us. I don't trust her. I have too much history with her, and I'm suspicious of whatever she says. Remember when she was in jail for forging that check, and she told us she was in the hospital?"

"Yes," I admitted, "but—"

"And the time she borrowed money for a medical bill and used it to go on a cruise?"

I sighed. "You're right about that, too, but—"

He silenced me with a quick kiss. "But you're doing what you believe in, China. I'm registering a protest, but that's as far as it'll go." Dodging Howard, he headed to the fridge to get the mayonnaise. "So okay," he said over his shoulder. "So she's here. Is that going to change anything about the holiday?"

"I don't see why it should. I thought we could lend her Brian's car, so she'll at least have something to drive." Brian doesn't have his learner's permit yet, but Blackie Blackwell, the Adams County sheriff and a friend of McQuaid's, gave us a deal on his used Ford that was too good to pass up. Brian sometimes goes outside and sits in the car and (when he thinks nobody is looking) pretends to be driving it. He's already saving his allowance for gas and insurance. I hoped he wouldn't mind if his mother borrowed it.

With a scowl, McQuaid added mayo, pecans, and vinegar to his coleslaw. Basil vinegar, which gives it a totally different zip. "Make sure her license is current. And that she's covered under our insurance."

"I will." I fished a chunk of sausage out of the chowder and gave it to Howard, who gulped it down. "About the holiday, nothing is going to change. She can go with us to take the kids out to get the Christmas tree tomorrow evening and—"

A stricken look crossed his face, and I stopped. "What? You forgot? You scheduled something else?"

"Yeah, I forgot," he replied glumly. "I'm sorry, China. I promised Charlie Lipman I'd fly up to Omaha to interview a guy. I'm going tomorrow. I'll be back on Friday night."

"Omaha!" I squawked. "But we agreed! The kids are looking forward to getting the tree, and Donna is planning a hayride and a bonfire, and caroling, too. It'll be something new for Caitie. She'll love it. I don't want her to miss it."

"I know," McQuaid said unhappily. "I screwed up, China, big-time, and I'm sorry. Look. Why don't we put the tree off a couple of days? Charlie's job is a quickie. I'll be back Friday night. We can get it on Saturday."

I shook my head. "Won't work. If we don't pick it up tomorrow, we won't get it decorated in time for the party Saturday night." We had invited a dozen friends and their children—a neighborhood get-together, potluck-style, nothing fancy. But we had to have a tree. I eyed him. "Don't tell me. You forgot about the party, too."

"Yeah, I guess I did." He sighed. "Well, maybe you could do it without me. Pick up the tree, I mean. It's no huge deal, I guess."

"Right," I said ironically. "Sally can go in your place and—"

"Yeah, sure." He threw his hands into the air. "Sally can take my place. I won't be missed at all."

I rolled my eyes. "You're the one who decided to go to Omaha—without consulting me. If you had asked, I would have been glad to remind you about getting the tree."

"And you invited Sally to stay here without consulting me." He gave me a lopsided grin. "So I guess we're even, huh?"

I went back to the chowder, sprinkling on minced chives and parsley. "No, we are not even. You owe me one. Your going to Omaha is worse than my asking Sally here."

"Sez you," McQuaid replied, nuzzling the back of my neck.

"Sez me." I pulled myself loose and went to the oven to take out the dinner rolls. "Go call the kids. We're ready to eat."

Howard gave a plaintive whine.

"And tell Brian to come and feed the dog," I added. "Please."

Howard wagged his tail hopefully.

THE kitchen table was a little more crowded than usual. McQuaid sat at one end, I at the other, Brian on one side, and Sally and Caitlin on the other. Since Caitlin is new to our family, now is probably as good a time as any to catch up on that part of the story.

53

Caitlin Danforth is my eleven-year-old niece, the daughter of the half brother I had never met until early last year. Miles was my father's son by Laura Danforth, the "office wife" with whom he spent all of his working days and many of the nights and weekends that he might have spent with my mother and me. If that sounds bitter, well, I suppose it is. Wouldn't you be bitter if you learned, out of the blue, that your dad had fathered a love child, and that he had lavished more attention on his secret son than he had on you? At first I tried to deny it, although one close look at Miles was all it took to see the undeniable family likeness. Then I was angry at the way Dad had abused my mother's trust. Would she have turned to alcohol as she did, if he had been a real husband and father?

But that's an unanswerable question. Anyway, as things turned out, there wasn't a lot of time for anger or bitterness. I worked through most of my feelings about my father as I tried to learn more about his relation-ship with Laura Danforth and the circumstances of his death. And any animosity I might have felt toward Miles was completely flushed away by his hit-and-run death—his murder—only a few months after we first met. The killer has pled guilty and is serving his sentence, and the man behind the whole sad business died last month, avoiding the messiness of a trial and the penalty that he, too, would have paid. But he paid in a different way. Before his death (and rather than face the wrongful death suit I threatened to file) he set up a very substantial trust fund for Caitlin's edu-cation. The money will never compensate her for the loss of her father, but whatever happens, her future is provided for.

The present is a greater challenge. Caitlin watched her mother drown during a family outing at Lake Travis a few years ago, and then had to deal with the terrible trauma of losing her father. A dark-haired pixie of a child, she is small for her age, fragile and very shy, and she has reacted to her loss by turning inward, away from everyone. The one bright spot in her life was her aunt Marcia, her mother's sister, who became her court-appointed guardian after her father died. Marcia would have been an ideal mother for Caitlin—except that she was diagnosed several months ago with a virulent form of breast cancer. It has already spread to her spine, and the prognosis isn't good. As if Caitlin hadn't faced enough losses, now she's losing Marcia.

There is no one else in Caitlin's life, so with Marcia's encouragement and blessing, McQuaid and I petitioned the court for appointment as her guardians. Our petition was granted a few weeks ago. Caitlin is our daughter now. And while I may not have much confidence in my ability to mother a young girl, we're all she has. Since this Christmas was the first one she would celebrate (if that was the word) without either her mother or her father, McQuaid and I were determined to make it as happy a holiday as possible, hence the Christmas tree outing, a planned shopping expedition, a neighborhood party, and a couple of big family get-togethers. I could only cross my fingers that Sally—or Juanita, or Hard-luck Hannah—wouldn't complicate the situation.

But tonight, at least, Sally was on her best behavior. She and Brian seemed to have come to some accommodation of her past failures and forgettings. As they came into the kitchen, he was telling her about his plan to get a job as soon as he can drive. McQuaid thinks that as long as Brian keeps up his grades, this is okay. I don't agree. I'm in favor of high-school kids focusing on their schoolwork, not dividing their attention between school and work—and certainly not plowing every penny of income into an automobile. But I'm not likely to have the last word on the subject, and from the snippets of conversation I overheard, Sally seemed to be endorsing McQuaid's position.

When she sat down at the table, she turned her attention to Caitlin, beside her. Sally and I hadn't had much time to talk, but I had briefed her on the situation. To her credit, she seemed to be handling it sympathetically, asking about Caitlin's interests (photography and fairies), her favorite subject in school (art), her least favorite (arithmetic—*yuck!*), and her favorite sport (soccer). Sally confessed with a sigh that arithmetic was her worst subject, too, but brightened at the mention of fairies.

"Really?" she exclaimed. "Oh, I love fairies, Caitlin! I used to adore the little Flower Fairy books that my grandmother gave me. And even now, I'm always on the lookout for a good fairy story."

"Honest?" Caitlin seemed intrigued. "I didn't know grown-ups believed in fairies." She slanted a resigned look at me. "Aunt China doesn't."

This is not exactly true. I happen to believe in the tooth fairy, for I have personally watched as he sneaked a silver dollar under Brian's pillow. However, I doubted that Caitlin would consider hairy, mustached McQuaid as qualified for the tooth-fairy position, and I didn't want to throw cold water—or too much realism—on the discussion.

"Actually, I try to keep an open mind on the subject," I said, feeling that I was being measured against an invisible (fairylike?) standard and found wanting.

"Everybody should believe in fairies," Sally said decidedly. "It would be a very sad world if there weren't any."

"Fairies are lame," Brian remarked, and made that *L* thing that kids do with their thumb and forefinger against their foreheads.

Caitlin looked crushed, and Sally came to their common defense. "That's all you know, buster," she said spiritedly. "And let me tell you, Santa had better not hear you talking that way. He just might decide to skip your presents."

I could see the phrase, *There's no Santa Claus, either—it's just parents*, forming on Brian's lips. I was riding to the rescue when McQuaid stepped in.

"Your mother's right," he growled. He leaned over and put a heavy hand on the top of Brian's head. "Anybody who thinks he's too big for Santa Claus can look for coal in his stocking."

"Coal?" Brian asked, distracted from making his case for the lameness of fairies. "You mean, like the kind of stuff they burn in dirty power plants?" He appealed to me. "Why would I get coal in my stocking, Mom?"

He stopped, biting his lip, obviously puzzled by differentiating between Mom One and Mom Two, or Old Mom and New Mom, or maybe even Usually Absent Mom and Always Present Mom. When Sally wasn't here, I could be pretty sure where I stood (Mom-in-chief, to borrow a phrase), but at the moment, I wasn't clear about my position.

"That's the stuff," I replied. "And you'll get it in your stocking if you bad-mouth Santa."

"Sick," Brian said admiringly.

"It is not *sick*," McQuaid snapped. "It's traditional. It's been happening for centuries. Good kids get presents. Bad kids get coal."

"No, I meant really *sick*," Brian insisted. "Beast. Cool. Awesome."

I was glad to have the explanatory synonyms. *Sick* was new to me, but *cool* I understood from my own youth and *awesome* from last year or the year before. I don't try to keep track of the evolving linguistic universe of young adults, however. I just listen and say "uh-huh" and try to catch the general drift.

"Young man," McQuaid said sternly, "you can leave that slang at school."

"Yeah," Brian said, leaning on his elbows. "Hey, Dad, I'd really like to have some coal. I could burn it and see if it's as bad as Mr. Nordyke says." He pulled down his mouth and said in a deep voice, presumably Mr. Nordyke's: "'There is no such thing as clean coal, boys and girls. It's all dirty.'" He popped back into his usual Brian voice. "I'd like to see how dirty. Measure the pollutants. You know, the particulates. Any idea where I can get some?"

I had nothing to suggest, but McQuaid did. "You might ride your bike over and talk to Mr. Rich. He's got a blacksmith's forge and does some horseshoeing. He could maybe give you a couple of lumps of the stuff."

"Or you could wait until Christmas," Sally said in a meaningful tone, "and check your stocking." She turned back to Caitlin. "You and I, on the other hand," she added sweetly, "will have candy and presents in our stockings. Because we're good girls."

Caitlin looked up at her, eyes wide, and I could see that she was smitten. "You're going to have a stocking, too? Here? With *us*?"

Brian looked at me, surprised and alarmed. I guess Sally hadn't told him that she was here for the duration.

McQuaid looked at his plate.

I looked around the table. "Yes, Brian's mom is going to have a stocking," I said brightly. "Here. With us. Isn't that awesome?"

And seeing Sally and Caitlin together, I had to agree with my somewhat optimistic remark: it was pretty awesome. Come to think of it, there was something about Sally that reminded me—and perhaps Caitlin, too—of Marcia, before she became so sick. Sally and Marcia were both perky and outgoing, with a cheerful, playful spirit. Both of them seemed to relate to Caitlin on her level, as if they were best friends or Barbie buddies, rather than adult and little girl. That takes a special flair, I think, and I'm not sure I have it. Caitlin misses Marcia terribly, and since she came to live with us, I've been trying hard to stand in. But let's face it. I'm not the playful type, and my experience of fairies is severely limited. If Sally could begin where Marcia left off, she might help to make the holiday fun for a lonely child facing the bitter realities of loss.

I smiled at Caitlin. "We'll put in an extra nail and you can hang Sally's stocking on the mantel, right next to yours. Would you like that?" We were out of Christmas stockings, but I'd bet Ruby would have an extra.

"Yeah," Caitlin said shyly. She dipped her spoon into her chowder. "Sure." She smiled again at Sally, a sweet little smile that always turns my heart inside out. "I'm glad you'll be here."

"Me, too." Sally looked around the table. "It'll be just like family. All of us together at Christmas."

McQuaid glanced up. He was opening his mouth to say something—I hate to think what—but Brian leaned over and whispered something, sotto voce. I'm sure I couldn't have heard it right, for it sounded like "Peace out, cub scout."

McQuaid sighed. "Pass the rolls," he said.

We were clearing the table when Sally turned to McQuaid. "I wonder if you and I could have a little talk this evening, Mike. I really need your help. I—"

"Sorry." McQuaid put his dishes in the sink, where Brian was rinsing, and went to pour another cup of coffee. "I'm grading exams."

"But it's important," she said in a low voice. "It's the reason I came to Pecan Springs—other than being with Brian, I mean," she added hastily, seeing his shoulders stiffen. "It's about what happened in—"

"I said I'm sorry." McQuaid's voice was hard. He picked up his coffee and headed for the door. "It can wait until I've turned in my grades."

"Can I help you?" I asked sympathetically, wishing that McQuaid had been just a little nicer, especially with Brian in the room. He knows that his parents aren't exactly good friends, and when the animosity gets ugly, he tries to tune it out. But it has to hurt.

"Help me?" Sally pressed her lips together. "I wish you could, China, but I don't see how. Mike is an investigator. I was hoping he would—" She stopped, sighing. "I guess I'll just have to wait and try again, when he's in a better mood."

Whatever it was, she wasn't going to tell me, but there was something in her voice that made me think she was telling the truth. I wondered what kind of trouble she was in this time.

A moment later, Caitlin bounced downstairs and asked Sally if she'd like to come up and look at fairy pictures. Which left Brian and me to do the dishes. It was actually Caitlin's turn to help Brian, but she and Sally were getting along so well. I was happy to promote the friendship by giving her a night off.

Brian had a different opinion. He didn't say anything until he had finished wiping the counter. I was putting soap in the dishwasher when he came to stand beside me. "Mom," he said in a low, troubled voice. "Do you think it's cool for Caitie to get involved with my mother?"

I looked up at him. Brian is two inches taller than I am now, and as he's grown older, he looks even more like his father. His craggy face is still unformed at sixteen, but has McQuaid's strong nose and firm jaw. They have the same shock of dark hair and the same steel blue eyes. Brian lacks his father's broken nose (courtesy of a quarterback sack at the ten-yard line) and the jagged scar across the forehead (courtesy of a druggie's knife in a parking lot arrest). Personally, I love McQuaid's crooked nose and even his jagged scar, and I would never deny Brian any of life's challenging experiences. But I secretly hope he manages to get through life without football, and I don't mind hoping out loud that he can avoid crazy, knife-wielding dopers, as well.

"I don't think we need to worry too much about involvement," I said judiciously, wondering if there might be some jealousy here. "I think they're just talking fairies."

"Maybe," Brian said in a serious tone. "But you know Sally." He looked at me to judge my reaction. It was the first time I had heard him call his mother by her first name.

"How do you mean?" I asked. Looking at him, I couldn't see any jealousy. His gaze was too direct, too serious.

"I mean—" He took a deep breath. "You can't count on her," he said, and in those five bleak words, I could hear the whole history of their relationship. "She says one thing and does something else. She promises, but she never comes through. She's here one day and gone the next." Another deep breath. "I know that you and Dad are doing your best, but Caitie is still pretty unhappy. I'd hate to see her start depending on my—on Sally. And be let down." Having delivered himself of this long speech in only two breaths, he stood watching me, a handsome, gangly boy who—sooner than I would like—was going to grow into a handsome, husky man.

I lifted my hand to his face, remembering how I once had to bend over to touch his cheek and brush his hair out of his eyes, when he was a little boy and I was his father's girlfriend. His mother had been gone then, too. In fact, his mother had been gone for most of his childhood. It wasn't—

He said it for me. "It's not fair!" he burst out angrily. "I wish she'd stayed away. She's going to spoil our Christmas, just you wait and see. Look at the way she's bugging Dad about helping her. She got herself in trouble, and she wants him to bail her out."

I dropped my hand. "Please be patient with her," I said. "Yes, she's in trouble right now. She's lost her house and her car and her job and—"

"So she shows up here, looking for a handout!" he cried. "She doesn't bother to come when she's okay, when she's got money. She only comes when she *needs* something."

"But that's what family's for, isn't it?" I asked reasonably. "To be there for you when you need something?"

He frowned. "I don't get this. I thought you didn't like her."

"I'm not sure I do, very much. I wish—" I stopped. There was no point in saying that I wished she'd stayed away, too. "But it's Christmas, and we need to help one another. And if your mom can help Caitie even a little bit, I'm happy to have her here. I hope you will be, too." I paused. This might not be the right time to bring it up, but I had to ask sooner or later. I might as well get it over with. "Oh, and we'll need the keys to your car, Brian. Your mother's going to use it while she's here."

"My car?" he squawked. "But Sally is a terrible driver. I don't want her—"

"Your father and I paid for that car, Brian," I said firmly, "and we all agreed that he and I would be using it until you start to drive. Your mom needs a car while she's here. She's going to drive yours. I'll tell her to be careful. Okay?"

He gave me a black look. "I hope I don't get to say 'I told you so.'" He turned on his heel and left the room.

I spent the rest of the evening making some Christmas simmer pot-pourri. I divided it among some small earthenware jars I'd bought from a potter in Wimberley and wrapped them for Ruby, Cass, Laurel, and Sheila. Then I finished a holly wreath I'd started earlier, hung it on the front door, and strung the icicle lights on the porch railing. While I was at it, I got out the boxes of Christmas tree decorations so they'd be handy when we decorated the tree. By the time I finished, it was nine o'clock, and I went to say good night to Caitlin, already in her pink flannel jammies, in her bed with one of her fairy books.

I sat down on the edge of the bed, noticing a bruise on her forearm.

"Where'd that come from, Caitie?" I asked, touching it gently. "Does it hurt?"

"Not much," she said, pulling up her sleeve and peering at it. "I got it playing soccer." She looked up with that smile that always goes straight to my heart. "Did you know that Uncle Mike is going to be one of our soccer coaches?"

"No, I didn't know," I said. "That's great, Caitie! He'll be very good." Privately, I hoped that he wouldn't yell too much. McQuaid puts all of himself into the game, even when he's not playing it. He has a tendency to get excited.

She turned a page of her book. "It'll be fun to have him there. Most of the other girls' dads are too busy."

"He might not be able to make all the practice sessions," I said, "but I'm sure he'll do his best." I smoothed her dark hair back from her forehead. "Don't forget about tomorrow evening. We're getting our Christmas tree."

Caitlin looked up at me eagerly. "Is Sally coming with us?"

"Yes, she is—at least, that's the plan. Are you glad?"

"Uh-huh." She nodded forcefully. "I really like Sally. She knows an awful lot about fairies, stuff I've never heard of. And she's fun, too. I'm glad she's going to have her stocking on our mantel. Right next to mine."

Our mantel. This time last year, I hadn't even known Caitlin. Now, she was our daughter. Brian's comment about his mother went through my mind, and I shivered a little. I wanted to be able to count on Sally, if only for Caitie's sake—and Brian's, too. Mentally, I crossed my fingers that Sally would behave herself.

"Well, good," I said cheerfully, and bent over and kissed her. "Now, let's put your book away and I'll tuck you in."

Caitlin put her book on the bedside table, then reached up and threw both arms around my neck. "I love you, Aunt China," she whispered in my ear, and kissed me on the cheek.

Some kisses and hugs you have to work for, or hope for. Others come as a gift. They're priceless.

Chapter Five

Heigh ho! Sing, heigh-ho! Unto the green holly:
Most friendship is feigning, most loving mere folly:
Then, heigh-ho! The holly!
This life is most jolly.

William Shakespeare,
As You Like It, Act 2

A lovely thing about Christmas is that it's compulsory, like a thunderstorm, and we all go through it together.

Garrison Keillor

On my way to the shop the next morning, I stopped off at Lila's Diner for one of Lila's lemon custard jelly doughnuts for me and a raspberry doughnut for Ruby. Neither of us are sugar addicts, but our morning always seems a little brighter when it begins with one of Lila's jelly doughnuts.

Lila's Diner is an old Missouri Pacific dining car, located on Nueces, catty-corner from Ranchers State Bank. Lila bought the old railroad car with her husband, Ralph, who fell victim to his two-pack-a-day habit several years ago. (Never believe that all herbs are warm and fuzzy. Tobacco is an herb. It kills.) The two of them scrubbed the old railroad car clean and furnished it with vintage items they picked up at going-out-of-business sales: 1940s and '50s red Formica-topped tables, chrome chairs with red vinyl seats, soda pop signs, and a Wurlitzer jukebox loaded with scratchy 45s featuring Elvis, Buddy Holly, and Patsy Cline. Lila herself wears a green puckered-nylon uniform, a ruffled white apron, a flirty white cap perched on her pageboy do, and cherry red lips and nails. She looks like something out of a fifties advertisement for the sandwich counter at Woolworth's. She is locally notorious for her coffee, which (for me, anyway) is like drinking pure adrenaline.

Unfortunately, what has been brewing at the diner for the past couple of months is mostly trouble. Docia, Lila's daughter and the culinary mastermind behind the diner's comfort-food menu, ran off to Waco with her boyfriend, taking with her all of the diner's culinary secrets. Lila has suffered through a series of temporary replacements, none of whom were half as talented as Docia. Lila's customers have suffered, too. They've complained long and loud about the startling decline in the quality of the meatloaf (Monday), fried chicken (Wednesday) and catfish (Friday). It has been reliably rumored that Lila has had it up to her painted eyebrows and is ready to sell out.

But this morning, Lila was beaming sunnily from behind the counter, while from the kitchen came the clang of banging pots and Docia's mournful rendition of "I Fall to Pieces." Docia, who is past thirty-five and on the chunky side, can really belt out a song.

"Docia's back," Lila confided. She shoved a white mug across the counter and picked up the coffeepot. She raised her voice, speaking to the customers at the counter. "Chicken and dumplings fer dinner today, boys." The announcement met with a murmur of masculine appreciation.

"That's great," I said approvingly. "I'll take the doughnuts with me," I added hastily, pushing the cup away just in time to stop her from splashing tar-black coffee into it.

"'Bout time she got her tail back here," growled Bubba Harris, our former police chief, sitting on his usual stool by the cash register. Mrs. Bubba was visiting the grandchildren, and Bubba had been batching it since Thanksgiving. "I'm ready for some o' them dumplin's o' hers. Ain't been the same 'round here since Docia left."

On the other side of Bubba, Tom Lancer sopped up the last of his fried egg with his toast. Tom works at the feed store, where he keeps abreast of the news. "You still thinkin' of sellin' out to Bert Dankins, Lila? Heard you was."

Bert Dankins? I gave an involuntary shudder. Bert owns a sandwich shop about a block from the campus. He makes a fair submarine sandwich, but I couldn't imagine him turning out anything remotely comparable to Docia's lemon meringue pie.

"I was considerin' it," Lila chirped, putting my jelly doughnuts into a brown paper bag. "Bert offered me a fair price, too. But now that Docia's back, I'm outta the mood to sell. Back t' stay, she says, and I b'lieve her. That'll be two fifty," she said to me, and punched my receipt. Ten punched receipts, and I get a free doughnut.

"How come she's back?" I asked, taking the bag and handing over my money. "Did she and her boyfriend split up?" The question may seem tactless to you, but Docia's boyfriend troubles are the stuff of legend. The customers know that she's in love when they hear her crooning "Love Me Tender." When we hear her singing "I Fall to Pieces" we know that her heart is broken, usually because she's been jilted.

This time, apparently, it was the other way around. "He's in jail," Lila replied shortly. "Good place fer him, you ask me."

"Ask her how come," Bubba prompted me. When I hesitated, he leaned over and nudged me. "Go on, Miz McQuaid. Ask her." Bubba knows perfectly well that I use my own name. Calling me "Miz McQuaid" is his way of reminding me that my husband is still the boss.

"Okay," I said. "I'll bite. Why is Docia's boyfriend in jail?"

On the other side of the kitchen partition, "I Fall to Pieces" was silenced in midverse.

"'Cause Docia snitched on him," Lila said.

I raised my eyebrows. This was something new. "Snitched on him for what?"

"Fer sellin' drugs to kids, that's fer what," Lila snapped. Lila almost never approves of her daughter's boyfriends. But since Docia is thirty-five and presumably an adult, Lila can't do much about it.

"Good for Docia," I said approvingly.

Bubba nodded. He raised his voice. "Good fer you, Docia."

"Fer shure," Tom Lancer agreed. "They oughtta give Docia a job over at the po-lice department," he added loudly. "Long as they let her out long enough to git over here'n make lunch."

In the kitchen, Docia slammed a pot. "Go to hell, Tom Lancer," she yelled.

"Not 'til I get me some o' them dumplin's," Tom yelled back and winked at me.

Bubba grinned, Lila smiled, and so did I.

The diner was back to normal.

It was still early when I got to the shop, unlocked the front door, and stepped inside. I took a deep breath of the mix of fragrances that greeted me and felt as I always do: deeply grateful for being able to work in a lovely, peaceful place, far away from the Houston rat race where I once made a high-powered living chasing low-life rats through the courts.

And it *is* a lovely place. Wooden shelves along the old stone walls hold large jars and massive stoneware crocks full of dried herbs, small bottles of herb tinctures, and tiny vials of essential oils and fragrance oils. There are herbal seasonings, vinegars, and jellies, as well as herbal soaps, cosmetics, and aromatic oils—oh, and those little squirt canisters of pure hot pepper. Books line the walls of a cozy reading corner that also features a red-painted rocking chair, in case someone wants to sit for a moment, and nearby there's a rack of handmade paper and cards. Baskets of pomanders and sachets fill the corners, dusty-sweet bunches of yarrow and tansy and salvia hang from the ceiling, ropes of pungent peppers and silvery garlic braids festoon the walls, and the walls are brightened by Donna's holiday wreaths, lending a sweet, spicy fragrance to the air. I've pinned up sprigs of holly and mistletoe everywhere, and there's a potted rosemary plant on one table, trimmed in the shape of a Christmas tree and decorated with handcrafted herbal ornaments. Looking around, I couldn't help smiling.

"Is that you, China?" Ruby called from the adjoining shop.

"It's me," I called back. "Brought you a jelly doughnut. Raspberry."

"Oh, yum," Ruby said. I went into her shop. She was sitting on a stool in front of her book rack, shelving books. Khat, our shop Siamese, was lying on the floor beside her. "Just put it on the counter, and I'll get to it in a minute," she said. "So how did it go last night?" she added over her shoulder. "Supper with Sally, I mean."

Ruby's bookshelves offer all the important New Age topics, from deciphering your horoscope to reading your runes, throwing the I Ching, channeling spirits, attracting health and wealth, understanding your dreams, and unearthing your past selves, as well as the usual yoga, meditation, and feng shui books. If you have a secret hankering to discover your inner person and learn your place in the Universe, Ruby can recommend a book that will show you how. Or she'll show you herself. Just sign up for one of her classes.

"Sally was on her best behavior." I put down the sack containing Ruby's doughnut and took an appreciative sniff. Ruby burns a different incense every day. Today, it smelled like cinnamon-spiced apple cider, a homey smell on a chilly December morning and a sweet accompaniment to the Christmassy fragrances in my shop. "She and Caitlin were soul mates from the get-go," I added. "They discovered a secret bond. Fairies."

"Fairies?" Ruby stood up and brushed her red velour skirt. She was wearing a black turtleneck with a red silk scarf and high-heeled black boots today—her skyscraper boots, I call them. Her mass of red hair was piled up on her head. She looked like a towering inferno. "Really? Sally is into fairies?"

Khat got up, too, stretched, and walked over to me.

"So it seems," I replied, bending over to stroke his dark ears. Ruby is another fairy aficionado. She has a shelf of fairy lore in the shop, a collection of fairy dolls in her guest bedroom, and a framed Tinker Bell poster in her bathroom. I chuckled. "Maybe you and Sally ought to get together and compare fairy tales."

"Maybe," Ruby said without enthusiasm. She's probably heard me complain about McQuaid's ex too many times. She gave me a look. "Is she coming with us tonight to get the tree?"

I nodded, straightened, and leaned against the door frame, taking an appreciative bite of my jelly doughnut. "But McQuaid isn't."

"Meow," remarked Khat in a meaningful tone. He much prefers eating (chopped liver or fish) to watching people eat.

"Uh-oh," Ruby said. "Because of Sally?"

"Because he promised Charlie Lipman he'd go to Omaha to find somebody. I didn't tell him so, but I'm glad he has the work, with Christmas bills on the horizon." I made a face. "And with Sally here, he's probably glad to get away."

Ruby went back to her bookshelf. "He won't miss Saturday night's party, will he?"

"He's coming home on Friday." I eyed her. "Are you still game for tonight?"

"Sure," Ruby said. "Donna's saving a tree for me, too. I may be a bit late, though. I need to stop at Castle Oaks. Mom's having a little trouble." She chuckled sadly. "A 'little trouble' is relative, of course."

Khat wound himself around my ankles, reminding me that it was cruel to eat in front of him.

"Relative." I ate the last of my doughnut. "I'll pretend I didn't hear that."

"Hear what?" She picked up a copy of *Rune Stones and Your Destiny*, considered it for a moment, then propped it, partially open, on the shelf where she displays rune stones and other divining tools. Turning back to me, she added, "I ran into Sheila and Blackie last night. Did you know they're seeing one another again?"

"You're kidding!" I exclaimed. "Really?"

"Truly," Ruby replied. "They were having supper at Beans' Bar and Grill. And if you ask me, Blackie looked as if Sheila was all he wanted on his menu. She seemed pretty happy about it, too. They were holding hands under the table."

I shook my head. "Will wonders never cease," I muttered.

My friend Sheila Dawson is Pecan Springs' chief of police, and a tough one at that. Since the city council appointed her to the job a few years ago, law enforcement funding is up and property crimes and motor vehicle accidents are down. Under Bubba Harris, the previous chief, the police department was a comfortable haven for good ol' boys on the verge of retirement. With the funding, Sheila is rapidly turning it into a younger, stronger force that the entire community can be proud of. Sheila has had to arm-wrestle the city council for every penny, but even the most miserly, antifeminist council member grudgingly admits that Chief Dawson has put the department on the right track.

Blackie Blackwell, on the other hand, is McQuaid's poker and fishing buddy, a friendship that goes back at least fifteen years. As the Adams County sheriff, Blackie carries on a proud Blackwell family tradition. His father was sheriff back when the county was still largely rural, and his mother cooked for the prisoners and cleaned the jail. Both are warmly remembered by longtime residents, who would probably like to go back to those peaceful days, when vacationing families from Dallas and Houston came to fish in the San Marcos and Guadalupe rivers and sail on the Highland Lakes, and cattle rustling was the most significant crime.

But Adams County is no longer just a scenic rural vacation destination. Pecan Springs is close enough to Austin (some forty minutes, depending on the traffic) to be considered a bedroom community, and urban sprawl is crawling in our direction. We're located on the busy I-35 corridor, along which illegal drugs and illegal aliens are daily smuggled out of Mexico, and there are plenty of remote hideaways in the Hill Country for crystal meth labs, which Blackie aggressively targets. He has a sterling statewide reputation as a lawman's lawman, and Adams County appreciates what they've got, which is why they recently elected him to his third term.

That may also be why, when Sheila and Blackie first got together, their friends gave an enthusiastic cheer. Not only are they decent, likable people, but it seemed like a perfect match: two fine law-enforcement professionals, one the popular county sheriff, the other the police chief of the county's largest town—but not always popular, partly because she's a woman, partly because she's had to clean house in the PSPD. Then they got engaged, and we were all delighted. But as time went on, Sheila began to back out of her bargain and finally broke off the engagement. It wasn't their relationship, she said. It was their careers. Two cops in one family was one cop too many.

Ruby raised her eyebrows at my lack of enthusiasm. "I thought you'd be happy to hear that they're back together again."

"I can't decide," I confessed. "If it lasts, sure, I'll be thrilled. But I don't think any of us wants to go through the misery of another breakup."

"I don't have anything to say about it," Ruby observed practically, "and neither do you. So we might as well be happy for them."

"I guess," I said and looked down at Khat, who was sitting on my foot, watching me with a plaintive expression. "Breakfast?" I asked.

To his credit, he didn't say "It's about time." He merely rose with dignity and led the way to the kitchen, where I warmed his chopped liver in the microwave and set it down in front of him. "Enjoy," I said. The bell over my shop door tinkled, and a customer came in, so I left Khat to his breakfast and went to help her.

The customer bought one of Donna's wreaths, a couple of Jim Long's cookbooks, and some of the handcrafted paper we made in our paper-making workshop last summer. The purchase turned out to be a promising start to a pretty profitable day, and by the time I locked the door that afternoon and closed out the register, I was happy to see a tidy bundle of bills in the cash drawer, as well as a respectable sheaf of credit card slips. (If you've ever been in business for yourself, you'll appreciate what that means.) Both the Crystal Cave and the tearoom did well, too, and Cass reported that the Thymely Gourmet had picked up another new client. A good day all the way around.

On the family front, too, it looked like things were under control, for a change. McQuaid had turned in his grades and gone to the Austin airport to catch his flight to Omaha. Sally had volunteered to pick Caitlin up at school, and I had promised Brian I'd be waiting when his science club meeting ended. The four of us would meet for a pizza at Gino's, then head out for Mistletoe Farm to get the tree and join the evening festivities.

I was still putting the bank deposit together when the phone rang. I debated whether to answer, since the Closed sign was hung on the door and I had to stop at the bank before going to get Brian. But thinking it might be McQuaid calling about something he'd forgotten, I picked up.

"Thyme and Seasons Herbs," I said, cradling the receiver against my shoulder as I stamped the last three checks. "How may I help you?"

There was a momentary pause. Then, "I'd like to speak to Sally," a male voice said.

"Sally?" I clipped the stamped checks to the bank deposit slip. "Sally Strahorn?"

"Yeah, right. Is she there?"

"Not at the moment." I reached for a slip of paper and a pencil. "Who's calling? Give me a number, and I'll have her call you back."

"Don't bother." Another pause. "Just tell her a friend called." The man's voice was mild and almost ingratiating, but I thought I heard an undertone of something else. In the next second, though, the tone was lightened by an ironic chuckle. "Tell her I've got her car. She'll understand."

"What was that again?" I asked, not sure I'd heard right.

"Her car. The yellow Mini. Just tell her I have it." There was a sharp click as the connection was broken.

I frowned at the receiver as I put it down. *A friend* had Sally's car? I thought back to our conversation the day before. She'd said it was repossessed, hadn't she? But there wasn't time to think about that now. I put the checks and currency into the blue bank deposit bag and zipped it shut. I just had time to drop off the deposit and drive to the high school for Brian.

IT doesn't take long to get from one end of Pecan Springs to another, even with a detour through the drive-through window at Ranchers State Bank, where Bonnie Roth (known to her friends as Loose-Lips Roth) took my money away from me. Bonnie and I are both members of the Myra Merryweather Herb Guild, and she is one of my most loyal customers. As she tallied my deposit, she handed over some of the local gossip. This kind of community service is not part of her job description, but Bonnie is a valuable employee in all other respects, and Helena Stubbs, her supervisor, knows it. Helena turns a deaf ear when Bonnie starts retailing the news.

By the time my money was safely in the bank's hands, I had heard two stories—that Sheriff Blackwell and Chief Dawson were secretly married and that Lila Jennings had sold her diner to Bert Dankins—both of which I seriously doubted. Sheila wouldn't get married without giving me a heads-up, and Lila had said just that morning that the deal with Bert was off. That's Bonnie for you, though. She passes along every little scrap of news that blooms in her gossip garden, true or not.

But as she handed over my deposit slip, she leaned forward and whispered into the teller's microphone something that I knew to be true: "Maybe you've already heard this, but Sally Strahorn is in town."

Pecan Springs is growing fast, but at heart it's still a small town, where everybody knows everybody else's business and is happy to share it with as many people as possible. McQuaid is something of an icon here, for he once served as the interim police chief and solved (with a little help from his friends) a particularly notorious local murder. His ex-wife has been around often enough for people to learn something of her history.

I smiled nicely. "Yes, I know. We've invited Sally to stay at our house for the holiday." There was no point in adding fuel to the fires of gossip.

"Oh, good." Bonnie breathed a gusty sigh of relief. "To tell the truth, I was a little worried when she cashed that big check this morning and drove off with all that money. You never really *expect* anything bad to happen, although it's certainly true that sometimes it does, don't you know?" She took a deep breath, getting wound up for more. "I mean, I know Hark Hibler hates to print those awful things in the *Enterprise*, but he can't just leave them out, now can he? Just last week, there was that piece about poor old Mr. King getting mugged on his way home from winning twenty-seven dollars playing bingo, and the week before, Betty Banning's car got broken into at the mall and somebody stole the new flat-screen TV she'd just bought." She fanned her hand, dismissing these ugly snippets of crime. "But now that I know Sally is staying with you and Mr. McQuaid—" She smiled broadly. "I'm just glad she's being taken care of."

I unzipped my bank bag and stuck the deposit ticket inside. "All that money?" I asked casually, latching on to the one new fact that Bonnie had handed me. Sally had cashed a check and driven away with a lot of cash? But she'd said she was broke. Where did she get the check? And how much money were we talking about?

But it had occurred to Bonnie, a bit belatedly, that she might have said too much. She glanced over her shoulder and gave a nervous laugh. "Guess I shouldn't have mentioned that check." She pursed her lips and made a gesture meant to suggest a key turning in a lock. "My lips are sealed. Definitely."

Well, heck.

But I smiled. "Very professional. We'll take good care of Sally," I added reassuringly. "Don't you worry about a thing, Bonnie."

TWENTY minutes later, Brian and I were settled in a booth at Gino's Italian Pizza Kitchen. This historic joint served up Pecan Springs' very first pizza sometime back in the 1950s, and in spite of the fancy franchises that have mushroomed along the interstate, Gino's pizza is still the best in town. It has the same delicious crust (thick or thin), the same tempting cheese that strings when you pick up a slice, and the same fresh mushrooms, anchovies, and Italian pizza sausage heaped generously over the top. Fads may come and fads may go, but Gino's just keeps keeping on.

Gino's interior hasn't changed much, either. It still has the same brown-painted wainscoting and fake beams across the fly-specked ceiling and the same uncomfortable fake leather cushions in the booths. Brian and I sat down, ordered iced teas, and waited, listening to the blare of music from the loudspeakers and the crack of billiard balls from the pool parlor in the next room. Gino's pool parlor is also a local family tradition, where kids play side by side with the grown-ups.

"She's late," Brian said with an exaggerated look at his watch. He added, unnecessarily, "I told you so. Didn't I tell you so, Mom? Sally never gets anywhere on time." He scowled. "I hope she hasn't wrecked my car."

I conceded that yes, he had told me so and no, she probably had not wrecked his car and was just about to point out that he was late half the time himself, when Sally and Caitlin appeared at the entrance.

"They're here," I said brightly. I waved, and Caitlin ran to the booth.

"We went to the petting zoo!" she cried excitedly, scooting onto the bench beside me. "I got to pet the alpaca!" She giggled. "He licked my fingers."

"He didn't eat them, did he?" I demanded with mock alarm, leaning over to look. I leaned back, as if in relief. "Nope. There they are. All ten of them. Glory be."

Caitlin giggled that delightful little-girl giggle of hers that always makes me smile. Brian rolled his eyes, big-brother style, and scooted over so Sally could sit beside him.

"We had fun," Sally announced as the menus were placed in front of us.

"I'm glad," I said. "But I'm even gladder that Caitie brought all her fingers back." I was rewarded by another giggle from Caitlin. "Okay, gang. Time to get serious. What kind of pizza do we want?"

The next few moments were filled with a spirited discussion of the relative merits of anchovies, jalapeño peppers, green peppers, and onions. After various negotiations, I signaled to the waiter, who took our order and left us with plates of salad and glasses of iced tea (the national drink of Texas, even in the winter).

Brian turned up his nose at the salad. "I'm gonna watch 'em play pool," he said, elbowing his mother to move, so he could slide out of the booth. "I'll be back when the pizza's here."

"Me, too," Caitlin said, jumping up. "I've never watched anybody play pool."

"No," Brian said, very big brother. "You're too young. You stay here."

"She is not too young," I said firmly. "But both of you keep your mouths shut and stay out of the way. Any complaints, you're in trouble." When they had left, I said to Sally, "Caitlin has led a sheltered life. We're trying to give her more experiences. Broaden her out a bit."

"Pool is definitely a broadening experience," Sally said and laughed. "She's a cute little kid, China. It's such a shame about her parents—and her aunt." She sobered. "I know what it's like to lose parents," she added, and I remembered that hers were dead. They'd been shot to death in their home, in a senseless robbery. But Sally had been an adult then, not a little girl.

"You just have to wonder how much one small child can handle," I said. "I'm glad that the two of you are getting along so well."

Sally nodded. "I thought maybe I'd pick her up after school tomorrow and take her to the mall to look for Christmas gifts for you, Mike, and Brian. Will that work for you?" She paused. "Speaking of Mike, I tried to talk to him again this morning, but he was in too much of a hurry to get out of the house. Do you suppose you could persuade him to sit down with me?"

"I'll try," I said, "when he gets back from Omaha."

"Omaha?" Her eyes widened. "He's in Omaha?"

"On business," I said, just in case she thought he had gone for the fun of it.

She leaned forward, urgent. "When will he be back? I really needed to talk to him last night. I'm afraid—" Whatever she was about to say, she bit it off.

"Friday night," I said.

"Friday night!" Her tone implied that it might as well be next year.

"That's the plan." I paused. "Is there something I can do, Sally?"

"I wish." She sat back in her seat, shaking her head gloomily. "No. I'm afraid Mike is the only one who can help me."

"What is it you want him to do? Of course, it's none of my business, but . . ." I let my voice trail off.

She looked away. "I need him to . . . to talk to somebody for me. It's . . . it's an investigative matter."

"Oh," I said. "Yeah, well, he's certainly the guy you want to talk to. Investigation isn't my line of work. So I guess you'll have to wait until he gets back. Or you could call. He's got his cell phone with him." I felt guilty suggesting this, although it was still my considered opinion that McQuaid could have found a few minutes to talk to her, especially since she seemed to think it was so urgent.

"Call him?" She brightened, then thought about it and got gloomy again. "I'd rather talk to him in person. This is pretty complicated. It would be hard to tell him over the phone. He might . . . He might not believe me."

I hate it when people reject suggestions as fast as you can make them. "Well, I guess it'll just have to wait, then. In the meantime, if you'd like to take Caitlin Christmas shopping, be my guest." A year ago I might have had reservations about trusting Sally to do something like this, but now she seemed almost normal. "Why don't you pay for what she picks out— within reason, of course—and I'll pay you back."

Sally ducked her head, looking embarrassed. "Could I maybe get an advance? As I told you, I'm not exactly rolling in the stuff right now."

No? What about the cash she'd picked up at the bank? I was troubled, but I didn't want to give Bonnie's information away—not just yet, anyway. I picked up my purse, opened my wallet, and handed over three tens. "This should be enough. We're not having a big Christmas this year."

"Tell me about it." Sally tucked the money into her purse, laughing wryly, then picked up her iced tea and took a sip. "While Caitie and I are at the mall, I was thinking I might see if anybody's hiring temporaries for the holiday. I could maybe earn enough to help with the groceries and pay for gas for the car."

A job? Well, then, maybe she had already unloaded the cash. But where? And how much? Which reminded me of something else. "I was closing up this afternoon when I got a phone call," I said, picking up my fork to begin on my salad. "It was for you."

She looked up, startled. "For me? But nobody knows where—" Her voice cracked. "Who . . . Who was it?"

"Some guy. He didn't give his name." I was watching her. There was something in her voice—apprehension? fear?—that didn't fit my casual announcement of the phone call. "He just said to tell you that a friend called, and that he has your car."

I can't say exactly what happened next, whether Sally dropped her full glass of iced tea, or whether it was wet and slipped out of her fingers. It didn't break—Gino's glasses are tough—but it made a large, messy splash all over the table. Hurriedly, we slid out of the booth and waited while the server jogged over with a towel to mop up the spill.

"Sorry, China," Sally muttered. "I didn't splash you, did I?"

"Even if you had, it wouldn't matter," I said. I was wearing jeans and a sweatshirt—my usual working garb. "I'm totally washable."

We sat down again. Our salads had escaped the deluge, and I returned to mine. Sally toyed with hers. I let the silence deepen, waiting to see what she would say next. After a moment, she took a deep breath.

"The man who called—did he say where he was calling from?"

"Nope. I asked him to leave a number, but he didn't do that, either."

I frowned at my salad. Throughout my whole life, I have staved off other people's efforts to dig into what I consider my personal business, and I don't pry into other people's private affairs. But this time, my curiosity was about to override my passion for privacy. And anyway, the guy had called my shop, which meant that Sally must have told him where she was going and probably given him my number. Which made it at least partly my business. Right?

"This guy," I said. "How did he get your car? Didn't you tell me it was repo'd?"

Sally didn't quite meet my eyes. "Yes, that's right. Maybe he . . . Maybe he bought it off a lot in Kansas City, and knew it was mine." She laughed a little, flushing. "I don't think there were any other yellow Mini convertibles in town. Wouldn't be hard to identify it."

That was probably true, although I had the uneasy feeling that there was more to this than Sally was telling me. "How did he know where to call you?" I persisted. "And why didn't he leave his name?" And then I got it. I chuckled. "A secret admirer, I'll bet."

I expected a chuckle in return, but Sally flung down her fork. "How the hell should I know?" she flared angrily, and pushed herself out of the booth. "I'll be back in a minute. I have to make a phone call."

She slung her bag over her shoulder and headed for the door, reaching for her cell phone as she went. She was in a hurry.

Puzzled, I returned to my salad. What was going on here? I hated to say it, but it sounded like Sally was up to her old tricks again. She knew the guy who had called and she was going outside to try to call him back. But if that's what it was, why get all steamed about it? Why lie?

Well, whatever was going on, it would stay a mystery for the moment. The pizza appeared (extra large, with anchovies on my portion, no jalapeños for Sally and Caitlin, and onions for everybody). I fetched the kids from the pool room, and Sally came back to the table.

"Everything okay?" I asked her, opting to act as if nothing had happened. I put a slice of pizza on Caitlin's plate.

Sally nodded and managed a smile, but there were worry lines between her eyes. Something was definitely not okay, but she wasn't going to talk about it in front of the kids. Caitlin was oblivious, but Brian picked up the signals—I could see it on his face. He was worried, irritated, too. I couldn't say that I blamed him.

We polished off our pizza and trooped out to the cars. The kids were excited about getting their tree, even Brian, who is not quite old enough yet to be cool about Christmas. Caitlin wanted to ride with Sally, but Sally shook her head and muttered something about having to make another phone call. So Caitlin joined Brian and me in McQuaid's old blue pickup truck, which I had driven today so we could haul the tree home.

Whatever was behind it, the phone call business went on all evening. When we joined the others on the hay wagon at Mistletoe Farm, Sally made at least two calls—attempts, rather. The person she was calling didn't seem to be answering. I saw her try again while we were singing carols around the big bonfire. And again as Brian and I roped our chosen tree—a fragrant, flawless, freshly cut six-foot Virginia pine—into the back of the truck.

"Oh, it's pretty!" Caitlin cried, dancing around. "Sally, look how pretty!"

"Very nice," Sally said. She frowned and pocketed her cell.

"You still haven't been able to connect?" I wasn't going to ask who she was calling, but she volunteered it, sounding anxious.

"No, and I don't understand it. She said she was going to be home tonight. Leslie. My sister," she added. "Remember her?"

Ah, yes. Of course I remember Leslie. She lives in Lake City, a pretty little town about forty miles north of Austin, where she teaches elementary school. Leslie visits us several times a year, primarily to see Brian, for whom she has a great fondness. She has no children of her own and is deeply disappointed (this is my take on the subject, anyway) by Sally's neglect of her son, so she tries to make up for it as much as she can. Brian doesn't do this much now, because summers are pretty busy with other things, but when he was younger, he used to spend a couple of weeks every summer with his aunt, who took him fishing and canoeing on the local lake and hiking in the nearby state park. Leslie keeps in touch with birthday and Christmas presents and playful surprise cards that she draws herself. And once, when Sally was on an extended detox "vacation," Leslie and McQuaid collaborated in an intervention—a wrenching experience for both of them, but helpful to Sally, at least for a while. McQuaid hasn't said much about Leslie, but I had the feeling that there might have been something between them once, before I came on the scene. Life is complicated, isn't it?

I wondered briefly why Sally wasn't spending the holiday in Lake City, but then I remembered McQuaid's saying that the sisters had never gotten along, even when they were growing up. Anyway, whatever the reason, it was none of my affair. Sally's business—the check she had cashed, the phone call about the car, her relationship with Leslie—all that stuff was *her* business, not mine. I wasn't going to meddle.

Sally still hadn't reached her sister by the time the kids finished popcorn and hot chocolate and settled down to their homework. Or by the time I shut myself in the bathroom for a long, steamy, lavender-scented bath and a phone conversation (also pleasantly steamy) with McQuaid, who had checked into his motel and was going through the background material Charlie had given him.

I don't know how you feel about this, but to me, a hot bath is the perfect way to end a good day, and this day had been better than most. The kids had had an enjoyable evening (Caitie had smiled a lot), we had bagged a stunning Christmas tree, and McQuaid had tracked down his quarry within a couple of hours after arriving in Omaha. Assuming that tomorrow's interview went well and a few other things checked out, he might even be able to take an earlier plane on Friday.

Feeling warm and cozy in my old blue terry robe and slippers, I padded downstairs to fill the coffeemaker and set it on autopilot for the next morning. The kids had gone to bed, but Sally was still in the kitchen, hunched over a sandwich and a mug of mint tea. Howard Cosell crouched at her feet, watching her enviously. He turned toward me, and I could read the urgent question in his mournful eyes. *Is this person really going to eat that whole sandwich and not offer me a single bite?*

"How about a cookie, Howard?" I asked, taking pity on him. He scrambled to his feet and followed me to the stoneware jar where I keep his dog cookies—healthy homemade treats. I gave him two, and he carried them back to his place beside Sally's chair, where he ate one and dropped the other one on the floor, putting his paw over it so it couldn't escape. As you may know, bassets have very large paws. The cookie didn't have a chance.

At the stove, I hefted the teakettle. Finding enough hot water, I made mint tea for myself and sat down across from Sally. "Did you connect with Leslie?" I asked, spooning honey into my mug.

She shook her head, clearly worried. "I know she planned to be home tonight. There are things we . . . need to talk about."

I sipped my tea, appreciating the sharp, minty fragrance and the warmth of the mug in my hands. The tea was like a tonic. "Well, I'm sure you can reach her in the morning, before school."

"I hope," she muttered. She finished her sandwich in silence. Howard Cosell, who had clearly been hoping for a bite, heaved a heavy sigh, lifted his paw, and nabbed his cookie as a consolation prize. Sally didn't even notice this little drama. She pushed back her chair and stood up.

"Time for bed, I guess." She sounded dispirited.

"I'm glad you and Caitie are getting along so well," I said, trying to lighten her mood. "That finger-lickin' alpaca was a huge hit. And when I said good night to her just now, she told me she was looking forward to going shopping with you tomorrow afternoon."

Sally managed a small smile. "She's a very sweet girl. I'm sure we'll have fun together." Then, unexpectedly, she bent and kissed my cheek.

"Thanks for being such a good mom to Brian, China. I've missed too many years. Which is nobody's fault but my own," she added ruefully. "It's easy to see how happy he is here, with his father and you. I couldn't have given him anything like this—not even close. I appreciate all you've done for him, a lot more than I can say."

I reached for her hand, deeply moved. "I know it's been hard for you, Sally. But I'm glad you and Brian are spending the holiday together." This wasn't something I'd ever expected to hear myself say, but I found myself meaning it. There was no point in letting the past poison the future, if only for Brian's sake. "I hope we can put all that old stuff behind us and be friends."

"I do, too," Sally said fervently. "I—"

The telephone caught her in midsentence. "Probably McQuaid," I said, as I got up to answer. "He's thought of something he needs."

But it wasn't McQuaid. "Put Sally on, please," a man said. His tone was mild, ingratiating, almost smarmy. "I need to talk to her."

Startled, I covered the receiver with my hand and turned to Sally. "It's the same guy who called about the car."

"The same—" Sally's eyes grew large, and her face paled. "I—I don't want to talk to him. Tell him I'm not here."

I turned back to the phone. "You've missed her." My voice sharpened. "Who is this? How did you get this number?" After McQuaid opened his detective agency, we decided it would be a good idea to unlist our residential telephone number, which we now give out only to our friends. McQuaid gave it to Sally so she could reach Brian. She must have given it to—

"Oh, please, China Bayles. Let's be straight with each other." The caller's voice did not lose its mildness, but it had a darkly ominous edge that made me shiver. "I know Sally is there, and I'm sorry she doesn't want to talk to me. Just tell her—" He paused, chuckling. "Tell her I'm looking forward to seeing her again. Soon, I expect. Very soon." The connection broke.

I hung up the phone and turned. "He says he knows you're here, Sally. He's looking forward to seeing you again. Soon."

"Oh, god." Trembling, Sally sank into the nearest chair, propped her elbows on the table, and covered her face with her hands.

The nighttime dark on the other side of the kitchen windows seemed suddenly blacker and more threatening. I closed the blinds and snapped the dead bolt on the back door. If this guy was lurking out there, that's where he was going to stay. Then I pulled a chair up next to Sally's and put my hand on her shaking shoulder. I was about to do something I find deeply offensive. I was about to pry into Sally's private affairs.

If you know me, you know that personal privacy has always been one of my major hot-button issues. In general, I believe that government should stay out of the private lives of ordinary citizens—I am opposed to most of the provisions of the Patriot Act—and I don't believe that people ought to meddle in other people's lives. I vigorously resist attempted invasions of my own personal privacy. I wouldn't invade Sally's—except that she had clearly gotten herself into some sort of serious trouble and needed help.

But this was no longer just Sally's business. I was being dragged into the mess, whatever it was. A strange man had called our private, unlisted number late at night, refused to identify himself, and addressed me by name and in a tone that sent cold chills up my spine. It was an unwelcome reminder of the kind of life I lived before I left the law firm, when the occasional colleague was ambushed by the occasional bad guy in a fit of pique over something untoward that had happened in court that day. Back then, stranger calls to my unlisted number made me exceedingly nervous. They still do.

But I kept that apprehension to myself. "Okay, Sally," I said in a voice that was meant to convey mild amusement (although this was not exactly what I felt). "Time to 'fess up. Who is this jerk? A boyfriend? A former boyfriend?"

Sally's past is littered with the wreckage of relationships with men of questionable character, like the stockbroker who gave her so much grief in San Antonio and the wannabe lawyer who peddled pot when he should have been studying for the bar. While some of these guys might have been more involved with Juanita than Sally, it was reasonable to assume—

Sally sighed and dropped her hands. "Not exactly a boyfriend. I mean—" She raised her eyes to mine. There was fear in them. No, not fear, panic. Sheer, unadulterated panic. "He's beyond creepy, China. I don't want to talk to him. Ever."

"Somehow, I got that idea," I said drily. "Then why did you give him our number?"

"I didn't!" she burst out wildly. "My son lives here, China! I would never put Brian in danger."

"In danger?" I frowned. "In danger of what?" This was beginning to sound even more threatening. Who was this guy, anyway? Some petty criminal she'd gotten herself involved with? Worse?

She chewed on her lip, thinking it over, then tried to dial down the panic. "That was a silly thing to say. There's no danger. Not really." She tried to laugh. "You know me. I'm always dramatizing things."

Not convincing. But I left it. "The phone number?" I repeated.

She looked away. "I totally don't know, China. Honestly."

"Then how did he know where to find you? Did you tell him?"

"Absolutely not!" she cried angrily. "I haven't spoken to him since—" A gulp. "I have no idea how he knew I was here, China. Maybe he followed us. Maybe—" She glanced fearfully toward the window. "Maybe he's out there, watching."

I didn't want to say so, but I was wondering that very thing. Instead, I said, "I don't think so, Sally. We would have seen his headlights if he'd driven down the drive."

"Not if he turned them off."

I'd thought of that, too. I got up. "If it'll make you feel better, I'll check the other doors. Just to make sure."

Everything was securely locked, but Sally's fear was infectious. Feeling exposed and vulnerable, I drew the living room and dining room draperies. Two women, two kids, alone in a remote house at the end of a long country lane, the nearest neighbors nearly a mile away. Howard Cosell would raise the alarm if somebody tried to break and enter, but he was too elderly to be of much help if it should come to apprehending anybody. I thought fleetingly of the Beretta, locked away in the top drawer of my bureau. My father had given me the gun years before and made sure that I knew how to use it. And McQuaid, who believes in being prepared for anything, made sure that I kept in practice. But I didn't think the situation had come to that point. At least, I hoped it hadn't.

Back in the kitchen, I sat down again. "Look, Sally. I make it a point not to get involved in other people's business. Whoever this guy is, he's your problem. But he has my business phone number and our unlisted residential number. He knows my name, and presumably, he knows where I live. So now he's my problem, too." I was speaking in my lawyer's voice, in the tone I reserved for recalcitrant clients who expected me to help them without giving me all the facts. "I want to know who he is and just how you're connected to him."

She was silent for a moment, staring down at her clenched hands.

"You're right," she said. "It's not— I'm not being fair." She looked up at me. "You guessed right. He's a former boyfriend, that's all, and he doesn't . . . want it to end. His name is—" She broke off, adding in a whimper, "I wanted to talk to McQuaid about him, but I never got the chance."

"His name," I prompted. "He knows mine, remember? Which gives me the right to know his."

She swiped her sleeve across her eyes. "Jess. Jess Myers."

"Where does he live?"

"Near . . . near Kansas City, on the Kansas side. In a small town. Sanders."

With much coaxing and prompting and in breathless fragments, the story came out. Sally had dated this guy—whom she described as "sort of a nothing-looking person"—a long time ago. "I only saw him a few times," she said, shivering. "He was . . . creepy."

I agreed with that already, but when I pressed her for more details, such as what "creepy" looked like, she could only say that he was dark-haired, with dark-rimmed glasses. Medium height. How old? Forty, forty-one. He had a mole under his right eye. She was vague about how long she had known him or where she had met him. When I asked why she stopped seeing him, she shrugged and looked away.

"I . . . I didn't trust him," she said. "There were things—" She stopped, lacing and unlacing her fingers. "I did a little digging. I found out some things that bothered me." A deep breath, an exhale. "I just didn't trust him, that's all. Okay?"

I watched her for a moment. "Has he been stalking you?"

"Stalking?" she asked tentatively, trying the word on for size. Then she seized on it quickly, as if that was the word she'd been looking for. "Yes. Yes, stalking. That's exactly what he's been doing, China. He's been stalking me."

"And that's why you've come here? To Pecan Springs?"

"Well, I wanted to see Brian. Really. And Mike—I needed to talk to him. And it was Christmas and—"

"Forget Christmas," I said impatiently. "You came here to get away from this guy, this ex-boyfriend. Right?"

"Not entirely, but—" She swallowed, then nodded mutely. "Yes," she whispered. "I had to . . . to get away. I was scared, China."

"And the business about your house getting flooded, and your job—"

"Well . . ."

"It's not true?"

"I had to have something to tell you. It's all I could come up with." Her eyes were brimmed with tears, and they were trickling down her cheeks. "I know it was totally stupid to lie. But I thought maybe you'd be more likely to let me stay here if you felt sorry for me. If I'd told you I was hiding out, you wouldn't have—"

"You damn betcha, I wouldn't have," I muttered. McQuaid had been right—about this part, anyway. I hate being lied to. Worse, I hate being taken in by a lie. It makes me feel stupid. "The car?" I asked. "What about the car? Was it really repo'd?"

Her gaze skittered away. "Well . . ."

"How did he get the car, Sally? Did you give it to him?" My voice was rough with anger.

She threw up her hands wildly. "How the hell should I know how he got the freakin' car? Why are you asking me all these questions? Why can't you just—" She broke down and began to sob violently.

Yes, I was angry, but I put my arms around her, anyway. I wish she hadn't lied to me. I wish I'd been smarter, less willing to be taken in. But she was being stalked, and it's not fair to blame the victim. I softened my tone.

"I'm sorry this has happened, Sally. And it's not your fault, so please don't beat up on yourself. But stalking is serious business. It's a crime. The kids are here with us, and we can't take any chances. I think we ought to call the police."

"No!" She wrenched herself away from me. "I don't want the police involved! I can't—" She gulped and tried to get control of herself. "I mean, this guy, Jess, he's not that bad, really. He just sounds . . . on the phone, I mean. He sounds kind of scary. But I'm sure he wouldn't—" She faltered. "Honest. I'm sure."

I wasn't convinced. Her fear—the panic I had seen in her eyes—had been genuine. And now I knew, or thought I knew, what she had wanted to talk to McQuaid about.

"It's stupid to want to protect this jerk, Sally. Maybe you still care for the guy, or think you do. But a man who goes to the trouble of acquiring your car, follows you all the way to Texas, and makes threatening phone calls—" I frowned. "Okay, tell you what. Tomorrow morning, let's stop at the police department and talk to Sheila Dawson. You remember Sheila, our chief of police?" They had met, although they hadn't exactly hit it off. But that didn't matter, not in this case. "She'll know what to do. You won't even have to be involved."

Sally jumped up, knocking her chair over backward. "No! I don't want Sheila Dawson involved—do you hear? And stop trying to tell me how to manage my business, China! If you keep after me about it, I'll . . . I'll leave. Then you can stop worrying."

Leave how? I wanted to ask. Was she planning to steal Brian's car, or what?

"But I can't stop worrying, Sally," I said in a reasonable tone. "Stalkers are dangerous. You don't just ignore somebody who—"

But I was talking to myself, for she was already out the kitchen door and halfway up the stairs, taking them two at a time.

I sat for a moment after she had gone, thinking. Then I got up and went to the phone. I hadn't promised not to talk to Sheila, but we lived outside of Pecan Springs, beyond her bailiwick. And anyway, Sally didn't want her involved. But as far as law enforcement was concerned, I had another ace up my sleeve.

I punched in Sheriff Blackwell's home number. It was the fourth ring before he picked up.

"Blackwell here," he said gruffly.

"Sorry if I woke you up," I said. "It's China."

"Not a problem." There was a chuckle in his voice. "I wasn't asleep—quite. What's up?"

I told him about the stalker's phone call and Sally's response. "I'm not sure there's anything to be seriously concerned about," I added. "But McQuaid is out of town and we're here by ourselves tonight. If any of your deputies happen to be out this way on patrol, could you ask them to keep their eyes open? I don't like the idea of this guy hanging around out there in the dark."

His response was immediate and comforting. "Sure thing, China. When's McQuaid getting back?"

"Day after tomorrow." I paused. "I hope I'm overreacting, Blackie. This is probably nothing."

"Doesn't sound like 'nothing' to me," he replied. "Get some sleep. And don't worry. One of our guys will be around to check. I'll have him blink his lights when he pulls up to the house, so if you happen to be awake, you'll know who it is."

I hung up the phone, feeling better. It helps when the county sheriff is a family friend.

Chapter Six

Since early times holly has been regarded as a plant of good omen, for its evergreen qualities make it appear invulnerable to the passage of time as the seasons change. It therefore symbolizes the tenacity of life even when surrounded by death . . .

Jacqueline Memory Paterson,
*Tree Wisdom: The Definitive Guidebook to the
Myth, Folklore and Healing Power of Trees*

Both Holly and Ivy were plants with power, and they were specially suitable for protection in the dead of the year . . . The red berries help, since red is a colour against evil.

Geoffrey Grigson, *The Englishman's Flora*

The rest of the night was uneventful, mostly. I woke up once to auto lights against my second-floor bedroom window, but when they blinked a couple of times, I went back to sleep, glad that somebody was keeping an eye on us. Howard Cosell sleeps on the floor most of the time, but he is an opportunistic dog. When he saw that McQuaid's half of the bed was empty, he claimed it, sprawling belly-up, all four large paws in the air and his ears flopped out on the pillow, an immodest picture of pure basset pleasure. I don't mind sleeping with him, but he snores, a rhythmic, blubbery wheeze, punctuated by short, sharp basset snorts. I had to roll him over twice.

Next morning, there was the usual hectic rush of school clothes, lost homework, and breakfast. I put a load of sheets and towels in the washer—after I had retrieved a small brown snake from the laundry hamper and instructed Brian to keep it in its cage or else. Over cereal, I told him and Caitlin to check their cell phones at noon for a message from me about after-school plans. I'm not a cell phone fan, especially where kids are concerned, but I've got to admit that I like being able to reach Brian and Caitie, wherever they are. These days, you never know what's likely to happen.

After the kids had dashed out the door, Sally came downstairs, dressed in a red long-sleeved sweater, jeans, and a navy blazer. She was subdued and silent. As she helped herself to coffee, the dark circles under her eyes were a silent testimony that she hadn't slept very well. I didn't intend to advertise the fact that I had called the county sheriff, so I didn't ask her if she had seen the deputy's car lights. The guest room is at the back of the house, so I was fairly sure she hadn't; if she had, she didn't mention it. She didn't say anything more about leaving, either. But I had something to say to her.

I waited until she was settled at the table. Taking a sip of coffee, she reminded me that she and Caitlin were going shopping that afternoon after school.

I didn't hesitate. I was troubled, not only by what had happened last night, but by the fact that Sally had lied to me. The flood that had taken out her house was a lie. The lost job, also a lie. The repossessed car, another lie. The only truth I could put my finger on was that somebody was stalking her. She'd claimed he was a rejected boyfriend, but that might be another lie. For all I knew, he could be an ordinary bill collector, a drug dealer, or a man carrying a serious grudge—and a gun. Whoever, I wasn't taking any chances.

"I've decided that's not such a good idea, Sally. Until I know what this stalking business is about—and until McQuaid is back home and can be part of this conversation—I'm making other arrangements for the kids." I wasn't sure exactly what those arrangements would be, but I had several possibilities in mind.

Sally put down her cup. "I told you, China. The guy is harmless. You don't really think—"

"I don't know what to think," I said, giving her a straight look. "All I know for sure is that I don't like it when strangers call my unlisted number late at night. And I definitely don't like your lying to me. It makes me feel that you're taking advantage, when I was only trying to help. Makes me wonder just how far you can be trusted."

She bit her lip and looked away. There was a silence. I hoped she was deciding to tell me the truth for a change, but that didn't happen. Finally, she said, "Fair enough, I guess. I'm sorry you feel this way, but you're entitled to your opinion."

"No argument there." I glanced up at the clock. "I need to be out of here in ten minutes. Anything else?"

"I'll just finish my coffee and be on my way, too," she said. "But maybe you and I could have lunch." She managed a smile. "Really, China—I'd like to know more about the things you're doing with your shop and your other businesses. I'm sure I could learn from you. How about it?"

I made myself sound cordial. "Come by the tearoom around one. We can eat there, and Ruby and Cass can join us, if they have time." I eyed her outfit. "You look nice. Where are you off to this morning?" We were acting as if everything was normal, which of course it wasn't.

"Following up on a job lead." She gulped her coffee and picked up her shoulder bag. "See you at one."

A job lead. It might've seemed like a good plan yesterday, but after last night, I wasn't enchanted with the idea of Sally's getting a job in Pecan

Springs. It seemed to suggest a certain permanency. But maybe not. Maybe all she wanted was Christmas money—although there was that mysterious bank transaction Bonnie Roth had mentioned. What was the purpose of the check she cashed? Was it getaway money? Was it a legitimate debt that Sally owed to the man who was trailing her? Or was he demanding blackmail?

Still turning these questions over in my mind, I fed Howard, tidied the kitchen, took the sheets out of the washer and dumped them in the dryer, and closed Brian's door to thwart any more animal expeditions. Then I gave my hair a quick couple of licks with the hairbrush, pulled on clean jeans and a sweatshirt, grabbed a jacket, and headed out to the car.

But before I left, I made a careful tour of the house, trying all the doors and windows once again, to be sure that they were locked securely. I wasn't afraid, exactly, but it doesn't hurt to double-check.

I didn't intend to find that stalker lurking in a closet when I got home that night. Sally might be right, and he was harmless. But somehow I didn't think so. And I wasn't going to take the chance.

IT was not quite eight when I unlocked the front door and switched on the lights in the shop. Outdoors, the temperature was in the forties, with the fresh smell of cold rain in the air, and I turned up the thermostat. Khat presented himself for breakfast, so I took care of that little chore first. Then I put the cash tray in the register, swept the floors, and straightened the shelves—my usual morning chores. Ruby came in about that time, so I left her in charge and went out to Thyme Cottage to make sure that Hazel, our current paying guest, had everything she needed. I caught her just before she left to go across the alley to fix her father's breakfast.

"Oh, hi, China," she said, answering my knock on the door, her hair-brush in one hand.

"I see you're getting ready to go out," I said. "I just wanted to make sure that everything is okay. Oh, and to let you know that you're free to use as much fireplace wood as you like. Take whatever you need off the stack beside the deck."

"Thanks. I will." She was smiling. "Actually, I was going to stop in at the shop this morning."

"Don't tell me the hot water heater is on the fritz again." The last time Hazel stayed in the cottage, the heater went out, and there'd been no hot water for baths until it was replaced.

"No, no, the hot water is fine." She swiped her hairbrush through her short gray hair. "I was just wondering if that man was able to reach you."

"That man?"

"Yes. The one who was looking for your friend. Sarah, I think he said her name was." She frowned. "Or maybe Sally?"

I pulled in my breath. "I'm not sure exactly who . . ."

"Maybe he wasn't able to find you, then," she said. "Yesterday evening, early, I took Dad out to supper. We got back a little before six. I drove down the alley to park beside the cottage, the way I usually do, but there was a car in the parking space already—and as you know, there isn't room for two. I parked in the alley for a minute, thinking maybe I'd just put my car in Dad's driveway. And then I saw a man coming around the cottage."

I was beginning to get the drift. "What did he look like?"

"Dark hair. Dark-rimmed glasses. Sort of ordinary looking, non-descript, forty, maybe. Fortyish. Oh, and he had these two big scratches on his jaw. And a mole under one eye."

I stared at her, feeling the apprehension knot in my gut. Dark-rimmed glasses, a mole. She was describing Sally's creepy ex-boyfriend—or whoever he was. "Did he . . . Did he say anything?"

"Well, yes. He was nice, actually, very soft-spoken. He came over to the car and apologized for taking the parking space. He said he was looking for you. He thought you might know where he could find someone—Sarah, I think he said. I didn't catch the last name." She frowned again. "Or Sally, maybe? Anyway, he said she was visiting in Pecan Springs, and you would know where."

"Ah," I said. "What did you tell him?"

"I said that this was your guest cottage, and suggested that he try at your shop tomorrow—that would be today. He said he was in a hurry, and wanted to know your address." She eyed me. "I told him I didn't know where you lived, but I thought you were taking the children out to the Mistletoe Creek Farm to get a Christmas tree. That's what you said when I picked up the key. Remember?"

Yes, I remembered. "And then what?" I prompted.

"Oh, he thanked me, very politely, then got into the car and drove off. So of course I pulled into the parking space." She fluffed up her hair. "I guess he didn't find you after all, huh? That's too bad. He seemed really anxious to get in touch with what's-her-name."

"What kind of car?"

The smile lines crinkled around her eyes, and she laughed. "That was the funny part, really. Funny ha-ha, I mean. That car was the cutest little yellow convertible—" She gave a shrug. "It's the kind of car I'd love to drive. A happy car. But it didn't fit him, somehow. Seemed out of character."

A yellow convertible. That clinched it.

"I wonder," I said in a conversational tone, "if you happened to check the windows here in the cottage. After you saw that guy, I mean."

A frown puckered her forehead. "Why, no, I didn't. You don't think—"

"Of course not," I said firmly. "It's a good idea to be sure, that's all."

Five minutes later, I was sure. The kitchen window—the one that looks out onto the alley—is a casement. I had noticed some time ago that the window doesn't fit tightly against the sash and intended to get it fixed. Now, I could see that the inside lock (not a very secure one) had been lifted, perhaps by the simple expedient of a credit card slipped through the gap.

Hazel frowned at the lock. "Really, that man—he was so nice. His voice was so soft. I can't imagine that he would—" She broke off, puzzled. "And why, for heaven's sake? It doesn't make any sense."

"I can't imagine it, either," I said lightly, refastening the lock. "I'm sure your mystery man had nothing to do with the lock being loose. But I'm glad we checked. I'll get the window fixed. Today."

I didn't say so to Hazel, but I was guessing that the man she saw—he had to be Sally's stalker, Jess Myers—had slipped this lock. Maybe he figured that Sally would be staying here, and an open window would give him easy access during the night. But then Hazel had showed up. When he understood that she was staying in the cottage, he realized he'd have to look elsewhere for Sally.

I repeated my promise to secure the window, wished Hazel a good day, and went back to the shop, where I put in a call to Jill, the gal who does repair work for us. She promised to get the window fixed before the day was over, which put my mind at rest—on that score, at least. I was still wondering whether Myers had managed to locate Donna's farm and how he had gotten my unlisted number.

But I had other things on my mind—the kids, first of all. I didn't want to take any risks with Caitlin and Brian, so I needed to make some changes in the day's arrangements. Caitlin is crazy about Grace, Ruby's year-old granddaughter, who lives with her mother, Amy, and Amy's partner, Kate, just a few blocks from Caitlin's school. It was easy to arrange with Amy to meet Caitlin after school and take her home for an all-girls' sleepover. A phone call to Sandy, the mom of Brian's best friend, took care of Brian. Sandy said she'd be glad to have him spend the night with Mike. That settled, all I had to do was text-message the kids and explain the change in plans, and I could relax.

The rest of the morning went quickly. By eleven, it was happily clear that we were going to need more holiday wreaths, so I phoned Donna and put in an order for another dozen. There were seven business days left until Christmas, and I figured I could sell at least that many, maybe more. But Donna works on consignment, and there's nothing sorrier than a Christmas decoration that doesn't sell, so my order was conservative.

"I'll bring them in tomorrow," Donna said. She paused, adding brightly. "I hope the kids had a good time last night."

"They did," I said. "Brian met a new girl on the hayride. And Caitlin thinks the tree is gorgeous. Hang on a minute, Donna."

I cradled the phone against my shoulder. A woman had come up to the counter with a purchase—two copies of my book, *The China Bayles Book of Days.*

"I love this book," she said. "I already have my copy, and these are Christmas presents for my sisters. One for Annie, the other for Janice. Could you sign them, please?"

I gave her an extra large smile, personalized and signed the books with a flourish, and ran the credit card, still cradling the phone. When you're in business, you learn to multitask. And I love selling that book.

On the other end of the line, Donna cleared her throat. "I won't keep you," she said. "I know you're busy. But I was just wondering—"

I put the book into a bag, mouthed, "Thank you very much!" to the customer, and closed the cash drawer. "Sorry, Donna," I said into the phone. "I'm back now. But I missed whatever you said."

"That guy," Donna said. "I was wondering if he called you."

I focused. "Guy?"

"Sally's friend. He was here last night. Said he'd been looking all over for her and happened to catch a glimpse of her sitting on the other side of the bonfire. But he lost her in the crowd, and she got away before he could connect. He seemed really anxious to reach her, and I knew she was with you." She chuckled. "I got the feeling that there might be some romance in the air."

I was very focused now. Things were adding up quickly. "Somebody did call last night," I replied. "Actually, I was wondering how he got our number. It's been unlisted for a couple of years."

"Unlisted!" Donna exclaimed, horrified. "Oh, my gosh, China! I'm sure you must have told me that, but I totally forgot. This guy—he was really very nice—he said he'd been looking all over for Sally Strahorn and just happened to see her, and wondered if I knew where she could be reached. As I said, I knew she was with you, so I just looked up the number in my Rolodex, and he wrote it down." She let out a noisy breath. "I hope I didn't—I mean, it *was* okay to give it to him, wasn't it?"

I didn't answer that. "What did he look like?"

"I dunno. Nothing special, I guess. Dark hair. Plastic-rimmed glasses. Very mild-mannered. Nice voice, polite." She gulped. "Gee, I hope I didn't—I would feel really bad if I caused any trouble."

"Don't worry about it," I said in a comforting tone. There was no point in blaming Donna. It was just one of those things. "You concentrate on those wreaths. Okay?"

She sighed. "Yeah. Okay. I really am sorry, though. Honest. I'll never do that again."

I hope not, I thought as I put the phone down. But I couldn't be angry at Donna, who hadn't done it on purpose. And at least I understood the sequence of events. Somehow, Jess Myers had got hold of my shop's phone number—after that, the shop's address would have been easy. He had come here after I left yesterday and investigated the cottage. Hazel had told him that he could find me at Mistletoe Creek Farm, where he had gotten my unlisted number by the simple expedient of asking Donna for it. I shivered. Myers was a purpose-driven man. He wasn't playing games or fooling around. Every step he took brought him a little closer.

And all of a sudden, I felt as if *I* were the one being stalked. Myers might be looking for Sally, but she was staying at my house. If she was a target, so was I. It wasn't a pleasant feeling.

I was dusting shelves, still thinking about this, when Ruby came through the connecting door carrying Grace, her daughter Amy's baby—the one Caitlin is so crazy about.

"Ooh, there she is," Ruby said brightly. "Say good morning to Gwamma's best friend, Pwecious."

Precious cooed and smiled at me, waving her chubby little hand. Laugh if you will, but I immediately felt better. I've never been the maternal type, but babies—especially plump little girls with pink cheeks and strawberry curls—are almost universally irresistible, aren't they? This one is especially beloved and especially pampered. Amy takes Grace to work with her at the vet clinic a couple of days a week, where she charms even the most savage beast. Amy's partner, Kate, an accountant, takes her to the office a couple of days, where she enchants both the staff and Kate's clients. Grandmama Ruby fills in whenever there's a gap. Lucky Grace, growing up with three adoring females and a gaggle of doting friends and admirers.

Make that four adoring females. I spent the next couple of minutes happily playing pat-a-cake with Precious, then remembered about lunch.

"Will you be here about one o'clock?" I asked. When Ruby nodded, I said, "That's good. Sally's coming by for lunch, and I thought maybe you'd like to join us." Earlier that morning, I had told her about the stalker's phone call and my plan for Caitlin to spend the night with Amy and Kate. Now, I filled her in on what I'd learned from Hazel and from Donna.

Ruby's eyes widened as I talked. "That guy was in the crowd last night, watching us?" she asked, shaking her head. "That is totally scary, China. He means business, doesn't he?"

"Sounds like," I said cautiously. Ruby read all the Nancy Drews when she was growing up and is now working her way through Kinsey Millhone's alphabet mysteries. Suggest that there is a crime in the neighborhood, and she immediately clicks into detective mode.

"I wonder where he's staying," she mused. "He shouldn't be too hard to find, if he's driving a yellow convertible. I don't think there's another one in town."

"Ruby," I said. "Don't."

She looked at me with her best, most innocent Lucille Ball, eyes-wide look. "Don't what?"

"Don't even *think* of doing what you are thinking of doing."

"How can I not think about doing whatever-it-is when I don't know what you don't want me to think about?" she asked reasonably. While I was trying to sort out an answer to that, she added, "Why don't you and Sally come over and spend the night at my house? There are neighbors all around, and old Mrs. Wauer and Oodles right next door. Oodles would never let a stalker come within a mile of the place without making enough racket to wake the dead."

I had to laugh at that. Oodles is a fat white miniature poodle attack dog with the heart of a pit bull, a maniac bark, and a bite like a snapping turtle. I once saw him go up against another of Ruby's neighbors. If Mrs. Ewell hadn't defended herself with an umbrella, Oodles would have had her for dinner.

"Thanks for the offer," I said, still chuckling. "I hate to leave Howard Cosell at home alone, though." When we all go away overnight, Howard goes to stay at the doggie resort hotel: the boarding kennel at the vet clinic where Amy works.

"Bring him along," Ruby said generously. "I'm sure Oodles would love to bark at Howard through the fence."

Another laugh. "I'll check it out with Sally when she comes for lunch," I said.

"That'll work," Ruby replied. She paused. "Have you told McQuaid about any of this?"

"There's no point in telling him. He's in Omaha. There's nothing he can do except worry about us." Which he would, of course. It's his cop personality shining through.

"I think you should tell him. If he knows there's a stalker hanging around, he might make a point of coming home early."

"Really? You think?" Somehow, this hadn't occurred to me.

"Sure. He's a detective, isn't he? Detectives like to detect, don't they? And he's an ex-cop. He's trained to protect. You've got his number on both counts." She patted Grace's cheek. "What a vewy pwetty girl you are, little sweetie-puss." Sweetie-puss giggled and flung both arms around her grandmother's neck.

I considered. Ruby was right. McQuaid is one of those guys who loves to dig up the answers to problems that nobody else can solve. It's what made him such a good cop. It also makes him a first-class private detective. When it comes to inquiry, he is both intuitive and relentless. He doesn't give up. And he is protective to the nth degree.

"Come home early," I mused. "Why didn't I think of that?" Because I'd been too busy handling it myself, that's why. But Sally is McQuaid's ex, not mine. He would probably be glad to take his share of the responsibility. "Thanks for the suggestion, Ruby." I glanced at the clock. It was eleven twenty. "I'll call him right now. If he's finished with his job, maybe he can get an early plane."

McQuaid came on at the third ring. It didn't take long to tell him the story, not including the part about Sally's lying about her house and her job, which I knew would set off an explosion. But even so, he did not immediately reply to my diplomatically phrased suggestion that he come home early. There was a noise like a car door slamming, and I pictured him with his cell phone to his ear, sliding into a car seat in a parking lot somewhere.

"Lord deliver us," he muttered angrily. "Every time that woman shows up, she brings along a truckload of trouble. I wish to hell she'd stay away."

That woman. How many times have I heard McQuaid say those words, in just that tone? What's more, there was part of me that agreed with him—the part that had her nose out of joint because Sally had lied about losing her house and her job. And her car.

But there was another part of me that disagreed violently, for my husband—who is as dear to me as myself—had just pushed one of my hot buttons.

"Hang on," I said hotly. "You're blaming the victim. This isn't Sally's fault. This man is a *stalker.*"

"Don't give me that BS," McQuaid growled. "Sally's got a track record, remember? If she's a victim, she's victimized herself. Every guy she's picked has been a loser. Every single guy."

"Present company excepted," I reminded him tartly.

"Yeah." He was heated. "All those other Romeos, they were rotten apples, every one of 'em. Remember the lawyer lover of hers? The one who was dealing? And the stockbroker who robbed her blind? God only knows what kind of bad-ass punk she's gotten tangled up with this time." His voice hardened. "Listen, China. I'm going to call Blackie and see if we can't get somebody to stay at the house tonight. Maybe he's got an off-duty deputy who can bunk on the sofa and—"

"We are *not* hiring a security guard," I snapped. "Caitlin will be with Amy and Kate. Brian is spending the night with Mike. And Sally doesn't want the police involved." I made my voice softer. "She's *your* ex-wife, you know. And she would have told you all this herself, if you'd taken the time to talk to her, the way she asked. Look, McQuaid. Why don't you see about getting an earlier plane? If you were home with us, this jerk wouldn't dare—"

"I am not coming home because I've still got stuff to do here," he interrupted sternly. "I have to finish an interview. I can't hop a plane every time Sally thinks she's got some sort of a problem. And she is my *ex*-wife, remember?" *Ex* got a strong emphasis. He was going to be stubborn about this.

"It's my problem, too," I pointed out in an acid tone. "And I am your *current* wife." *Current* got an even stronger emphasis.

There was a momentary silence, then, "Hang on." I heard the car engine starting. He probably wanted to run the heater. According to the Weather Channel this morning, the temperature in Omaha would stay below freezing all day, and there was a snowstorm on the way.

"Okay," he said, on the line again. "If you don't want somebody hanging out at our house, why don't you and Sal spend the night at Ruby's? She's got plenty of room." He chuckled. "You could have a girl party. Put grease on your face, drink piña coladas, talk about guys."

I resisted the impulse to tell him to stuff his "girl party." "I'd rather you come home early, McQuaid. It might be a good idea anyway. I heard on the news that there's a snowstorm heading for Omaha. If you wait until tomorrow, you might not be able to get home."

"You're right about that," he said ruefully. "It's colder than a witch's tit here, and the local forecasters are saying ice, as well as snow."

"Then come home."

"I told you," he said, in the long-suffering tone he uses when he's being asked to do more than two things at a time. "I can't. Not yet." He sighed. "Okay. This guy, this stalker. What's his name again?"

"Myers," I said. Why is it that men can't multitask? "Jess Myers. He's from Sanders, Kansas, according to Sally. What time do you think you can come home?"

"Sanders?" His voice rose.

"Right. Do you know the place?"

He grunted. "You bet I know it. Sally's parents were living there when we got married. She went to high school in Sanders. She and her sister grew up there."

"Really?" I was surprised. "She didn't tell me that he was a hometown guy."

"Why would she? She's playing Little Miss Innocent, China. She wants to get your sympathy. She's probably been stringing this smitten schmuck along for months, then got tired of him mooning around after her and dumped him. So this poor joe is not only besotted but pissed. He wants to find her, talk to her, try to get her back."

"Being besotted does not justify stalking," I retorted.

"No, but it *explains* it," he replied, irritatingly patient.

"Maybe. But pissed-off people can be dangerous. She is genuinely afraid of him, McQuaid. She says he's creepy." I thought of his voice, of the ominous edge that had sent chills up my spine. "He sounded plenty creepy to me, too. And he has her car. Her yellow convertible. Hazel Cowan saw him driving it."

"I am calling Blackie." McQuaid's tone was firm.

I know when I'm defeated. "Okay, you win," I conceded. "Don't call Blackie. Sally and I will spend the night with Ruby."

"Promise?"

"Promise."

"Good," he said, gamely trying not to sound triumphant. "My flight is scheduled for tomorrow evening. I'll see you then." He paused and added, gruffly. "Sorry to be the bad guy, China. Tell Sally to suck it up. And when I get home, the three of us are sitting down for a serious talk. I don't want to have to spend the holiday worrying that some love-struck stalker is out there, casing our house."

I hung up, feeling that I hadn't accomplished very much. But there wasn't time to think about it, because the lunch crowd was beginning to trickle in. Ruby parked Grace's baby bouncer in a corner where I could keep an eye on her until her mother came to pick her up, and went to help Laurel in the tearoom. Cass was serving one of her famous quiches today (Garden Quiche, with tomatoes, basil, and garlic), which always draws a crowd, mostly tourists or women from neighboring businesses on their lunch hour.

From that moment on, we were so busy that I didn't stop to look at my watch. At some point, Amy (who still wears the silver nose studs, multiple earrings, and intriguing tattoos that have earned her a reputation as Ruby's wild child) stopped in to pick up Baby Grace, who loves her mother just as she is, undomesticated hair and all. I confirmed that Amy would meet Caitlin after school and got a text message from Caitlin saying that she'd love to stay all night at Amy's, and maybe she could give Baby Grace her bath. With so much going on, it was nearly one thirty when I realized that Sally was a half hour late for lunch. And I was hungry. In fact, I was ravenous.

I hunted through my purse until I found the scrap of paper on which Sally had written her cell number. I picked up the phone and was about to punch it in when Ruby came in from the tearoom, pushing her hair out of her eyes and looking frazzled.

"I just got a call from the nurses' station at Castle Oaks," she said. "Mom's MIA again. Looks like she's gone on another walkabout."

"Oh, no!" I exclaimed, putting the phone down. "Oh, Ruby, I'm sorry."

"Me, too." She sighed. "I really, really, *really* need this not to be happening right now."

Ruby's mother, like many dementia patients, is prone to wandering. The nurses at Castle Oaks try to keep a close eye on her, but she's a wily old lady and occasionally gives them the slip. The last time she escaped by filching a coat from her roommate's daughter and slipping out the front door in the company of several other visitors. She got as far as the neighborhood supermarket, where she liberated three Hershey's chocolate bars and a bottle of apple juice. She was just finishing her snack when a clerk asked for money. When she said she had twenty-three million dollars in the bank but had forgotten to bring any of it with her, he called the cops. Doris was thrilled when she got an armed escort back to the nursing home.

"What can I do?" I asked with genuine sympathy. Ruby took on a big job when she moved Doris to Pecan Springs. I try to pitch in.

"Can you watch the shop? I have to go over to Castle Oaks and help them find her. I hope she had the sense to snatch a coat before she left. And a hat and gloves. It's cold outside." She started for the door to her shop. "Oh, and Laurel had to go home early. She and her husband are going out of town for the holiday. And Cass has already left, too. She had to go to the doctor."

"Sure, I'm not planning to go anywhere." I frowned. "Laurel won't be here to help out tomorrow?" So who was our backup, in case things got out of hand?

"Nope," Ruby tossed over her shoulder as she left. "Laurel is gone until after the first of the year."

Rats. No Laurel, and Cass was on the wounded list, and this was the holiday. We were definitely short-handed.

Ruby put her head through the door again. "Oh, and tell Sally I'm sorry I missed her. I'll catch her later."

"You didn't miss Sally. She missed us." Which reminded me that Sally was late, and that I really needed to talk to her about my conversation with McQuaid. And that I was really, really hungry. I reached for the phone again. No answer. I got voice mail.

"Where the heck are you, Sally?" I demanded. "I thought we were having lunch together."

By this time, I was seriously irritated, as well as hungry. Ruby's shop and mine were temporarily empty, so I made a quick expedition to the kitchen in search of leftover quiche. I put a slice on a plate, alongside a helping of chicken salad and a handful of blue corn chips, and took the food back to the shop, where I sat on the tall stool behind the counter and snatched quick bites in between phone calls and customers. The shop had emptied out and I was just finishing the last chip when the bell jingled and the door opened.

I looked up quickly, thinking it was Sally at last, and opened my mouth to give her a piece of my mind. But it wasn't. It was Sheila Dawson, our police chief—Smart Cookie to her friends.

"Hey, Sheila!" I said with a grin. "Nice to see you. It's been a while."

"It's our busy season," she said. "The mall is full of shoplifters, and every Christmas party seems to uncork a slew of drunk drivers." She took off her cap and returned my grin. "How are you, China?"

Sheila was uniformed in her usual natty blue and gray jacket, shirt, pants, and cap, her blond hair scooped into a bun at the back of her head. Even so, and with a radio on one hip and a holstered weapon on the other, she's beautiful. Somehow, it doesn't seem fair that there's so much firepower—intelligence, competence, confidence, and damned good looks—loaded into one woman. But while Smart Cookie might look like Miss Dallas costumed for the cover of *Law Enforcement Magazine*, I wouldn't mess with her, if I were you. She's an experienced cop with over a decade of law enforcement experience, not to mention being a crack shot. She can outshoot any of her officers, any day. And she don't take no sass, as the locals say.

"How am I?" I might have given other answers to that question, but I settled for the simplest. "Not too bad, I guess. We had a full house for lunch in the tearoom, which is good. But Doris went AWOL again. Ruby's out on patrol, looking for her."

Sheila rolled her eyes. "Poor Doris."

"Poor Ruby. Doris gets a kick out of it, if you ask me, especially when she's driven back to Castle Oaks in a squad car. Your uniforms ought to make her walk. There's nothing wrong with her legs, Ruby says."

Sheila chuckled. "Probably a good idea." She glanced around the shop. "Is Sally here?"

I raised my eyebrows. "Sally who?"

She turned back to me. "Don't give me that. You know who I mean. Sally Strahorn."

"Gee," I said, hamming it up. "I wonder how you found out that Sally's in town. Is it possible that when Sheriff Blackwell picked up the phone last night . . ." I let my voice trail off suggestively.

She ducked her head, coloring. "Yeah, you're right. I was with him when you phoned."

"Figures." I grinned, remembering that Blackie had sounded a bit groggy. Maybe I had caught them in flagrante delicto. "I won't ask what you were doing when I phoned. I wouldn't want to embarrass you. Anyway, I'd already heard that you two are a couple again. Ruby told me she saw you at Beans' the other night."

"News gets around, doesn't it?" She gave me a challenging look. "Okay with you?"

I held up both hands. "As long as you're happy, I'm happy, Smart Cookie. And I figured you wanted folks to talk, or you and Blackie wouldn't have showed up at Beans'." Everybody who is anybody in Pecan Springs hangs out there, and when two people are noticed to be a couple—especially when one is the police chief and the other is the county sheriff, and each was previously engaged to the other—the news spreads out like a tsunami. I added, "We're looking forward to seeing you and Blackie at the party on Saturday night."

"We're planning on it." Sheila put her palms on the counter, and I noticed, enviously, that her nails were beautifully manicured. Mine are not. I work in the garden every day. What Sheila mostly does is fill out paperwork. "What about Sally?" she repeated in a businesslike tone.

"I wish I knew." I pushed my empty plate away. "She was supposed to meet me here for lunch, but she didn't show. I got hungry and gave up waiting." I tilted my head, feeling curious. "What's up with you and Sally?

As I recall, the two of you didn't exactly hit it off the time or two you were together." Sally hadn't hit it off with any of my friends, actually. Sheila wasn't the only one.

Sheila was watching me. "How long has she been in town?"

This did not sound like an idle inquiry, and I felt a nudge of apprehension. "Why are you asking?" I countered.

"Official business," Sheila said crisply, and straightened, giving her gun belt a hitch. "How long?"

Uh-oh. Official business. A police matter. Maybe Sally had been involved in an accident before she showed up in Pecan Springs. Maybe this had something to do with Myers. Maybe—

But given Sally's previous record of weird behavior, there was no point in guessing. "Here's the straight scoop," I replied, equally crisp. "She showed up day before yesterday, around eleven, here in the shop."

"That would be Tuesday. Right?"

"Right. She was lugging a duffle bag. She said she'd ridden the bus into town. She didn't have a car or a place to stay or any money—"

I stopped, remembering my encounter with Bonnie Roth at the bank. Not having money was another one of the things Sally had lied about.

"She *said* she didn't have any money," I amended. "No money, no car. Which meant no motel. So I invited her to stay with us for the holiday."

The phone rang, and I picked it up quickly, thinking it might be Sally. "Is my mother there?" Ruby asked plaintively.

"I'm sorry, Ruby, she isn't. Why are you asking?"

"Because somebody saw her heading in that direction, walking fast," Ruby said, sounding disappointed. "Phone me if she shows up there—okay?"

"Okay." I glanced at Sheila. "Smart Cookie is here. Have you already called the cops?"

"Castle Oaks called when they first missed her," Ruby replied. "It's standard operating procedure. But tell Sheila, will you? Just in case."

"I already did," I said. "I also told her that her officers should make Doris walk back, just so she doesn't get too used to riding in those squad cars."

"Good idea." Ruby chuckled sadly. "Call me if you see her." She hung up.

"Ruby says Doris is hotfooting it in this direction," I reported. It would be funny if it weren't so sad.

Sheila took her radio off her belt, spoke into it briefly, and replaced it. "We're putting another car on this side of town. We'll find her." She went back to the subject. "I'm surprised to hear that you invited Sally to stay at your place over the holidays, China. I thought you weren't a big fan of hers."

"I'm not," I admitted. "But she seemed . . . well, different, I guess. Not quite the same old Sally. Ordinary clothes, no makeup, a little less attitude." Unfortunately, there was still some of the old Sally, the part that told lies, but I didn't see any point in going into this with Sheila. "Anyway, it's Christmas," I added. "Be of good cheer and all that. And she is Brian's mother, after all. He doesn't like to make a big deal about it, but he's glad to have her here." I looked at Sheila. "Why are you asking? What's she done?"

Sheila was matter-of-fact. "I don't know that she's done anything, China. But her sister is dead. I was notified by the Lake City chief of police about an hour ago."

I stared at her. "Leslie? *Dead?* Oh, god, Sheila! When? How?"

Leslie, dead. It was hard to believe. Leslie was a couple of years younger than Sally, which made her, oh, six or seven years younger than I am—a young woman, with most of her life ahead of her. Hearing something like this always stops me in my tracks. First there's a sweeping wave of regret and sadness, and then something else, something less noble, a great gratitude that I am still alive. What had happened? Some sudden illness, maybe, or an accident?

"You knew her?" Sheila asked.

I nodded. "Not as well as McQuaid or Brian. Leslie is—was Brian's favorite aunt. But yes, of course I knew her. She's visited us quite a few times." I paused. What was I going to tell Brian? He would be terribly upset. "How did it happen?"

"Sorry. I don't have the details."

"Well, I'm sure we'll fill in the gaps." I gave her a sadly grateful smile. "I appreciate your stopping by to tell Sally in person, Smart Cookie. Next-of-kin notification is no fun. Thank you for doing this."

I was already beginning to make mental lists. Leslie was divorced, no children. Sally was her only sister, and their parents were dead. Sally would have to go up to Lake City and do all the unhappy things that need to be done when a family member dies: make funeral arrangements, deal with the house and the furniture and the bills, notify people in the deceased's address book—all that difficult, painful stuff. I know how hard this is because I am still cleaning up my brother Miles' estate after his death last spring. It takes a long time and it hurts the whole while. Sally would want to leave for Lake City right away, and she might not be back for Christmas. She'd have to take Brian's car, I guessed. Or maybe she could wait until McQuaid got home, and he could drive her there. I was sure he would want to go to the funeral.

But Sheila was shaking her head. "I'm not here for next-of-kin notification, China. The Lake City police have named Sally Strahorn as a person of interest in her sister's death. They've requested that she be detained. They'll send an officer to interview her."

"A person of interest?" My head jerked up. "You're kidding. Why in the world—" I took a deep breath. A person of interest. This was not sounding good. Not good at all. "Okay, Sheila. Exactly how did Leslie die?"

Smart Cookie and I have been close friends for several years. What's more, I have been involved in several of her local cases—not, I hasten to add, as a person of interest, merely as an interested person. From time to time, I have even assisted the police, as the news media are fond of saying, in their investigations. Not that I go around inviting these things. They just happen. But still—

"I'm sorry, China." Sheila looked me straight in the eye. "It was a homicide."

Chapter Seven

McQuaid: Omaha

With a frown, McQuaid said good-bye to China, clicked off his cell phone, and sat back in the seat of his rented Chevy compact parked in the snowy lot outside the offices of Nebraska Asset Management Services in downtown Omaha.

A little while ago, he had concluded a preliminary conference with Peter Kennard, the man Charlie Lipman had sent him to track down and interview. Their conversation had been unexpectedly informative, and he'd gotten at least some of what Charlie was looking for—enough to know that there was more good stuff there. They might have wrapped things up this morning, but Kennard had a tight schedule. They couldn't complete the interview until tomorrow afternoon, which would give McQuaid just enough time to get to the airport, drop off the car, and catch a plane home.

McQuaid glanced at his watch and sighed. Eleven thirty. Over twenty-four hours to kill until tomorrow's interview. So how was he going to spend the time? Omaha had an art museum, the Joslyn, but museums weren't exactly his thing. It was too cold and snowy to go for a walk in the park. Hole up in the motel and watch TV? The prospect didn't fill him with enthusiasm. Maybe he'd stop by that little mystery bookstore over on Thirteenth. They might have a new Steven Havill or one of Bill Crider's mysteries. A couple of police procedurals, popcorn, crackers, cheese, a few beers—might not be a bad twenty-four hours after all.

He turned up the heater to high, feeling the warm air on his feet. He would've brought his boots if he'd known there'd be this much snow on the ground. Gloves, too, and a warmer coat. He looked out the window at the metallic sky, the dirty drifts along the perimeters of the parking lot, the leafless, spindly trees planted in gray cement containers, the racks of newspaper vending machines, the parking meters like iron soldiers lined up in military precision, wearing caps of melting snow. Not an inspiring view.

The bleakness outside the window matched the way he was feeling. He felt bad about the brusque tone he'd taken when China asked him to come home early. She phoned because she was trying to handle a bad situation—although probably not a dangerous one—and he'd all but bitten her pretty head off. He hoped she wasn't too mad about spending the night with Ruby. But that business with Sally's ex-boyfriend had pissed him off, and with good reason, too, damn it. Sally had a long history of sicko relationships. Sounded like this jerk was more of the same.

Angrily, he smacked the steering wheel with the flat of his hand. Whenever that woman was around, there was trouble, sometimes less, sometimes more, but always trouble. Like the time she snatched Brian and took him to the *Star Trek* convention without telling anybody, setting off a police manhunt. Or the time—

He grimaced, making himself stop. If he started down that road, he'd be there the whole freakin' day. He and Sally had been through a lot of ugly stuff in the few years they were married, and the divorce hadn't ended it. You could get a divorce, but when there was a child, you were still connected, like it or not.

He rubbed his hands together and held them briefly in front of the heater panel, frowning at the scrap of paper on which he had written the name China had given him. *Myers, Jess.* He hadn't needed to write *Sanders, Kansas,* because he knew the town, knew it from the dozen or more times he'd gone there with Sally when they were still married, when the Strahorns were still alive, before—

He shook his head, not liking to think of that, either, and pulled up a pair of happier images from his first visit there. He was still a Houston PD rookie with a shiny badge, Sally was just out of college, and they were too young to have a clue to what marriage was all about and whether they were right for each other, which they weren't, as it turned out. But Sally was pregnant with Brian. When she said she was going to get an abortion, he'd put his foot down, fast and hard. Not that he was opposed to abortion in general—women had a right to choose, and he had no problem with that. But this was his kid, by god, his boy. His just as much as hers, which meant that he had every right to insist. That was the way he saw it, anyway. If she'd do her part and carry the child, he'd do his part and marry her. What's more, he'd try his damnedest to make it work.

So Sally had bought a fancy dress, they'd driven up from Houston to Sanders, and the Strahorns had arranged a ceremony in the First Methodist Church and a big party at their house afterward. The whole town showed up with wedding presents and best wishes—more for the sake of Mr. and Mrs. Strahorn than for Sally or him, he thought, but whatever, it was nice. It was Christmas then, too, and there had been a fresh snow and carolers in the yard and a Christmas tree with lights and tinsel and a big

121

holiday dinner, and Sally's parents and her younger sister Leslie had been graciously welcoming to their unexpectedly married daughter and her newly minted husband, who felt out of place and a little bit alone in the midst of all this family and small-town camaraderie.

But not for long. Mrs. Strahorn—Mama Lucy, she liked him to call her—was a pretty, petite lady with a sweet voice and a cap of iron gray curls precisely arranged at the local beauty parlor every Wednesday morning. She made a big fuss over her new son-in-law, asking him what he liked to eat and fixing it for him. Old Mr. Strahorn, as Kansas as they came, was a bluff, cordial man with rough, red hands who sold crop insurance for a living and knew every farmer in a fifty-mile radius of Sanders. He invited McQuaid to go with him on his business calls, introducing him with pride as "Sally's husband, he's a big-city cop and a tough son of a bitch, so you better not hand me any of your usual flimflam when he's around." McQuaid had enjoyed meeting the people, likable, salt-of-the-earth Kansans, had even enjoyed—more than he expected—being the Strahorns' son-in-law. In fact, he had thought even then (and kept on thinking it) that he liked being their son-in-law more than he liked being Sally's husband.

The Strahorns, a prosperous couple, lived in a white frame house with green shutters and screen doors, pretty in the way of old farmhouses, with a wide porch and elm trees around it and a stretch of grass out front, and a big vegetable garden and a red barn in the back, although the house was in town. Sanders was fairly small, maybe forty-five hundred people, and its citizens went in for barns and gardens and chickens and even pigs. That was part of its charm. Real down-home America, as solid as the high-school homecoming dance and church suppers and the Fourth of July parade down Main Street. That's why it was so hard to accept what had happened to the Strahorns. Something like that doesn't happen in down-home America.

Except that it had. It had happened.

McQuaid's mouth tightened, and he put the car in gear. He'd been a cop for a long time, and he'd seen more than his share of brutality. But what had happened to Sally's folks wasn't something he liked to think about, ever. He checked his rearview, and backed out of his space. It was time to get some lunch, and since he had so many hours to kill, he could blow off the usual fast food and have a real meal. He had noticed a promising-looking Italian restaurant down the street, so he pulled out of the lot, swung around the corner, drove a couple of blocks, parked, and went in.

After the chill wind sweeping down the street, the restaurant was warm and fragrant with the spicy smell of tomato sauce. He bought a copy of the *Omaha World-Herald* and took a seat by the front window, his back to the wall, a habit from his days on the force that he'd never quite been able to break. The lunch special was spaghetti and meatballs, which suited him just fine, with fresh, hot garlic bread (there were other herbs in it—China could have told him which ones), the house salad (marginally acceptable), and a glass of red wine.

He caught up on the sports, football mostly, while he lingered in a leisurely fashion over his meal, finishing off with cannoli (first rate) and coffee. No point in rushing, since he had nothing else to do but pick up a book or two and head for the motel. Anyway, it had started to snow, and he was enjoying the sight, since it rarely snowed in Pecan Springs. Oh, maybe once in a blue moon, although he remembered one year, before he and China were married, when they got a four-inch snowfall the week the students came back for January registration, and everything on the campus came to an icy stop. Outside the window, the fat white flakes were falling fast and faster, swirling through the air on eddies of wind, tossed and tumbled like feathers. It looked like they'd be getting a helluva lot more than four inches.

He had just eaten the last bite of cannoli when his cell phone rang. He flicked it open, saw the number, and sighed. Sally. Damn. Good thing she hadn't called before he'd eaten. Might've lost his appetite.

"What's up, Sal?" he asked shortly. She hated being called Sal, so he did it whenever he got the chance.

"Are you where we can talk?" she asked hesitantly.

"Yeah. Just finished lunch." He paused. "Heard you had a little problem last night. Old boyfriend, huh?" He let her hear the barb. "Some poor schmuck who just can't bear to let you walk out of his life, I suppose."

If it stung, she didn't let on. "China told you, I suppose."

"Yeah. So who is this jerk? Anybody I know?"

Probably not. He'd tried not to keep track of Sally's boyfriends, unless Brian was somehow involved in the situation. Then he felt obliged—although there was precious little he could do to keep her out of bad relationships. That was her modus operandi, one no-good bum after another. She had tried to blame it all on that Juanita character, that "personality" she had invented. Dissociative identity disorder, the therapist had called it. But he was skeptical about that kind of stuff, at least as far as Sally was concerned. He didn't dispute the diagnosis, but this multiple personality business might be just a convenient way for her to do whatever the hell she wanted to do and let Juanita take the blame.

"That's what I need to talk to you about, Mike." Her voice was wire-thin, tense, and he pictured her clenching her hands. "I tried to get you to sit down with me the other night, but you wouldn't. Now I have to get you to *listen* to me. But please do it without getting mad."

"Mad? What's there to be mad about?" He chuckled sarcastically. "You don't write to your son, don't phone, don't even shoot him an email. You show up broke, on foot and without a vehicle, and announce that you're moving in for the holidays. And then this meathead starts making threatening phone calls to our unlisted number. And now you're telling me not to be mad? Come on, Sal. Get real."

He knew he shouldn't be doing this, shouldn't let her know that she could still get under his skin. But he couldn't help himself. It wasn't that he cared about her any longer. That feeling, strong as it once had been, was dead and buried. The trouble was that he still felt responsible for a lot of what had happened to her. His being a cop, but worse, his liking for being a cop, his insistence on being a good cop, the *best* cop—that had changed her, hurt her, in big ways and small. Too many ways, too many hurts.

China said that Sally should have been stronger, should have coped. But China was tough, competitive. She'd been one of the best criminal attorneys he'd ever seen, and he'd seen plenty. When she left the law and put her money into her shop, she was still competitive: sharp, smart, focused, determined. She'd made it work against all the odds. When times were tough, China just got tougher and smarter. He loved her for that.

Sally had never been tough. When he married her, she was still just a vulnerable kid. He'd known that, known how fragile she was, and still—

Sally broke into the silence. In a small voice, she said, "Just listen, please. The man who phoned your house last night—his name is Jess Myers. Does that ring a bell?"

Jess Myers. The name he had written down on the scrap of paper. "Nope. Should it? This is somebody I'm supposed know?"

"He lives in Sanders. He came to our wedding."

"Yeah, well, if I remember right, several of your old boyfriends came to our wedding." Another sarcastic chuckle. "They were first in line to kiss the bride. Remember? In fact, one of them spent quite a few minutes kissing the bride, enthusiastically, as I recall. Was that Myers? Did he finally figure out that you're single again and decide to get back in the game? I guess some guys never learn."

"Please, Mike, stop." She was speaking just above a whisper, and her voice was raw and edgy. "This isn't easy for me. I need you to do something, and I don't quite . . . I mean, I know I shouldn't . . ." She swallowed audibly. "You're in Omaha. Right?"

She needed him to do something for her. Something she knew she shouldn't ask. How many times had he heard that? And when he did what she wanted (which he almost always did, even though he damn well knew better), what did he get? More freakin' trouble, that's what.

Cautiously, he said, "Yeah, I'm in Omaha. On business. What about it?"

"I need you to drive down to Sanders, Mike. I want you to talk to somebody."

Sanders? Now, that was a joke. A real side-splitter. "You gotta be kidding, Sal." He looked out the window. "It's snowing here, and colder than the north end of Hades. I'm not going anywhere except to the bookstore for a couple of books and then back to the motel. I've got a meeting tomorrow afternoon, and then it's out to the airport and home. And when I get there, you and I are going to have a talk about that jerk who called the house last night."

She ignored that. "Really, Mike, it won't take you that long to drive." She was using the tone she always used when she was trying to work a con job on him. "It's only a hundred and twenty miles. Two hours, tops. It's one o'clock now. You could be there by three and back to Omaha by bedtime. All I need you to do is talk to this person. Her name is Joyce Dillard."

"You want to talk to somebody, pick up the phone and talk to her yourself. Anyway, it's a hundred and *forty* miles." McQuaid glanced through the window. "And it's snowing like a blasted sonuvagun. The roads will be a mess. Why in the world would I—"

"Not I-29. It won't be bad at all. They keep it plowed because of the trucks. And I've tried calling Joyce. She doesn't answer. Anyway, I want somebody else to hear what she has to say. I mean, I want *you* to hear it. You're a cop. You'll know what to do next."

A cop? "Hear what? What's all this about, Sally?"

"It's complicated. I can't go into it over the phone. You'll understand when you . . . when you talk to her."

He frowned. "Does this have to do with Myers?"

"Please, Mike. Just say you'll talk to her. Please."

"Myers," he persisted. "You told China that he's a former boyfriend. Is that true?"

"Yes, sort of. I mean, I dated him, a long time ago." There was a pause on the other end of the line. Then Sally said, very low, "You have to talk to Joyce Dillard, Mike. She . . . She says she knows who killed my parents."

Everything around him seemed to become very still. No sound, no motion. He held the phone to his ear, staring at a reddish brown spot on the tablecloth. Spaghetti sauce. Next to the spot was a second, orangy yellow. Italian dressing. The two spots blurred, merged, went out of focus.

Sally's parents were killed ten years ago. No, more like eleven, because Brian was four or five and he and Sally were breaking up. He was still with the Houston PD, and she was drinking and taking antidepressants in those wildly dangerous up-and-down cycles that usually end up all the way down, with a fatal overdose and a cold body on a slab in the morgue. Juanita was around sometimes, too, going on buying binges, filling the closets with expensive clothes and dozens of pairs of shoes. He'd stuck with it as long as he could, hating to admit that his marriage was a failure, bitterly ashamed that he hadn't been able to give Sally enough of what she needed and she'd had to make up for it by buying all those clothes. But he'd finally reached the point where he couldn't stand it any longer. He'd taken Brian to Seguin to stay with his parents, got a cheap apartment closer to the station, and filed for divorce.

That's when it happened, a couple of weeks after he moved out. The word hadn't come from Sally but from Leslie, who called him at work to tell him that the Strahorns had been shot to death and their sizable cash stash stolen. He was used to death—in fact, that was one of the bitternesses Sally kept throwing up to him when they argued, that his skin was a cop's skin, bulletproof, tough as rhino hide, and that none of her suffering ever got through to him. Maybe she was right.

But this got through like a knife in the gut. He had loved Mama Lucy for her sweetness and patience, and respected Mr. Strahorn for all he knew about Kansas crops and weather and the tough times farmers faced. He had admired them for making a life where life had put them, and loving their kids and supporting the town. And now they were dead, senselessly, stupidly, brutally dead, in an apple-pie, lace-doily, flag-flying town where everybody square-danced at the VFW on Saturday night and worshipped in church on Sunday.

Sally hadn't handled it well, of course. The murders had spiraled her into an even wilder tailspin, and she had forbidden him to go to Sanders for the funeral: "Not *your* family," she had spat at him. "Not anymore."

Leslie had felt differently. She had begged him to come, but he hadn't, since the sight of him would have sent Sally over the edge for sure. Leslie was a good girl, the apple of her parents' eyes, and Brian loved her because she read to him and made him laugh in a way his mother never did. Later, after Leslie moved to Texas, to Lake City, she always invited Brian to spend a summer month or so with her. For a while, McQuaid had even thought that the two of them—he and Leslie—might get romantically involved, which would have made Brian happy. But they'd held back because of Sally, and then he'd met China, and that was the end of that.

Anyway. After the murders he had kept in touch with the Strahorn case—through Leslie, since Sally hadn't wanted anything to do with him. When Les reported that the Sanders police seemed to be pretty much out of leads, he'd toyed with the notion of taking a couple of weeks off and driving up there to see what he could dig up. But he'd decided against it. Sanders wasn't his turf. He'd only antagonize the local police, and likely for nothing. If the murders could be solved, they'd do it. And then the divorce had gone through and he'd brought Brian back from Seguin to live with him, and life had gotten so complicated that everything else— Sally's latest follies, Juanita's wildness, even the Strahorns' murders— faded into the background.

And now the murders were foreground again, front and center. The two blurry spots on the tablecloth separated, became what they were, spaghetti sauce and Italian dressing. A dish clattered in the kitchen. The restaurant door opened and a woman in a green coat came in, her hair dusted with snowflakes. She said something to the hostess, and they laughed.

"Dillard claims she knows who killed your parents?" McQuaid demanded roughly. "Did she say who? Does she have any evidence?"

"She gave me a name, but I'd rather not say. She told me where to find the gun, and some other evidence. But I don't want . . ." She stopped. "I'd rather you talked to her."

"When did she tell you this?"

"Not long ago. A few days."

"Where? How did you connect with her?"

"I went to Sanders. I was trying to—that is, I was hoping to . . ." Sally's voice trailed away.

"Hoping to what?"

The words came out in a rush, propelled by (he thought) her effort to overcome her natural propensity to lie. "I was working for the newspaper in Kansas City. I was stuck in Advertising, but I heard about a reporting job opening up. I've always wanted to get back into reporting, and I thought if I could write a really good story, a true-crime story with a local angle, I'd maybe have a shot at it. Sanders is local to KC—it's in the same media market. So I went back home and talked to a few—"

"You were using your parents' murders to get a *job*?" McQuaid demanded incredulously.

"Not their murders." Sally was heated. "That would be despicable."

"Yeah, it would," McQuaid said, disgusted. But despicable wouldn't keep Sally from doing whatever the hell she wanted to do. Wouldn't keep her from trying to rope him into it, either.

"I wouldn't do that, Mike, honest," she said plaintively. "I was going to focus on the police investigation, from a human-interest point of view. *My* point of view, as a daughter. That's entirely different. And totally legitimate. Lots of books get written by family members after a tragedy."

Oh, so it wasn't just a job she was after, he thought in even greater disgust. It was a book contract. Next to being an actress, being a writer had been Sally's dream. Trust her to have her eyes on the grand prize, always. And he didn't buy her claim that she was focusing on the investigation. If she wanted a book deal, or even just the job, she'd have to include the lurid stuff, the murders. The bodies, the blood, the sickening horror of it. That would be her hook—that, and the fact that she was the victims' daughter. Sally, poor, poor Sally, the victims' grieving daughter.

So what exactly did she want from him? He scowled, thinking back over what she had said.

"This Dillard woman," he said. "How'd you get connected with her?"

"She's a friend of . . . She's somebody I knew in high school. Most of us left Sanders. You know what it's like—there's not much opportunity if you want to make something of your life. But Joyce stayed. Her father is on the town council, and the family is connected with just about everything. That's why—" She cleared her throat. "I mean, I think she really does know, Mike."

"So what did she tell you?" He didn't try to keep the skepticism out of his voice.

"Uh-uh. *You* have to talk to her, Mike. You're a cop. An ex-cop, I mean. You'll know how to handle it."

Yeah. That was Sally for you. Wanting to rope him in on her literary project. Wanting him to do the investigating for her, so she'd have something more to write about. God only knew what else she wanted. He took out his pen and wrote *Joyce Dillard* on the paper napkin. "Give me her number."

"Wait a sec, and I'll get it." There was a short pause. "Here it is."

He wrote it down. "Okay," he said. "Anybody else in Sanders you'd like me to talk to?"

That got her attention. Her voice was suddenly eager. "Then you'll go to Sanders? You'll talk to Joyce?"

"I'll *call* her," McQuaid said firmly. He looked out the window onto the rapidly drifting street. "I told you, Sal. It's snowing like hell here. The roads will be a mess."

"But calling won't work. You won't be able to find out—"

"You'd be surprised at what I can find out. I'm an investigator, remember?" He paused, thinking about the stalker. "Where are you?"

There was a momentary silence. "In Pecan Springs," she said guardedly. "Where else?"

No matter. He had her cell number. "Okay. You sit tight and stay out of trouble. You hear?"

Another silence, and then the connection was abruptly broken. McQuaid stared at the phone, tempted to call her back and make her say good-bye, like a grown-up. But she'd just say he was treating her like a child (which he was, because she was), so he resisted. He thought for a moment, then clicked on Sheriff Blackwell's number. He got him on the second ring.

"China told me that you sent somebody out to have a look at the house last night," McQuaid said. "Thanks, buddy."

"No problem. Glad to do it." Blackie paused. "Everything okay?"

"Probably. Hard to tell with Sally." He reported what China had told him, ending with, "I don't know what Myers is after. But to be safe, China is sending Caitie to Amy's for the night, and Brian's sleeping over with a friend. China and Sally will be at Ruby's. Thought you ought to know—in case your deputy happens to notice any action out our way tonight. The house should be empty, except for the dog." Howard could batch it for one night. He had his dog door for the necessities. He'd be okay.

"Will do," Blackie said. "It's a good idea to get the kids out of there." He paused. "Are you thinking that this is maybe just another one of your ex's little parlor games?"

McQuaid smiled crookedly to himself. He and the sheriff had played poker and fished together for years, and Blackie had heard too many of his tales about Sally's wild antics. "Who the hell knows?" he replied. "Where Sally is concerned, there's no predicting."

"Yeah," Blackie said. He paused, as if there might be more to say on the subject, then asked, in a different tone, "Did Sheila call you?"

McQuaid heard the tone. Something there. "No," he said. "Why?"

"No particular reason." Blackie cleared his throat. "Sheila and I are making another run at it." Blackie was a man of few words, but McQuaid knew him well enough to know that this made him happy.

"Glad to hear it," McQuaid said warmly. Blackie hadn't been the same since he and Sheila split the year before. He had seemed lonely, almost desolate, not quite sure where he was going or why. "Hope it works out for you this time."

Blackie chuckled. "Yeah. Me, too. It's a risk. But in this life, everything's a risk. Get a couple of good days, you feel like you hit a gold mine."

"Amen to that," McQuaid said. "Is that why you asked if Sheila had called me? To tell me that the two of you are back together?"

"No," Blackie said. His voice changed. "Something else. I'll let her tell you. Catch you later, buddy."

McQuaid frowned as he clicked off the phone and slipped it into his pocket. Maybe he'd call Sheila. But maybe not. Sounded like trouble, and he was in no mood. He finished his coffee, settled with the waitress for his lunch, and shrugged into his coat. Outside, the snow was beginning to pile up on the roofs of parked cars and drift against the buildings. The temperature was dropping, the sidewalk glazing with ice. In the distance, muted by the snow, traffic growled on the freeway, punctuated by the wail of a siren, an accident, most likely. Bound to be plenty of that today.

McQuaid was glad he didn't have far to drive—just to the bookstore and back to the motel, where he'd make that phone call for Sally. To tell the truth, he was intrigued at the idea that somebody in Sanders might be holding on to information about the Strahorns' murders. But he'd be damned if he'd help Sally dig up information for some sensational book she wanted to write. Hell, no. He'd make the call, then stretch out on the bed to read. Might even catch a few z's.

Yeah. He shoved his hands into his pockets, whistling cheerfully, and set off in the direction of the car—walking carefully, because of the ice. It was going to be a good afternoon, after all.

Chapter Eight

In Wales, the celebration of Boxing Day (the day after Christmas) included the tradition of "holly-beating" or "holming." (*Holm* is the Welsh word for holly). Young men and boys would teasingly slap the unprotected arms or legs of young women and girls with holly branches (perhaps a means of getting the girls to lift their skirts a few inches?). In some areas it was the custom for the late-risers to be swatted with sprigs of holly—a good reason for getting up early on Boxing Day.

China Bayles, "Hollies for Your Garden,"
Pecan Springs Enterprise

"Homicide? Leslie?" I stared at Sheila, still trying to comprehend what she had said. "What kind of homicide? How was she killed? A gun? A knife? A blunt object? What?"

The chief frowned and gave her head a warning shake, meaning that this was cop stuff, confidential, top secret. If Smart Cookie knew the inside story, she wasn't going to tell me.

I swallowed hard, still trying to come to terms with what I had heard. I thought of Leslie, pretty, petite, perky, the third-grade teacher you always wished you'd had, who could turn the times tables into a giggly game or teach a kid how to hold a rabbit or build a drum out of an oatmeal box. If Sally had been the bad girl of the very proper Strahorn family, the wayward, not-quite-respectable daughter, Leslie had been the good girl, the solid citizen, respected schoolteacher, apple of her parents' eye.

And now Leslie was the victim of a homicide. And crazy Sally—Sally/Juanita, she of the multiple identities—was a "person of interest." Why? What had she done that made the cops want to come after her?

Sheila was watching my face, reading my feelings, which were naked and exposed. "Did the two of them get along? Sally and her sister, I mean."

I didn't answer immediately. I could see where this was going. Sheila—who was a very good cop, trained to do her job—was pumping me for information. Anything I told her that was relevant to the case would be relayed to the Lake City police, to assist in their interview with their "person of interest."

But I have a problem with this, a big problem. The words "suspect," "subject," "target," and "material witness" are defined by law, and everyone knows what they mean. The phrase "person of interest," on the other hand, lacks any legal definition or evidential standard. It can mean anything the authorities—local, state, even federal—want it to mean. Sometimes they use it to keep their guy from lawyering up, as sensible people have a natural tendency to do when they find themselves in the clutches of the cops. Other times, they use it to let the media know that they're on the lookout for someone they can't immediately lay their hands on, who just might be involved with a case they're pursuing, although they can't specifically tell you how or wouldn't if they could. The media puts the word out, and the next thing you know, the "person of interest" is either reported to be "cooperating" with authorities or prudently leaves town, which is taken, both by the media and the cops, as an admission of guilt.

Now, you might not immediately see a problem with this—until *you* become a "person of interest," that is. Imagine that your next-door neighbor is found dead in her garden, killed with a sharp whack from her garden spade. Imagine that the two of you have had a few unneighborly disagreements over the years—she has a dog and the dog has a habit of digging up your rosebushes, say—and that these little squabbles have been witnessed by other neighbors.

Now imagine that you pick up the local paper and find your photograph on the front page. The cops want to find out what you know about this homicide. You're a good citizen, so you go in for an interview, and then you're called back for another and another. Imagine that the cops turn up no other leads for weeks and weeks, and that they—and the newspaper and the local television channels, which seem to have no other news but *your* news—continue to regard you as the only "person of interest" in the case.

What happens if this cloud hangs over your head for days, weeks, months, for a year? How are your friends going to feel? Your neighbors? Your boss? Your mother? After a while, in the mind of the public, you become the prime suspect without a single charge being filed or a single hearing held. Tragically, the term "person of interest" has the potential to tar and feather innocent people who have nothing to do with a crime.

And if you think this can't happen, think again. It happens, and far too often. "Person of interest" has wormed its way into the national lexicon in recent years, and has been used in several high-profile cases seized on by the national media. In some instances, the "persons of interest" have filed lawsuits and won them, sometimes for hundreds of thousands of dollars. All of us, including the media and the cops, have to remember that *all persons* are innocent until they are proven guilty. And that includes Sally Strahorn—or Juanita or whoever else she may be.

I took a deep breath, composed my features, and said, very deliberately,

"Afraid I can't be of much help, Chief. Sally has never told me how she feels about Leslie."

Sheila sighed. "Oh, please. Don't go getting all lawyerly on me, China."

"Hey," I countered. "I *am* a lawyer. Remember?"

This is true. I may not be in practice at the moment, but you never know. I keep my bar membership current, just in case the shop goes under or there's a sudden family crisis. It's good to have a backup.

"As if I could forget," Sheila muttered, rolling her eyes.

"And why do the cops want to talk to Sally?" By this time, I had fully switched into what McQuaid calls my *hackles-up mode*. My defense-attorney mode. "Why are they calling her a 'person of interest'?"

Another sigh. "Sorry, China. I honestly don't know, and even if I did, I couldn't tell you. But since you're a lawyer, you already know that."

"Yeah, I do." I got off the stool and stood facing her, hands on my hips. "But here's something I can tell *you*, Chief Dawson, and please take notes. Since you were at Blackie's last night when I called, you already know that Sally is being stalked."

Her eyebrows went up. "Really? I thought it was just a matter of a former boyfriend on the phone, wanting to give her a hard time."

"He might be a former boyfriend, but he is also a stalker," I said with emphasis. "His name is Jess Myers. He's from Sanders, Kansas, the same town where Sally—and Leslie, too—grew up. The Lake City police ought to know about this man, in case there's a connection to Leslie. To her *homicide*," I added firmly. "Maybe they should add him to their 'persons of interest' list."

"Thank you, Counselor," Sheila said steadily. "I'll pass along the tip." She took a small notebook out of her pocket and flipped it open. "Jess M-y-e-r-s?"

"I think so. There's a good chance that he's driving Sally's car. A yellow convertible. Hazel Cowan, who's staying in our bed-and-breakfast, saw him last night, hanging around the cottage. He may have tried to force the kitchen window."

She scribbled for a moment longer, getting it all down. "Description?"

"Dark hair, dark-rimmed glasses, medium height." I thought for a moment. "And a mole. Under his right eye."

"Tags on the convertible?"

"Kansas, I suppose. You could run the registration. Hazel Cowan saw him driving it." I took a breath. "There's more, too. I don't know the whole story, but this isn't the first homicide in that family. The Strahorns—Leslie and Sally's parents—were shot to death about ten years ago. Just before McQuaid and Sally were divorced."

Sheila frowned, her attention now fully focused. "Where was that?"

"In Sanders, where they lived. I don't know the details, but McQuaid does. You can ask him."

She nodded, looked over her notes, and said, "How about Sally's cell phone? Do you have the number?"

I was saved from answering by the bell over Ruby's shop door, which chose that auspicious moment to jangle. "Excuse me," I said. "I'm the only one here this afternoon. I need to go next door and take care of Ruby's customer."

"No problem. I'll be right here." Sheila reached for her radio, switching it on. I hoped she was going to pass on the information about the Strahorns.

But the customer wasn't a customer. She was Ruby's mother. Doris was wearing a green sweater over her cotton print dress, a red coat three sizes too large (obviously borrowed) over the sweater, and fluffy pink rabbit slippers with floppy ears. Her sparse gray hair was disheveled, and her nose was red with cold. As I came in, she was slipping a box of rune stones into the pocket of her coat.

"Ramona," she said querulously, and pointed toward the stairs that go up to the loft. "I saw Ramona go up there. Tell her to come down. I've been standing here waiting for her."

"Ramona isn't here," I said. "You mean Ruby." For the past year or so, Doris hasn't been able to keep her daughters straight. Ruby is the one who looks after her, making sure she has what she needs and that she is well cared for. Ramona (Ruby's sister) lives in a posh north Dallas suburb and stays away as much as possible. Daughters are not created equal—at least, not created with an equal sense of obligation to their mothers. "But Ruby didn't go up the stairs," I added. "She's out looking for you."

Doris gave me a withering look. "It wasn't Ruby. I know Ruby. She's tall and thin as a rail. She needs to eat more. And stop doin' those things to her hair. She looks like a scarecrow wearin' a red dust mop on her head. I know my own daughters, don't I? It was Ramona I saw." She scowled. "Who the hell are you?"

Doris has known me for years. "I'm China," I said patiently. "Are you cold, Doris? Let's get you a cup of hot tea while I make a phone call." I took her by the elbow and began to steer her toward my shop.

She pulled away. "China," she said scornfully. "You think I just came in on the turnip truck? You're no more from China than I am. Your eyes are all wrong." With her fingers, she pushed up the corners of her eyes to show me what mine ought to look like. She puckered up her mouth. "Shame on you, lyin' to a poor old woman."

The door burst open again, and Ruby rushed in. "Mom!" she cried, gathering Doris into her embrace. "Oh, thank God you're safe! We've been looking everywhere for you."

"Well, you weren't lookin' for me very hard, I guess," Doris said critically. "I've been standin' right here on this very same spot for the past hour, waiting for Ramona to come down those stairs." She glowered at me. "Something was said about tea quite some time ago, but I haven't had it yet. More lies," she added contemptuously. "That's folks for you. Always lyin' to old people. Ought to be ashamed."

Three minutes, I mouthed to Ruby, over her head.

Ruby nodded, understanding. "Tell you what, Mom. We'll go back to Castle Oaks and get you a cup of tea there—and some cookies, too. Everybody's been so worried."

Doris pulled herself up. "I'm not going back there," she said with great dignity. "That's why I'm here. So Ramona can take me home." She pointed up the stairs. "That's where she is—up there. I saw her with my very own eyes. You go and get her. Make her come down here and take me home."

"Ramona is in Dallas right now, Mom," Ruby said, putting her arm around Doris' shoulder. "I talked to her on the telephone not ten minutes ago. I'm afraid she can't—"

At that moment, two orderlies from the nursing home, wearing jackets over their scrubs, appeared in the door. "We've brought the van," one of them said to Ruby. "We'll take her back to Castle Oaks."

"No!" shrieked Doris, when she saw them. "Stay away from me. I'm not going back there!" She flung out her arms and backed into a display, which went over with a crash, spilling china angels and fairy tree ornaments onto the floor. "Ramona!" she screeched. "You come on down here and save me! I'm being kidnapped!"

The connecting door opened and Sheila appeared. "Do we have a problem here?" she asked pleasantly. "May I help you, Doris?"

Doris stopped screeching and brightened. "Oh, there you are. I knew you'd come. You'll take care of me. The police always take care of old folks when they're lost."

"Of course we'll take care of you," Sheila replied gently. "But I'm afraid I'm here on business, so I can't give you a lift back to Castle Oaks."

"Oh, pooh," Doris stamped one pink-rabbit-clad foot. "I saw your car outside and I thought you'd take me."

Ah, I thought. Sheila's police car. Yes. This visit had nothing to do with Ruby or Ramona. Doris was looking for a ride in a squad car—that was all.

"I'm very sorry. But please let me make sure that you get safely out to the van." Sheila extended her arm to Doris. "Shall we?"

"Well, since you're being so kind." Doris gathered her too-large coat around her, lifted her chin, and accepted the chief's arm with an imperial smile. Trailed by the orderlies, they left the shop. It was a bizarre parade.

"Thank heavens," Ruby muttered. She turned to me. "Has Sally shown up?"

"No," I said. "Not a sign of her." I took a deep breath. "And something awful has happened, Ruby. Sally's sister Leslie was killed, up in Lake City where she lives. The Lake City police have named Sally as a person of interest. Sheila is here, looking for her. She hasn't asked me yet, but I'll have to tell her that Sally's driving Brian's blue Ford. I'm sure they'll put out an APB on it."

Ruby paled. "Leslie, dead? Omigod, China, I can't believe that!" The two of them—Ruby and Leslie—had met several times during Leslie's visits here. "She's such a lively young woman, so pretty and—"

"Lively young women can get dead, too," I said glumly. "It happens all the time."

"But why are the police interested in *Sally*?" Ruby cried. "They can't think . . . They couldn't possibly believe that she would kill her *sister*! Not even Sally would do a thing like that." She put her hand to her mouth. "Unless—"

"Unless what?"

Ruby's eyes were huge. "Unless Juanita did it."

"Ruby, I really don't think—"

"You don't know about split personalities? One part of the self can do something that the other part of the self would never even imagine—like pick up a gun and shoot somebody, for instance."

One of the nursing home orderlies opened the door. "Are you coming back to Castle Oaks, Ms. Wilcox? We're ready to go."

"Yes, I'm coming," Ruby replied in a harried tone. To me, she said, "This is something you need to think about, China. Split personalities are—" She gulped.

"We'll be in the van," the orderly said, and left.

"I am so sorry about Leslie." Ruby hugged me. "I'll be back as soon as I've got Mom settled."

"Better lock her in," I said and went to get the broom. I had finished sweeping up the pieces and replacing the ornaments on the display when I thought I heard a thump upstairs in the loft. I was about to go and investigate, but Sheila came back at that moment.

"Poor old thing," she said, shaking her head sadly. "I hope I go before my mind does."

"You should have seen her in her heyday," I said, giving one last critical look to the display. "All starched and buttoned up to the chin, spine stiff as a board, voice like a drill sergeant." The old Doris had no sense of humor, was right about everything, and always had to have the last word. The new Doris is sometimes a little hard on the nerves, but I think I like her better. She has more humanity.

The bell over my door jingled, and Sheila followed me back into my shop, where two older ladies, coiffed in delicate blue white curls, courtesy of the stylists at Bobby Rae's House of Beauty, had paused to look at the last two of Donna's wreaths. I recognized them as members of the Pecan Springs Book Club, which meets for lunch on the third Wednesday of the month in the tearoom. The two Bookies (that's what they call themselves) gave Sheila's uniform a quick, curious glance, exchanged disapproving looks, then turned their backs.

"I've already passed on the information about the Strahorn murders to the Lake City police. Myers' information, too," Sheila said in a low voice. "But we need to talk to Sally as soon as possible. Do you know what she's driving?"

Asked directly, I had to answer. I nodded. "We loaned her the car Blackie sold us for Brian. Dark blue four-door Ford, five years old. Dented left rear." Minor damage. We'll probably let Brian drive it as is, on the theory that a few more dings will follow.

"License number?"

Talk to Sally. What Sheila really meant was that she needed to pick Sally up and park her in one of the PSPD's interrogation rooms until the Lake City police could get here to question her. I considered telling the chief I didn't know the license number, but my better angel told me she didn't think this was such a hot plan. It wasn't, either. I didn't like the notion of Sally being apprehended as a person of interest, but I liked the idea of Myers catching up to her even less. If the cops had Sally, at least she'd be safe. And Sheila already knew what the car looked like—she'd ridden in it often enough. They'd pick Sally up, sooner or later. Sooner would be better.

I reached under the counter for my shoulder bag and dug the insurance card out of my wallet. "You're putting out an APB on the convertible, too, I hope." I handed her the card.

Without answering, she copied down the tag and handed the card back to me. "If Sally shows up here, give me a call."

It was a command, not a request, and I muttered something that might have been a yes, might have been a no. I was once again chewing on the phrase "person of interest," and it didn't taste good. If I were Sally (thank God I'm not), maybe I'd sit tight until the Lake City police were ready to name me a "material witness," a "target" of their investigation, or a "suspect." But those terms aren't very appetizing, either, so maybe I wouldn't. Maybe, if I were Sally, I would tell them everything I knew about Myers, so they would turn their attention from me to him, where it belonged. Anyway, the word "cooperating" has such a respectable ring to it.

Sheila put her cap back on, nodded and smiled in the direction of the Bookies, and left. As she went out the door, I remembered that she had asked for Sally's cell number—that was before Doris interrupted us. I hadn't given it to her, and she hadn't asked again. I considered running after her with the information, which I had on a scrap of paper on the counter, but I didn't. Instead, I picked up the phone and punched in the number. Still no answer. Damn. I left another voice mail message, a much more urgent one this time, telling Sally to call me as soon as possible.

The Bookies had finally decided that they would take both wreaths. They brought them to the counter, where they argued for a moment more about which of them was buying the wreath as a Christmas present for the other. They finally settled the matter by agreeing that each Bookie would buy one wreath and then give it to the other Bookie. (You'd be surprised at how often this happens when two people are shopping together.)

"I suppose some of your customers might be glad to see that law enforcement is watching out for them," the first Bookie remarked to me, adding, "although I personally find it a little . . . well, nerve-wracking to try to shop with the police looking over your shoulder, watching your every move, as if you were a common shoplifter."

The other Bookie was shaking her head. "I wonder what her mother thinks. A beautiful woman like that, and she's a policeman." She sniffed. "I'm surprised that she can't find some other line of work."

"Police*woman*," I corrected cheerfully, handing the credit cards back. "And her mother thinks it's just great, actually."

"Oh, really?" Bookie Number One did not quite believe me.

I nodded. My better angel had abandoned me, and my worst instincts were about to take over. "They're in the same business, you see," I added confidentially. "Sort of."

Bookie Number Two frowned. "What sort of business is her mother in?"

"She's the director of the state penitentiary at Huntsville," I said. I leaned forward and lowered my voice. "She runs Death Row."

Both Bookies' eyes grew round as saucers, and one of them raised her hand to her mouth. I repented of my folly immediately.

"Sorry," I muttered. "Just joking."

"If that was a joke," Bookie Number Two reprimanded me sharply, "it wasn't in very good taste."

"Not at all," Bookie Number One agreed wrathfully, taking her wreath. She didn't say, *You ought to be ashamed of yourself,* but she looked it.

"You're right," I said humbly. "I don't know what got into me. I apologize."

But I knew very well. I had been standing behind the counter all day, and I wasn't going to get a break anytime soon. I was irritated at Smart Cookie and ticked off at the Lake City police. I was seriously ticked off at Sally, too, but I was also seriously worried about her. As a result, I had alienated two customers, who would probably go straight home to their telephones (Bookies are not the sort to use cell phones or the Internet) and tell all the other Bookies that they'd been insulted by one of the own-ers of the tearoom and that they should find another place to meet for their monthly lunch.

The minute the two Bookies were out of the shop, I reached for the phone. There was no point in trying Sally again. She had either turned off her phone or . . . I didn't want to think of the other possibilities.

But there was somebody else I needed to talk to. McQuaid had to know that Leslie was dead and that the police had named Sally a person of interest.

And after that, I had another call to make. I was calling a lawyer.

the place, especially on the icy overpasses, where they executed elephan-tine 360s, like Sumo wrestlers on ice skates. A couple of eighteen-wheelers had jackknifed across two lanes, and another skidded onto the median and flipped onto its side, right in front of him.

But if the interstate heading south had been a skating rink, Route 36 heading west was a helluva lot worse, with only one lane plowed and the visibility deteriorating as the twilight deepened, so that by the time he'd reached the turnoff, he was barely creeping, the car rocking with every blast of the crosswind. The rented Chevy didn't have snow tires or chains, so he was pretty much at the mercy of the blizzard, which wasn't showing any mercy at all. It was after six o'clock now, and dark, and if he hadn't spotted the red neon sign, Joe's Feed Lot, bleeding blood-red onto the snow, he'd have missed the narrow Sanders turnoff altogether. Joe's Feed Lot. Any port in a storm, although as ports went, Joe's was better than some.

Wearily, he switched off the ignition. He had not planned to make this trip. He had meant it when he'd told Sally that he was going to pick up a couple of good books, a bag of snacks and a few beers, and head for the motel, where he could turn up the heat, stretch out on the bed, make a couple of phone calls, and spend the next twenty-four hours reading and snoozing and getting pleasantly blitzed.

That was the plan, anyway. He'd already gotten as far as the books, the snacks, and the beer. He'd even put in a call to Joyce Dillard. No answer, which took him off the hook until the evening, when she'd more likely be home. After the call, he picked up one of the books and settled himself on the bed to read, with the television tuned to a NASCAR race rerun on ESPN. And then the rest of the plan got deep-sixed in a hurry, because China had called with the staggering news that Leslie Strahorn was dead, a homicide, and the Lake City cops were looking for Sally as a person of interest.

Chapter Nine

McQuaid: Joe's Feedlot

McQuaid pulled up next to the black-and-white police cruiser in the parking lot of the hamburger joint outside of Sanders and unclenched his hands from the steering wheel. He flexed his stiff, cadaverlike fingers and sucked in a ragged breath. The drive from Omaha had taken over four hours, twice as long as it should have. The snow had never stopped, blinding white, blowing, flying, pinging pellet-hard against the car windows, clogging the windshield wipers, a blizzard if there ever was one. It had been a slick trip, too, hazardous and nerve-wrenching. Interstate 29 had been plowed, all right, but the snow was coming so furiously that the plows didn't have a prayer.

The blowing pellets were mesmerizing, and he had driven mostly by focusing on the taillights of the vehicle ahead of him, hoping there wouldn't be some sort of pileup and they'd all end up in one huge bumper-to-bumper chain collision. That hadn't happened, luckily, but otherwise it was bad enough. Cars and trucks were swerving and fishtailing all over

Leslie's death was a sucker punch in the belly, knocking the wind out of him, and it had taken him a minute to get his breath. He could picture her, pert, perky, sweet. He remembered kissing her once, months after the divorce. They'd just been playing around, but the kiss had delivered such an unexpected wallop that he'd decided he wouldn't do it again unless he was looking for something serious, which he wasn't and couldn't, as long as Sally was in the picture. And then there was China, who was even more of what he was looking for, so Leslie had become more of what she had always been: Brian's favorite aunt, his own friend, even sometimes—when things with Sally were at their worst—his confidant.

And now Leslie was dead, and her loss left him stripped down, raw, helpless. But what was this crap about the Lake City police being interested in Sally? What the hell was going on? Had Sally been staying with Leslie in Lake City before she'd come to Pecan Springs? If so, she hadn't said anything about it. Why? And why did the cops think she had anything to do with Leslie's death?

Hell. He sat up and swung his legs over the edge of the bed. The two sisters had had a strained relationship for a long time, going back to before he and Sally were married, for reasons he'd never quite understood and didn't especially want to. He didn't think it was Leslie's fault, since she was even-tempered and accommodating. But whenever Leslie and Sally were together, their animosity crackled like heat lightning, making it uncomfortable to be in the same room with them. Still, he didn't think it would get to the point where Sally would actually—

What the hell do you know? asked a voice in the back of his mind. *Sally is volatile. Too much alcohol, too many drugs, Juanita—a potent mix. Maybe she showed up at Leslie's house drunk or stoned out of her mind, and the two of them got into a shouting match. Maybe Juanita showed up, and things escalated. Push came to shove, and Leslie ended up dead.*

Dead. Despairingly, McQuaid shook his head. No. No. No. It hadn't happened that way. He knew Sally, and he knew it wasn't possible.

Not true, said the voice. *When people get angry enough, anything— from a fast, hard stab with a kitchen knife to an overhand hit with a fireplace poker—is possible.*

Maybe. But China wasn't buying it, either. She hadn't been in a courtroom for a while, but she still had the instincts of a criminal defense attorney. She had already convinced herself that Sally was innocent of whatever crime had been committed in Lake City. She thought Myers— the stalker—might have had something to do with Leslie's death. And when McQuaid told her about Sally's phone call and her story that she had been looking into her parents' murders, China had jumped on it with both feet.

"Sally was conducting a murder investigation?" she asked sharply. "In Sanders?"

"If that's what you want to call it." McQuaid gave a sardonic chuckle. "If you ask me, she was playing another role. This time, she was Lois Lane, crack investigative reporter. Using her parents' death as a springboard to career fame and fortune. And a book deal. A bunch of crap, if you ask me."

He rested his elbows on his knees and rubbed his forehead with his hand. A damn book. It made him so mad he couldn't see straight. Sally wanted to write a goddamned book about the murders. Her parents didn't deserve that.

China was silent for a moment. "Wait, McQuaid," she said, in her let's-consider-this-carefully tone, the tone she used when she was addressing a jury. "Myers lives in Sanders, right?"

"I guess so. He came to our wedding. That's what Sally says, anyway. Can't prove it by me. There were a lot of ex-boyfriends lined up to kiss the bride."

"Then what if—" China cleared her throat. "What if *Myers* is the guy Joyce Dillard suspects of being involved with the Strahorns' murders? The one she named to Sally but Sally won't name to you?"

McQuaid stopped rubbing his forehead. "That's a reach," he said cautiously. But he could see how China got there.

"Do you know if the Sanders police questioned him?"

"I don't know anything about the investigation, who they questioned, what kind of evidence they turned up."

"Or overlooked," China said. "From what you've told me, it's a small town, right?"

"Yeah. Maybe three thousand, tops."

"Which means that they've got how many investigators? One? Two? I don't imagine they were accustomed to carrying out an investigation into a double homicide. Who knows what kind of evidence they overlooked— hair, fiber, tissue. Probably didn't have access to any up-to-date forensic technology."

He was still thinking about that when she went on, even more urgently. "You have to drive down there and interview the woman Sally talked to, McQuaid. Joyce what's-her-name. Find out what she knows. If the suspect she has in mind is Jess Myers, we're not dealing with a simple stalker here. And there's another homicide to consider. Leslie. Don't forget Leslie."

Leslie. What he remembered was kissing her and wanting to do it again. His gut clenched at the thought of her, dead. He felt a numbing pain.

"Dillard," he said. He picked up the remote and turned off the sound. "The woman's name is Joyce Dillard."

"Right. Joyce Dillard. Talk to her, McQuaid. Find out if she has any reason to suspect that Myers killed the Strahorns."

He got off the bed, walked to the motel window, and yanked the drape open. "It's snowing like crazy here, China. This morning, you wanted me to come home. Right now, this afternoon. Now you want me to drive a hundred forty miles in a freakin' blizzard."

"I'm sorry it's snowing." She paused. "I can't make you do it, McQuaid. But I think you should."

He dropped the drape, still thinking of Leslie. But he gave it one more shot. "If you ask me, there's a damn good chance that Sally is making this whole thing up, starting with this woman in Sanders."

Yeah, that would be just like Sal, wouldn't it? the voice put in. *Invent a story about some woman who has incriminating information about this guy Myers, who is stalking her. Morph the unpleasant ex-boyfriend into a killer, make him dangerous, a menace to society. If Sally was looking for a hook for a book, what could be better?*

"I don't know about Dillard, but Sally is not making Myers up," China said firmly. "I talked to this guy myself, remember? He's creepy, I tell you. And he's purposeful. Determined."

McQuaid sighed. He was glad that China and Sally would be at Ruby's tonight, out of harm's way. And by this time, he very much wanted to know just what the hell kind of game Sally was playing. But he wasn't going to let China know it. He sighed loudly.

"This is something you really want me to do, huh? So what'll you give me if I do it?"

She thought for a moment. Then, "Sex," she promised provocatively. "All the sex you want."

He played innocent. "Don't I get that anyway?"

"More. You'll get more. Lots more. Whenever you want."

"I'm making notes." He sighed again, overdoing it for effect. "Okay,

154

you've twisted my arm. But you owe me big-time. And if I end up frozen stiff in a ditch on I-29, it's on your head."

"Thanks," she said. "I mean it."

"You'd better. And don't forget. You're spending the night with Ruby. You and Sally."

"Sally may be spending the night in jail," China replied in a meaningful tone.

They'd said good-bye then. He had checked out of the motel—there'd be no hope of making it back to Omaha tonight, not in this storm. He'd bagged up his books, beer, and snacks and taken them with him to the car. The temperature was dropping, too, and he wasn't dressed for it. So he'd stopped at the first discount store he'd seen and bought a fleece-lined corduroy jacket, a decent pair of boots (which he needed, anyway), a sweatshirt, a wooly blue hat, a pair of gloves, several bottles of water, and an emergency kit with hazard markers, flares, and a flashlight. He didn't intend to get stuck in the snow, but if he did, he'd at least be prepared.

Now, he glanced up at the sign. Joe's Feed Lot. It was years since he'd been here, but the place hadn't changed, at least on the outside. He reached for his cell phone to call China, tell her where he was. No answer, so he left a brief message.

"Just got to Sanders. Bitch of a drive. Hope to hell this is worth it, China. You and Ruby be good tonight. Keep Sally out of trouble. Call me when you get a chance."

He clicked off the phone, pulled on his gloves and his hat, yanking it down over his ears, and got out of the car, thinking that the weather might be doing him a good turn. Joyce Dillard wasn't likely to be out and about on a night like this, and somebody here could tell him where she lived. The temperature had dropped sharply in the past couple of hours, and the cold air slashed like a knife in his lungs. There were three other vehicles in Joe's parking lot: the black-and-white cruiser, its hood still steaming; a red Ford pickup, the driver's side door bashed in, the window crisscrossed with duct tape; and an old green Buick, heavily mantled with snow. McQuaid noticed these as he noticed most things, cataloguing them without being consciously aware that he was doing it, a habit learned early in his cop career and never forgotten.

The concrete apron, lit by a blazing Coca-Cola sign, had been recently shoveled and sanded. But the blowing snow was already beginning to pile up. It crunched icily underfoot as he trudged to the door. Inside, it was blessedly warm and half-dark, with a jukebox in the shadows off to the right—Dolly Parton belting out "Oh by gosh by golly, it's time for mistletoe and holly." The smell of hot grease and hot coffee was heavy on the air, like syrup. McQuaid had been here often when he and Sally had come to Sanders to visit her folks, and he remembered Joe as an affable guy with a beer gut who liked to talk to the customers.

There weren't many tonight. A couple of kids—teenagers—were making out in one of the booths, what was left of one of Joe's pizzas on the table in front of them. A heavyset man was sitting at the counter. He wore jeans, a red-and-black plaid shirt, a khaki hunting vest, and a black cap with the red letters SPD. The cop who belonged to the police cruiser, McQuaid thought, off duty. He was hunched over a double-decker cheeseburger and crisp fries, with a giant pickle, a substantial side of slaw, a second side of beans, and a mug of steaming black coffee.

McQuaid sat down a couple of stools to the right of the cop. Joe turned around from the coffee machine, wiping his hands on the white towel he wore like an apron over his jeans. He was round-faced and red-cheeked, nearly bald, with gold-rimmed glasses, ten years older but not much changed. Behind him was a green-painted partition with an open pass-through shelf to the kitchen. The partition was plastered with autographed photographs of football and basketball players in their uniforms and signs: purple and white Go K-State Wildcats! and Jayhawk Victory! banners and green Beat 'Em Badgers! bumper stickers. Joe's Feed Lot catered to the sports crowd, which was pretty much everybody in Sanders, as McQuaid remembered it. Football and basketball were about it where local entertainment was concerned, unless you wanted to count the Rotary Club and the Ladies' Auxiliary.

"Cold out there?" Joe inquired hospitably.

"Brisk," McQuaid replied. "Snowing like blue blazes." He pulled off his hat and gloves, stuffing them into his jacket pocket. "I-29 was a skating rink. Thirty-six wasn't much better."

"Bad all day and gettin' worse." Joe grinned, showing a broken front tooth. "Nobody's drivin', everybody's eatin' at home. Even the county snowplows are headin' for the barn. Figgered I'd be here all night with nobody but them two," he added, nodding toward the couple making out energetically in the booth. "I was fixin' to close after Hank here cleaned his plate, but I'll be glad to take care of you, if you're wantin' to eat." He pointed to a chalkboard menu hung on the wall, offering meatloaf, fried catfish, and burgers.

McQuaid unzipped his jacket and nodded toward the cop's plate. "I'll have what the man's got, but skip the coleslaw. Just beans and java."

"Comin' up." Joe pulled a mug of hot coffee, set it in front of McQuaid, and disappeared around the partition into the kitchen, where he was visible through the open pass-through.

"You won't be sorry," the cop said in a gruff voice. He was a big guy, beefy, maybe six three, with graying hair a tad shaggy on the collar of his

157

plaid shirt, and dark eyebrows that met over a battered nose. "Joe makes the best cheeseburgers in Kansas." He raised his voice. "Hear that, Joe? Best cheeseburgers this side of the state line. Real Kansas beef. None of that rain forest crap."

"I hear you," Joe said and dropped fries into a sizzle of hot fat. "Bet you think I'm gonna give you a discount, huh?"

The cop laughed, and McQuaid put out his hand. "McQuaid. Houston PD, Homicide. Retired."

"Oh, yeah?" The eyebrows went up, the hand came out, a thick hand with a hard grasp, a weight lifter's grasp. "Jamison. Hank Jamison. Me, I think about quittin', too. I ain't as crazy about night work as I used to be. So what's it like, bein' retired?"

"Dunno." McQuaid gave him a rueful grin. "I didn't say I quit. Just moved over to the private side. Investigations."

Jamison nodded. "Thought of that myself. But I figger I'd hafta move somewheres else to do it. KC, maybe, or Tulsa. Not much call for that kinda work around here. O' course, I could do security. I'd still be workin' nights, prob'ly, but there'd be less time on the road."

Dolly Parton quit singing. The boy and girl got up from their booth, exchanged one last kiss, and struggled into heavy coats. McQuaid saw with some surprise that they were two girls. Jamison followed his glance with a disgusted look.

"Yeah. Kids these days. Makes you sick, don't it? Wonder if their folks know what they're gettin' up to." He dipped a fry into catsup, popped it into his mouth, chewed. "So where'd you drive from? KC?"

"Omaha." McQuaid cradled his coffee mug, warming his hands. "Way I remember, used to be a motel this end of town, west side of the road. Still there?"

"Yeah. Clarks' Sycamore Court. Changed hands, though. The Clarks sold out a few years back. Some Ay-rab owns it now." Another disgusted look. "Guess there ain't no red-blooded Americans wantin' to get into the motel bizness these days."

"I don't care who owns it so long as there's hot water, the bed's clean, and the TV works." He raised his voice. "Hey, Joe. I'll have everything on that cheeseburger. Heavy on the onion."

"Onion, huh?" Joe raised his head from whatever he was slicing and peered through the pass-through. "Guess you and Hank don't have no dates tonight." He frowned. "McQuaid, you say? Any relation to the fella who married that girl of Gene Strahorn's a few years back? The oldest one," he amended. "Sally."

"I am that fella," McQuaid said, "and that was sixteen years ago. We're not married any longer."

Joe whistled. "Sixteen years? That long ago? Hard to believe. Leslie— Sally's kid sister—used to work here when she was in high school. Pert little girl, right promisin'. Always found something good to say about folks."

McQuaid flinched. It hurt to hear her name. He might have said then that Leslie was dead, but he held his tongue. No need to give away information that might come in handy later.

"Helluva thing about the Strahorns," Jamison remarked around a mouthful of pickle. "Couldn't ask for no nicer folks."

"You said it," McQuaid replied. "Helluva thing, especially in a town like this. In Houston, maybe. Not in Main Street America." There was a silence, broken only by the sizzle of the burger on the grill. Easing into it, he added, "You in the department then, when they were killed?"

"Yeah. I was chief." Jamison chewed reflectively. "All four of us worked on it, worked hard, too. But there wasn't much to go on. Never really had a case."

Four. McQuaid remembered what China had said and knew she was right. They'd probably never had a double homicide before—at least, one where the shooter wasn't standing over the bodies with the gun in his hand when the cops arrived. "Heard from somebody that you maybe had a suspect at one point, though," he said. "Some guy named . . ." He frowned, pursing his lips. "Byers, was it? Something like that."

Joe came around the partition, a plate in one hand, a dish of beans in the other. "That'd be Myers. Jess Myers."

"Yeah," McQuaid said. *Score one in China's column.* "Myers. That was it."

"But Jess wasn't really a suspect, was he, Hank?" Joe set the plates down in front of McQuaid, who saw with appreciation that the burger was thick and juicy, the slab of cheese was ample, and the tomato slices looked like they came from a real tomato, not that cardboard stuff you got in the fast-food places.

"Yeah, we had Myers on the list for a while," Jamison replied. "Plenty of opportunity. Mr. Strahorn had him do some repair work in the upstairs bathroom, so he knew his way around the place. Would've known where to find the gun, maybe the money, too. Other'n that, we couldn't find anything to tie him to the killings. If he was the one, he never spent a dime. Not around here, anyway." He turned to look at McQuaid, squinting a little. "We had another suspect, though. A serious one."

"Yeah?" The look was deliberate, a shove, a preliminary move in a sparring match. McQuaid held it for a second and turned away, picking up his coffee cup. "Who would that be?"

"Your wife." Jamison grinned bleakly. "'Scuse me. Ex-wife."

McQuaid swallowed wrong, sputtered, coughed, and washed down the cough with another gulp of hot coffee. "Sally? You're kidding." *Subtract the score from China's column.*

Jamison chuckled. "You got more than one ex?" He paused. "Never told you, I reckon."

No—but she wouldn't, of course. Leslie hadn't mentioned it, either. McQuaid picked up his cheeseburger and made a show of taking a bite out of it. "You cleared her, I guess." They must've. She'd gotten her share of the payoff from her parents' insurance, which wouldn't have happened if she'd continued to be a suspect.

"Yeah, finally," Jamison replied, half-regretfully. "Took a while, though. Opportunity, y'see. She was in town when it happened—acting a little goofy, too. She knew where he kept the gun. She knew he kept it loaded. And then there was motive."

Sally was here in Sanders when her parents were killed. He hadn't known that. But he'd been living in a new place and working on a big case. And she had forbidden him to come to the funeral. Was it because she was a suspect, and she didn't want him to know?

McQuaid picked up the catsup bottle, lifted the bun again, and gave the burger a healthy squirt. "Okay, opportunity, motive. Motive?" But the minute he asked the question, he knew the answer.

"Insurance," Jamison replied offhandedly. "A cool couple million, split between her and her sister. The company wouldn't pay her share until we cleared her."

A couple of million? McQuaid hadn't known there was that much. All he'd known was that she had burned through the money pretty fast. Juanita had, anyway—that was Sally's explanation for where it had gone. One or two of her boyfriends had been glad to help, of course. He frowned. Was that where Myers came in? The money?

He lifted his cheeseburger, took a bite. It was even better than he remembered, which (as China would no doubt tell him) meant that it had plenty of sodium and artery-clogging fat. "Under that theory, Leslie should have been a suspect, too. How come she wasn't?"

"Because she wasn't all the time fightin' with 'em," Jamison replied, going back to his meal. "She wasn't all the time tryin' to borrow money, or givin' 'em hell when they turned her down. Wasn't actin' goofy, either."

"Acting goofy. Like how?"

"Like buyin' stuff from the local boutique, tryin' to use credit cards that were declined. Then writin' checks that bounced, that her dad had to cover." He eyed McQuaid. "Like flirtin' with the mayor to the point where His Honor's wife had to have a talk with her mom."

McQuaid winced. Juanita's behavior, familiar. But he'd never known that Sally brought Juanita to Sanders. She was strictly the big-city type. But maybe Sally hadn't been firmly in control. Maybe Juanita had been calling the shots, which was where Myers came in.

Jamison chuckled wryly. "Maybe you didn't know your wife very well, huh?"

McQuaid felt suddenly cold, as if the door had blown open and an icy wind had swept through the place. "Why'd you clear her?"

"New county attorney came in, didn't feel like there was enough evidence." He shrugged casually. "A few folks said that the attorney should take himself out of the loop—a Strahorn cousin, it seems. But he didn't." He slid a look at McQuaid. "You know how that goes, I reckon."

McQuaid knew. He also knew, without hearing it said, that in Jamison's mind, Sally was still a suspect and would be, until somebody else was charged with the murders. There was nothing wrong with that, of course. It was the way a good cop thought, especially with a Strahorn cousin in the county attorney's office. Contemplatively, he returned to his cheeseburger.

Joe turned back to the pass-through shelf and produced two more plates, with large pieces of apple pie. "On the house," he said. "Yesterday's pie, but that's not gonna hurt the taste none. I'm closin' early, with this snow, so you might as well help me get rid of it." He picked up McQuaid's coffee mug and went to refill it.

"Well, hey, Joe," Jamison said with approval. "You ain't gonna find me turnin' down no free pie, yesterday's or last week's."

"The gun that killed the Strahorns," McQuaid said. "Luger, wasn't it?" Leslie had told him that much.

"Yep." Jamison spooned up beans. "Belonged to Mr. Strahorn. Guess he picked it up when he was in Germany, during the war. The shooter took it out of the gun cabinet in the basement. Strahorn had a few old pieces that'd been in the family awhile. A pump-action twenty-two, an old single-shot twelve-gauge, nice old Model 94 lever-action thirty-thirty. They were all in the cabinet, which was conveniently unlocked. Odd, according to your wife's sister. She insisted that her dad kept it locked."

"Was the gun found? Did the shooter take the Luger with him?" *With her,* the voice said, inside his head. *Or maybe the shooter was in her employ.* Joe pushed his cup across the counter, and McQuaid reached for it. *Not Sally,* he thought. *Not Sally.*

You sure? the voice said, and chuckled. McQuaid swallowed hard.

"No gun," Jamison replied. "Found the casings, is all."

McQuaid put down his cup. "Prints on the casings?"

"Strahorn's. Kept it loaded, Leslie said." He swiveled on his stool. "You here on bizness, McQuaid?"

"Personal." McQuaid began on his beans. "Actually, I'm doing a favor for Sally."

Joe turned around from the coffee machine and slid McQuaid's cup across the counter. "Can't get away from the exes, can we." It wasn't a question.

McQuaid shook his head. "Not when you've got a kid."

"Boy? Girl?" Joe asked, interested.

"Boy. Sixteen. Brian. His grandpa used to take him out on claim calls." McQuaid remembered the old man's pleasure in his grandson and was surprised at the pain he felt. "Thought he'd make a crop insurance man of him. Teach him to take over the business when he grew up." Almost regretfully, he added. "Brian would be good at it, actually. Has a head for numbers."

"Hell." Joe sighed. "Too bad what happened. Whole family's gone from here now, 'cept for that cousin. The house was sold, and the girls—Les and Sally—never do come back home. Guess they figger there's nothin' for 'em to come to." He settled down on his stool, his back to the partition, and began to eat his pie. "Most young folks do leave these days. Not much here for 'em to do."

"That's not quite right," Jamison remarked. He picked up his fork and pulled his pie toward him. "McQuaid's ex was here in town not long ago. Saw her myself, drivin' a little bitty yella convertible. Joyce Dillard was with her." He forked up a slug of pie. "Any idea why she came back here, after bein' so long away?"

"Sorry," McQuaid said. "I guess I don't."

Yeah, you do, the voice in his head said. *She wanted to write an article, maybe a book. Only maybe she didn't, not really. Maybe it was something else she was after. Somebody knew something, and she had to find out what and how much.*

Jamison's voice was flat. "You said you was here to do a favor for her. Anything we can help you with, McQuaid?"

"Maybe." McQuaid heard what was behind the question and understood. He'd be asking the same thing, if he were Jamison, if this were his case. If Sally wasn't his ex-wife.

He polished off his beans and turned his attention to the apple pie. "You mentioned Joyce Dillard. Sally went to school with her. She asked me if I'd give Ms. Dillard a message. So maybe you can tell me where to find her. I've tried calling her house, but she doesn't answer." Actually, he'd tried twice, no, three times. Once from the motel in Omaha, twice during the drive. "Probably at work," he added. "Figured she'd be home tonight, bad as the weather is."

Jamison and Joe exchanged glances. The silence lengthened. At last, Jamison said, "Well, that's an interestin' question, McQuaid, especially seein' as how it's the same question lots of folks around here have been askin'."

McQuaid picked up his fork and pitched into his pie. Not as good as China's, but fruity, spicy. "Out of town, maybe?"

"Could be, I reckon." Jamison didn't look up. "Nobody knows. Just gone."

Joe filled a cup of coffee for himself, reached back to the pass-through, and picked up another plate of apple pie. He hooked a stool with one foot and sat down on the other side of the counter. "Real odd, though," he said softly. "Got people worried."

McQuaid heard the tone and was wary. "Ms. Dillard do this kind of thing often?"

"Not hardly," Jamison said, pushing his plate away. "Joyce is the town librarian, only one we got. When she misses work, the library don't open unless somebody from the Friends comes in. Old Miz Cramer has been mindin' the desk in Joyce's place, but she don't open the library until noon, and from what I hear, she don't know where things are or how to get the computer turned on. Folks'd like to get their librarian back." He picked up his coffee mug. "So you can see why that's such an interestin' question, McQuaid."

McQuaid looked from one to the other. "No idea where she is?"

Joe shook his head. "Car's at the house. Dinner on the table. House is unlocked. Was," he amended. "Reckon her dad's locked it up by now." He glanced at Jamison. "Am I tellin' tales outta school, Hank?"

Jamison shrugged. "That was in last week's paper, so I reckon the chief released the details." He turned, watching McQuaid steadily now. "Just what kinda business you got with Joyce Dillard, McQuaid? I'd appreciate a straight answer, if you don't mind."

McQuaid was not surprised. Out of the corner of his eye, he could see Joe's shoulders tense. He didn't want to give up too much, but he'd need to put down enough to keep him in the game.

"All right. When my ex-wife was here in town, Joyce told her that she had some information—might've been just a suspicion, maybe more than that—about who killed the Strahorns. Sally asked me check it out, see what I thought of Dillard's story. Whether she knew what she was talking about. Whether there was any truth to it or not."

"Oh, yeah?" Jamison asked. His voice was cooler now. "Did Joyce tell your ex-wife who this mystery killer might be?" He didn't ask why Joyce hadn't gone to the Sanders police with her suspicions, but McQuaid knew that's what he was thinking. He was also wondering why Sally had kept this information to herself, why she had commissioned her ex-husband—a private investigator—to come nosing around instead. McQuaid found himself asking the same uncomfortable questions. He didn't have any answers, either.

"Nope, she didn't," McQuaid said. "I wasn't too keen on getting out in this weather, but I was up in Omaha on business, with a day to kill." He shrugged. "Hell. You know how women are. Sometimes they get hold of you in a place where it's kind of hard to say no."

"You sure got that right," Joe said, twisting his mouth.

McQuaid looked at Jamison. He knew, but had to ask it for the record. "Is Joyce Dillard's disappearance under investigation?"

"You bet it is," Jamison said.

"Her daddy's a town councilman," Joe put in. "Organized a search, been puttin' up flyers, gettin' it on the KC TV channels, even posting a reward. Twenty grand, dead or alive."

"Forty," Jamison said sourly. "He doubled it last night." To McQuaid, he said, "The money's good, but it brings in tips, a ton of 'em, most completely phony."

"Makes it hard on you," McQuaid said.

"Yeah." Jamison's mouth tightened. "We're doin' all we can, fast as we can, but there's a limit to what we can follow up on."

McQuaid knew. This was the sort of crime—if that's what it was— that gave every policeman a serious headache. Abduction? Amnesia? Staged disappearance? By this time, the Sanders cops would have gone through the house carefully, and just as carefully, they'd have gone through Joyce's relationships—or they would've, if they had the manpower to do it, which maybe they didn't. This kind of investigation would be out of the usual for them, and the reward would bring out all the crazies. Too many tips, ninety-nine out of a hundred phony.

Jamison cleared his throat. "So you can see why it seems just a little coincidental, you might say. Here's your ex-wife comin' back to town and drivin' Ms. Dillard around in her car. Then here you come, wantin' to talk with Ms. Dillard and find out what she knows about the Strahorn murders. Unfortunately, Ms. Dillard isn't around to give you any answers." He paused, let the silence lengthen. "Get my point?"

McQuaid got it. He was about to answer when the door burst open behind him with a crash.

"Joe!" a girl cried. "Joe, you gotta help us!" It was one of the two girls who had gone out together.

"What is it now, Annie?" Joe asked with infinite patience. "How often I gotta tell you, it's time for a new batt'ry? We can't go pushin' you two kids every time that ol' clunker won't start."

Now, all three of them were looking at the girl. She was covered with melting snow, her boots and pants crusted with snow to the thighs, her hair spilling out from under the hood of her coat.

"It's not the truck!" she cried, holding out her mittened hands, covered with snow, as if she had been digging with them. "We were headed back toward town when Meg spun out, and we went into the ditch. We were trying to dig ourselves out and we uncovered—" She gulped and closed her eyes.

Jamison got up from his stool and strode toward her. "Uncovered what? What've you found?"

"We found her!" the girl cried. "We found Miss Dillard, under the snow." She burst into noisy tears. "We tried to dig her out, but—but we couldn't!" The last was a wail.

"You poor thing," Joe said sympathetically. "You get on over here and have a hot cup of coffee and some pie. You must be half-froze."

Jamison had his jacket on and McQuaid was reaching for his. The girl sat down at the counter. She stopped crying, sniffled, and swiped her sleeve across her nose.

"Do you think we'll get the reward?" she asked.

Chapter Ten

Holly is still the most popular of all evergreens used to decorate homes at Christmas, although in the past a variety of branches were used:

> Spread out the laurel and the bay,
> For chimney-piece and window gay,
> Scour the brass gear—a shining row
> And holly place with mistletoe.

Nevertheless the holly must be hung before the mistletoe, otherwise ill luck will come down the chimney on Christmas Eve.

Josephine Addison,
The Illustrated Plant Lore

No doubt a function of Holly inside the house was to deal, not only with demons and witches, but with the house goblins . . . Holly and Ivy would have subdued the house goblin precisely from Christmas Eve, when the decorations went up, to Candlemas Eve, when they were taken down.

Geoffrey Grigson, *The Englishman's Flora*

After McQuaid agreed that he would drive down to Sanders and talk to Joyce Dillard, I clicked off, then punched in Justine Wyzinski's number. McQuaid might be able to dig up the backstory, but if anybody could get Sally out of her current fix, it was Justine.

A couple of centuries ago, Justine and I sat next to each other in first-year criminal law at the University of Texas. Envious law students nicknamed her the Whiz, because she could whip a recalcitrant collection of facts into a comprehensible legal theory and persuade you of its validity while the rest of us were still trying to find our notes. I was wildly jealous of her and worked like hell to keep her from getting too far ahead—which earned me the nickname of Hot Shot. After a couple of years of competitive craziness, the Whiz and I both made Law Review, where our rivalry ripened into wary respect and eventually into friendship, which we continued when we graduated, passed the bar, and went into practice—I in a large Houston firm, Justine in private practice in San Antonio. When I left the law some years later, the Whiz publicly expressed the conviction that I was non compos and ought to be crated and shipped to the loony bin, while I told her that she was certifiably crazy to stay. But we haven't let that little difference of opinion sabotage our friendship. I have called Justine when I needed her help. She's asked me for a favor occasionally, too. I keep score. And if my tally was correct, she owed me one.

She recognized my number on her caller ID. "How the hell are you, Hot Shot?"

"Can you spare a minute, Justine?"

"I'm in court and whether I can spare a minute depends on when Judge Paulson shows up. You got something, give it to me quick." Justine is a speed demon and a specialist in multitasking, but even she has to stop talking and texting once the judge takes the bench. I'd better make it snappy.

"It's Sally."

"Ah, yes, the inimitable, incomparable, unrivaled, one and only Sally."

The Whiz chuckled. She has suffered with me through several unfortunate episodes in Sally's checkered past. "What's she done this time?"

I was succinct. "She's a person of interest in her sister's homicide."

The Whiz whistled. "That's a biggie, even for Sally. An elephant on steroids. So tell me about it."

It didn't take long, because I was lamentably short on facts. I concluded with "She's going to need somebody with her during the interview. When they find her, that is." I looked at my watch. It was nearly two. Where *was* she?

"You don't need me for an interview," the Whiz replied. "You can handle this, Hot Shot. Time you got back in the ring, anyway."

"I can handle it, but I won't. Sally is Brian's mother. I'm too close to the situation."

Justine snorted. "Don't tell me you're emotionally involved with this woman."

"I'm emotionally involved with Brian," I said. "And if things don't go well—"

"Sally is Sally, China. Things will not go well. In fact, things will go as badly as it is possible."

I sighed. The Whiz has a way of putting her finger on the pulse of the problem. "That's why she needs you, Justine. I need you. Will you?"

Justine sounded reluctant. "My plate is heaped and overflowing right now. 'When they find her,' you said. Your local gendarmes haven't nabbed her, then?"

"I'm out of the loop. If they have, they haven't told me. What I know is that she was supposed to meet me for lunch, and she didn't show up. Sheila has put out an APB on Brian's car. That's what she's driving."

"I see. Well, when they find her, phone me, and I'll let you know whether I can take the case—if it is a case. Which of course it might not be. Maybe they just want to ask her what her sister had for breakfast. In the meantime, dig up the facts, will you? Our friend Sally is like a piñata full of nasty little surprises, bugs and worms and things that bite. I don't want to do this if I have to jump into it naked." She paused. "Any chance she did it, China? Knocked her sister off, I mean."

The word *no* leapt to my lips, but I bit it back. I had seen Sally act rashly, impulsively, angrily. I had hated her for it, and for the disruptions she had caused in Brian's life. But still, I didn't believe she had killed Leslie, for the simple reason that over the past couple of days, she had not given a single indication of sadness, guilt, remorse—any of the horrific emotions that would swamp anyone who had killed a member of her family. Would swamp even Sally, who could hold her head above the tides of guilt longer than most people.

But I know the Whiz. I knew that she was much more likely to agree to take Sally's case if I gave her a different answer. So I lied.

"Yes," I said. "Sally has an alter ego, somebody named Juanita, who sometimes does crazy things. She was diagnosed a couple of years ago."

"Aha," Justine exclaimed, and I pictured her snapping her fingers and coming to full attention, all systems alert. I had punched her Intrigue Me button. "The dissociative identity disorder defense."

"Exactly," I said. Justine is always three leaps and a bound ahead of any developing situation. In her mind, she was already reviewing the list of expert witnesses—psychiatrists, mental health authorities—she would call. She was already in front of the jury box, making opening arguments. "Then you'll do it?"

"Probably," the Whiz said. "But right now, I gotta do this. Oh, and don't forget about those facts, China."

There was a stirring in the background, and I heard the bailiff's distant command: "All rise." In the old days, this was a battle cry that made me leap to my feet, my blood racing and my pulse quickening. Not anymore. I was just glad it was Justine in that courtroom, not me. I'll settle for Thyme and Seasons, any day.

I said, "Thanks, Justine." But she had already clicked off.

I sat there for a moment. While I'd been talking to the Whiz, three people had come into the shop. Customers. Not that I wasn't glad to see them. I was, especially if they had come to buy. But I was here all by myself. Ruby was trying to manage her unmanageable mother, Cass was at the doctor's, Laurel was unavailable. All of which meant that even if I'd wanted to, I couldn't start digging up facts for Justine. I couldn't even think where to go or what kind of shovel to use.

And there was more. During my life as a lawyer, I had a very simple rule. I advised potential clients that you never launched an investigation unless you know what you're going to do with the information you dig up. If you can't or won't live with the answers—*all* the answers—forget all about asking the questions. And here I was, promising to look for answers that might not be in Sally's best interests.

After a flurried fifteen minutes, the shop was empty again, and I had time to think about the matter at hand: Sally. But then there was another little rush, and another, and before I knew it, an hour had flown past, dropping tidy little deposits of fives and tens and even a couple of twenties in Ruby's register and mine. The phones in both shops hadn't stopped ringing, either—usually, music to my ears, except that today, I had something else to worry about, and I was beginning to think I wasn't going to get there from here. And then my phone rang again. It was Ruby.

"I've just left Castle Oaks," she said breathlessly. "I got Mom settled again and—"

"Super," I said. "Then you're heading back to the shop, I hope?"

Ruby cleared her throat apologetically. "Actually, I'm doing surveillance."

"Surveillance? Don't tell me. I don't want to hear this."

No, wait. Whatever Nancy Drew was up to, I'd better hear it now, before she got herself into some really serious trouble and had to be bailed out.

I gave a resigned sigh. "All right, tell me, Ruby. Who are you surveilling?"

"Not a who, a what. Brian's blue Ford. The one you loaned to Sally. It's parked in the First Congregational lot, just off the alley behind McMasters Office Supply."

Brian's car? Ruby had located Sally? But I had to register a protest. "I thought I told you not to go looking for—"

"I didn't go looking for anything. Brownie's oath, China! I got Mom settled in her room and started back to the shop, and on the way I remembered that we're nearly out of adding machine tape, so I stopped here at McMasters. While I was at it, I bought some folders and pens and rubber bands and talked to Peaches—you know, Peaches McMasters. Her sister just had twins, two girls, and she had to tell me all about it. They named them Zoe and Zora."

"I know about Peaches' sister's twins," I said impatiently. "Get to the point, Ruby."

"Well, the point is that when I finished buying the tape and the folders and pens and rubber bands and talking to Peaches about the twins, I came back to the car. I was getting in when I just happened to glance across the alley, and there it was, on the other side of the hedge. In the First Methodist parking lot. Is, I mean. It's still there. I'm looking right at it."

"How do you know it's Brian's car? There are lots of blue Fords around."

"Dented left rear? I remembered that. And here's the license plate." She rattled it off. It was the same one I had given Sheila. It was Brian's car, all right. So where was Sally? Shopping?

Ruby answered my unspoken question. "I've been watching for ten minutes or so, and there's no sign of Sally. She wasn't in McMasters, and there's no other shopping or food places nearby. There's nothing but residential around here."

Ruby was right about that. McMasters isn't a mall business, it's a local business, patronized by other local businesses. It's about six blocks from here, off by itself. There wouldn't be any reason for Sally to be in that area.

"And what's more," Ruby went on, "the car is cold. I walked over there and touched the hood. It's been parked there for a while, China."

"Okay," I said. "Stay where you are and phone the cops. And keep out of sight, okay? If Sally comes back and sees you, she's going to wonder what the heck is going on."

"I will, definitely." In a lower voice she added, "Does Sally know that Leslie's been murdered?"

"Not unless she did it herself," I said.

"Weeeellll . . ." Ruby dragged out the word.

"She *didn't*," I said firmly. "She could not have murdered her sister and then sat at our dinner table with the kids and McQuaid and me without giving us some sort of clue. It's just not possible, Ruby." As a former criminal attorney, I've seen my share of killers, some of them pretty cool characters. Sally was an accomplished liar, and she had already fooled me once. But I didn't think she was capable of killing someone—especially her sister—and then acting normally afterward.

"Mmmm," Ruby replied in a thoughtful tone. "Well, maybe it was Juanita."

I closed my eyes. Juanita. I didn't want to think about Juanita.

"In which case Sally would have been there," Ruby was saying, "but she might not know what happened. That's why she could act normal, sort of." She paused. "As normal as Sally ever acts. Remember what they call it? Dissociative identity disorder? It means that you dissociate. And when you dissociate, you might as well not be there, because you don't remember."

I opened my eyes again. "If the case goes to trial, which it won't, that will likely be the defense." Insanity is a very hard row to hoe in Texas. It's the defense attorney's last resort, when nothing else will work. "But I still don't believe it," I added stubbornly. "I can't believe that the Lake City police have anything concrete against her."

"That's because you have a defense attorney's mind-set. You're used to rooting for the underdog."

"It is *not*," I snapped. "I don't believe it because . . . because I don't believe it," I finished lamely.

Ruby didn't respond to that, for which I was grateful. "When is McQuaid coming home?" she asked.

"Tomorrow. He's on his way to Sanders right now."

"Sanders? Where's that?"

"Kansas. Sally's hometown."

"For pete's sake." She was surprised. "Why?"

"Because Sally asked him to, and I thought it was a good idea." I didn't want to go into the whole story just now. It was too complicated. "He wants me to spend the night with you. And Sally, too—if she's not in custody. In case Myers decides to show up at our house."

"Works for me. You know you're always welcome. Both of you— although Sally has to promise to send Juanita somewhere else."

"Thanks." The bell over Ruby's door jangled. "Listen, Ruby, I've got to hang up now and check out a customer in your shop. Phone the police about that car right now. Okay?"

I went next door and sold Ruby's customer two books on astrology, a folder of blank birth charts, and a Capricorn T-shirt. After that, I came back and waited on two customers of my own, which took a little time, because they wanted to find out about natural dyes, a fairly complex subject. I discouraged them from buying dried herbs, since from my experience, it's much better to work with fresh material you can grow or gather. I also suggested that if they wanted to try some easy vegetable dyes, they might experiment with onion skins and tea leaves for beige, coffee grounds for brown, red cabbage leaves for blue and purple, carrot tops and spinach leaves for green. Oh, and turmeric, a spice that makes a vibrant orange. They bought a book—*A Dyer's Garden*, by Rita Buchanan— that will help them decide what to plant in the spring garden, and left happy.

By this time, I was seriously worried about Sally. I tried calling her cell again, but there was no answer. I didn't bother leaving a message—I'd already left several, and none had been returned. I called the police department, but all they would tell me was that she hadn't been located yet.

Ruby returned a half hour later, bubbling over with excitement about her surveillance adventure.

"Sheila has assigned somebody to stake out Brian's car," she said. "They're hoping Sally will come back to get it. Then they'll take her into custody."

I frowned. I was wondering whether Sally had deliberately left the car there. The church is on a quiet street, in a quiet neighborhood, and that blue Ford hardly calls attention to itself. If she wanted to stash it there, it might not be noticed for a couple of weeks.

Of course, there was another possibility, one that I didn't much like to think about. Maybe Jess Myers had spotted Sally and grabbed her—assuming that their relationship was adversarial. Or (assuming that it was collaborative) she had gotten in touch with him, and the two of them had gone off together somewhere. Either way, now that I knew about Leslie's death, finding Myers seemed every bit as urgent as finding Sally, perhaps even more.

Ruby was apparently thinking along the same lines. "How was Leslie killed, China?"

"I don't know," I replied. "Sheila either doesn't know the facts or has decided that I'm too close to Sally, so I'm not to be trusted with them. And without the facts, I have no idea whether the Lake City police have even a shred of a case against Sally. Maybe she was in Lake City before she came here. Maybe they just want to talk to her. Anyway, I called Justine Wyzinski."

"Oh, good," Ruby exclaimed. She's a fan of the Whiz. "I was just about to suggest that. Will she help?"

"She's agreed to consider taking the case—if there is one—and she'll sit in on Sally's interview. But she's asked me to 'dig up the facts,' as she put it, so she doesn't have to jump into the interview 'naked.'" I chuckled. "I know she meant it metaphorically, but still, it's an interesting thought."

Ruby snickered at the idea of Justine—who is short, shaped like a fireplug, and twenty pounds overweight—jumping into an interview stark naked. Then she frowned.

"Dig up the facts," she said thoughtfully, tilting her head to one side. "Maybe we should—" She paused, tapping her long, scarlet-painted fingernail against her teeth. "Lake City," she mused. "I know that town. It's a cute little place. Shannon taught there for two semesters a couple of years ago." Shannon is Ruby's younger daughter. She teaches high school girls' phys ed and coaches girls' basketball and track. "It's not much more than an hour and a half from here, depending on the traffic. Maybe we should—"

"Ruby," I said warningly.

She didn't pay any attention. "I think you and I should drive up there and do our own investigation." She paused, her eyes seemed to glaze just slightly, and an intent, listening look came over her face. I knew that look. It signals that she's got a hunch—one of those skyrocket bursts of intuition that Ruby gets every now and then, and always insists on acting upon, for better or worse.

"No, Ruby, no," I said. "You don't go jumping into an investigation without some idea of what you're going to—"

"Yes, China, yes." She looked at her watch. "If we leave now, we can be there by six."

"We are *not* going to Lake City," I said firmly. "For one thing, there's the kids. They'll be home from school in an hour. I need to fix supper and—" I stopped, remembering.

Ruby said it for me. "Not tonight, you don't. Caitlin is staying with Amy and Brian is sleeping over with a friend. You've already made the arrangements. It's all set."

I backed up and regrouped. "Well, then, what about Sally? We can't just go off and leave her to—"

"Of course we can. For one thing, we have no idea where she is. For all we know, she could have ditched Brian's car and caught a bus to San Antonio or Houston or El Paso. Or maybe she and her stalker connected and they're taking a lovers' holiday—or something. For another, if she walked in the door right now, you would call the police, and Sheila would come and take her off to the hoosegow." She eyed me. "Wouldn't you?"

I sighed. Fair point. I'm no longer in practice, but I'm still a member of the bar and an officer of the court. Which means that if I don't stay on the right side of the law, I risk losing my privileges. And anyway, I had already decided that Sally in custody is safer than Sally on the street. Ruby was right. I'd call Sheila.

"But what do we do about the shops?" I asked. "Cass isn't available, and Laurel's out of town. We'd have to close early."

"So what's wrong with that?" Ruby replied. "It's after three o'clock. We'd be shutting up shop in a couple of hours, anyway. Let's just put up the Closed sign and be on our way—or you could add 'Family Emergency,' if you want to include an explanation. Sally is family, sort of, and this is definitely an emergency." She looked at me, straight and hard. "Something is telling me that we should do this, China."

I shook my head. But after a number of years hanging around with Ruby, I have learned to honor her hunches. And I definitely wanted to find out what had happened to Leslie, although that might be easier said than done. As far as the Lake City police were concerned, we had no authority whatever. They wouldn't give us the time of day, let alone hand out information about a homicide that was under investigation.

Still, it was worth a shot. I wasn't going to get any information for the Whiz hanging around Pecan Springs. And Ruby was right. It wouldn't kill us to close the shops early for once. Lake City wasn't that far. And the kids were settled for the night.

"Okay, we'll go," I agreed reluctantly. "But I'll need to let Justine know. She can contact the Pecan Springs police and have them telephone her directly when they pick Sally up." *If* they picked her up. As the afternoon wore on, that *if* was looming larger and larger.

"Are you going to call McQuaid, too?" Ruby asked.

I hesitated. "Yes, but maybe I'll wait until we get there, so he can't tell me not to go." Or rather, he could tell me and he probably would, but it wouldn't do any good, since I'd already be there. Anyway, he wanted me to spend the evening with Ruby, didn't he? So I was spending the evening with Ruby—in Lake City.

"Good plan," Ruby said with satisfaction, "but we'll need a cover story."

"A cover story?" I asked warily.

"Well, yes," Ruby replied in a sensible tone. "You don't expect us just to barge into the Lake City police station and tell the cops that we're there to investigate Leslie's death. That'll get us nowhere fast. Kinsey Millhone would have a reason, you know. A cover story."

I regarded her suspiciously. "What do you suggest?" Ruby has roped me into more than one crazy adventure. "And it had better be a reasonable reason," I added. I wasn't eager to try out another of her idiotic schemes.

"Give me a minute," she said, casting her eyes to the ceiling, as if inspiration might be waiting somewhere above, in the loft. And maybe it was, for within thirty seconds, she had concocted a plan. We would drive the Party Thyme van and take a couple of boxes of Cass' Thymely Gourmet dinners to go, with Leslie's name and address written on the boxes. That way, we could say we were delivering a special order.

"A couple of boxes of takeout, all the way to Lake City?" I scoffed. "Come on, Ruby, get real."

"I am real," she insisted. "It's a surprise, you see. One of Leslie's friends wanted to give her a holiday gift. And you and I just happened to be going up to Temple, to cater little Mickey Hitchcock's afternoon birthday party. We told Cass we'd deliver her dinners to Ms. Strahorn on the way back."

I regarded her. "Temple?" It's a small city halfway between Austin and Waco, on I-35. "And who's Mickey Hitchcock? I've never heard of him."

"Of course you haven't. I just made him up. The decorations from the party Cass and I catered for Janine Kelly's little boy's birthday are still in the van. If somebody—a nosy cop, say—wants to check us out, he'll find boxes of crepe paper, a dartboard, a couple of piñatas, and the railroad caboose we made to hold the gifts. How's that for a cover?"

I resisted the urge to roll my eyes, which I often do when Ruby comes up with one of her wild ideas. But since I thought the Lake City cops had better things to do than check us out, and I couldn't come up with anything better on such short notice, I nodded, humoring her.

"Good." Ruby reached for the phone. "You call Justine. I'll call Amy. I always let her know when I'm going somewhere. Oh, and we also have to do today's deposits."

A half hour later, phone calls completed and the cash deposits readied, we were in Big Red Mama, with two Thymely Gourmet boxes we had filled with Cass' croissant sandwiches, salad, chips, and cookies. Mama is the red shop van that replaced our beat-up old blue van two years ago. Her former owner was a hippie artist named Gerald who lived in Wimberley until he was arrested for running a crystal meth lab, and the Hayes County Sheriff's Office impounded and sold his van. Ruby and I bought Mama primarily because of the imaginative, Art Deco designs of blue, green, and yellow that Gerald painted on her sides, probably under the influence of a certain hallucinatory herb. Mama looks like a cross between a Crayola box scuttling down the road and a Sweet Potato Queen float in a Mardi Gras parade.

Mama rolled out of the alley, and we turned left. "I need to go to my house and change," Ruby reminded me. "We're headed in the wrong direction."

"We have to go to the bank first," I said, nodding to the deposit bag, although the deposit wasn't the only thing on my mind. Five minutes later, we were there, and in luck. Bonnie Roth was working the drive-through window. I dropped the deposit bag into the automated box below the window. Bonnie zapped it inside and got to work.

When she had counted the cash and was noting the amount on the deposit ticket, I said into the mike, "Oh, I almost forgot, Bonnie. Remember that check you mentioned yesterday? The one Sally cashed?"

"Sure," Bonnie said absently, turning to the checks in our deposit. She began keying them rapidly into her adding machine. "What about it?"

"McQuaid was curious. Did you happen to notice whether it was drawn on her bank up in Kansas? Sanders is the name of the town." I was only telling part of the truth. I hadn't mentioned the check to McQuaid, but if I had, I knew he'd be curious. And if I mentioned McQuaid to Bonnie, she'd be more likely to answer the question.

"Not Kansas," Bonnie said, concentrating on her work. "It was a Texas bank. Lake City, I think. Her brother's bank."

"Her brother?" Then it dawned, and I felt my stomach clench. This wasn't what I wanted to hear, but I couldn't let Bonnie know that. "Oh, sure. Leslie. That's her sister."

Bonnie looked up and rolled her eyes. "Don'cha just hate those names that can be both? I have this second cousin—my mother's brother's daughter's daughter—who sent me a baby announcement for their second. Taylor." She went back to her adding machine, fingers flying. "They named their first one Logan. Logan, for pete's sake!" She snorted. "How am I supposed to know whether to buy blue or buy pink? This is a big thing with me. Parents ought to name their kids so you know whether they're boys or girls."

"I agree a hundred percent," I said. "Listen, Bonnie, I hope you don't think we're prying, but McQuaid thought he ought to know how big the check was, just in case."

Anybody else might've asked, "In case of what?" or "What makes you think I'd give out private financial information?" But not Bonnie.

"Well, I'm glad Mr. McQuaid is thinking about this," she said, jiggling the checks into a neat stack. "Five thousand dollars is a lot of money to be carrying around, and of course, the bank manager had to approve it. I believe she called the other bank and found out that there was enough money in the account to cover it. Of course, if it had been someone else, we'd probably have held it. But seeing that it was covered, and that it was Mr. McQuaid's ex-wife, we figured it was okay." She stamped the deposit ticket with vigor and tucked it in the bag. "I'm just concerned for safety. These days, you just never know."

"Oh, right," I said. "Better safe than sorry any old day of the week. I'll let Mr. McQuaid know how helpful you've been. Thanks a bunch." The automatic box slid out, and I took my bag. "You have a great day, Bonnie."

"You, too, China." She might think later that she shouldn't have been so generous with that information, but by then, it would be much too late.

But as we drove away, I was frowning. Five thousand dollars. Surely Sally wasn't carrying all that cash around with her. But if she wasn't, where had she stashed it? And the check itself—had Leslie actually written it? Or was Sally—or Juanita—practicing her forgery skills on a stolen check? There had been one other instance of forgery in Sally's checkered past. I corrected myself. There was only one that I knew about, but that was because she got caught. There might have been more. McQuaid and I didn't know all that much about Sally's life.

Ruby had been listening, naturally. "Five thousand dollars?" she asked incredulously, as we drove away. "Sally's sister wrote her a check for *five thousand dollars*? And I thought Sally told you she was broke. What is she planning to do with all that money?"

"I don't have a clue. But I'm wondering whether Leslie actually wrote that check."

I told Ruby as much as I knew about the check and then about Sally's phone call to McQuaid, asking him to go to Sanders to talk to Joyce Dillard. I finished the story just as we pulled up to Ruby's house, where I waited in the van—still thinking about Sally—while she went in to change into something "more appropriate," as she called it. The fact that Sally had one of Leslie's checks—legitimately or not—suggested to me that she had been with Leslie in Lake City before she came to Pecan Springs. Since this was definitely something Justine ought to know about, I phoned, got the Whiz's answering machine, and left a message. I added that Ruby and I were on our way to Lake City to dig up the facts and promised to call again when—no, make that *if*—I had news.

It didn't take long for Ruby to change. She came back wearing yellow jeans, a Big Bird canary-yellow sweatshirt, and a Big Bird hat, crocheted in yellow wool and complete with a brown beak and big round eyes. Her jacket and sneakers were yellow, and she carried a yellow Big Bird tote.

"That's some getup," I said. "Especially if you're fond of yellow."

"I'm glad you like it," she said, pleased. "I wore this costume when Party Thyme catered PattiAnn Parker's birthday party last summer. The kids loved it, especially because I'm tall. One of them said I was almost as tall as Big Bird himself, and that I should eat lots of worms so I could grow some." She adjusted her hat. "Anyway, I thought it would be more appropriate."

I cleared my throat. "More appropriate than what?" I turned the key in the ignition. Mama coughed once, politely, and began humming.

"More appropriate than plain old everyday street clothes. You know what Kinsey says. 'Being a private investigator is made up of equal parts ingenuity, determination, and persistence, with a sizable dose of acting skills thrown in.' I act better when I'm in costume."

"I suppose there's something to that," I said.

"I have a hat for you, too." Ruby reached into the tote bag and held up a shaggy electric-blue hat with two large eyes, the size of Ping-Pong balls, the black pupils pointing off in different directions. "There's more to the Cookie Monster costume, of course. There's a shaggy blue oversize shirt and pants. Blue mittens and booties, too. But I didn't think you'd want to wear those."

I shuddered. "You got that right, Ruby."

She put the Cookie Monster hat back into her tote. "I figure the hat alone will be enough to convince them," she added complacently, fastening her seat belt. "You won't need the rest of it. They'll know who you are."

"Convince *them*?"

She gave me a look that said she was surprised that I wasn't smart enough to figure this out for myself. "The Lake City police. With me dressed up as Big Bird and you wearing your Cookie Monster hat, they've got to believe we've been catering a party, instead of on our way to solve a crime." She pulled down the visor mirror and adjusted her hat. "Nobody in her right mind would go out looking like this unless she got paid for it."

"You have a point there." I shifted into first gear. Mama hummed louder and began to move. "But we are not going to come anywhere near the Lake City police, Ruby. In fact, we are not going to solve a crime. We are only trying to find out what kind of crime was committed." I pushed down on the accelerator, and Mama got rolling. "I have to tell you that

I'm not optimistic, though. I doubt that we will discover any significant facts." I wanted to add, *Particularly with you looking like Big Bird.*

But that would have been cruel, so I didn't. I love Ruby dearly, even though I sometimes wonder if she isn't almost as loopy as Doris.

Anyway, as things turned out, I was wrong. We were going to learn quite a few facts, although not all of them would be helpful in Sally's defense, if it came to that. In fact, most would not.

And Big Bird herself was going to unearth the most crucial fact of all.

Chapter Eleven

McQuaid: A Body in the Snow

McQuaid followed Jamison outside, shrugging hurriedly into his coat as he ran. The snow had lightened a bit, and the flakes were no longer blowing horizontally. They were falling lazily now, swirling like white moths through the blue light cast by the single mercury lamp at the edge of the parking lot. The deep marks left by McQuaid's tires when he drove in were already softened by a fluffy white layer.

Jamison jammed himself into his cruiser, put on the red and blue strobe and siren, and blasted out of the lot, spewing snow and shattering the quiet night. McQuaid followed, knowing that the cop was already on the radio, calling for EMS, for backup, for all available officers. Joyce Dillard was the town's librarian, the daughter of a councilman. If that was her in the ditch, she'd be big news, probably the biggest news of the year.

The road had been plowed a couple of hours ago but was already drifted heavily on the curves, narrowing it to one lane. Driving was hazardous. The cruiser had snow tires, and Jamison knew where the hell he was going. All McQuaid could do was keep the taillights in view and stay as close as he could, even though it meant pushing the Chevy harder than he should in these marginal conditions.

The wind was whipping, the snow came in brief, hard spurts, and yet the full moon rode through the broken clouds, lighting up the silvered fields and woods like an intermittent beacon, throwing everything into a glittering patchwork of bright and dark, dark and bright. In better weather, when he didn't have to keep his eyes on the road, McQuaid would've enjoyed seeing the snow-covered landscape: the bare, ice-coated willow trees lining the river that wandered through the fields to the west; the snow-clad sycamores marching single file along the east side of the road; the old red barns, stalwart shelters against the glacial sweep of winter winds. He had liked it here in Kansas, had liked the seasons, even the winters. In early times, in the first days—the youthful, hopeful days—of his marriage to Sally, he had even entertained the thought of coming to Sanders to live. He and Sally could settle down, buy a house with enough room for a garden, and have a passel of kids and a couple of dogs. He would become a small-town cop, or maybe he'd go into business with Sally's dad. They would hunt and fish together, play poker, run the horse-shoe tournament at the Fourth of July picnic every year.

But Sally had made it clear that while she didn't mind coming back to Sanders to visit every now and then, she had no intention of leaving the city. And as far as being mom to a gang of kids and wife to a small-town cop—well, forget that, buster. No garden, that wasn't her thing. And no dogs, either. She was allergic, she said, which of course wasn't true.

So McQuaid had tabled his hopes—regretfully, because he'd thought Brian would be happier in Sanders. He'd never really given up the idea of living in a small town, though, and it came back in a warm flood when he met China Bayles and learned that she was planning to leave her law firm and open some sort of shop in Pecan Springs, not far from another small town—Seguin—where his parents still lived. A few months later, with Brian and their newly acquired basset hound, Howard Cosell, he had left the Houston PD and moved to Pecan Springs. Never regretted it. Not once.

He was less than a half mile from town when the cruiser ahead of him swerved to an angled stop, blocking the road, and McQuaid made himself focus on what was in front of him. Off to the right, in the bright pool of Jamison's headlights, he could see the red pickup blocking one lane of the two-lane road, its back wheels in the ditch, its lights punching holes in the sky above the trees. Jamison himself was out of the cruiser and running toward the truck, where a girl, probably Meg, was hunched over, throwing up into a snowbank. The other girl, Annie, was still back at Joe's, probably also throwing up. Teenage girls were a helluva lot tougher than they were when McQuaid was their age, but they didn't find dead bodies every day of the week. Chicago, L.A., maybe, but not out here in the middle of Kansas, in the middle of winter.

McQuaid got out of the Chevy and went toward Jamison and the girl, the wind pushing at his back. Straightening up, hand over her mouth, she was pointing to a heap of red wool, some strings of dark hair, loose. A pale, empty face, upturned, framed by mounded snow.

McQuaid stopped. Jamison turned to look at him. "You stay back," he said gruffly.

"Not a problem," McQuaid said. He stopped where he was and shoved his hands in his pockets. "That her?"

"We didn't touch her, honest," Meg cried. "Just enough to brush off the snow and see who it was. Ms. Dillard's dead," she added unnecessarily. "Froze to death." Her hand went over her mouth again and her shoulders heaved.

"That's okay, Meg," Jamison said. "How about if you go sit in my car? I left the engine on, and the heater's goin'. Except don't throw up in it. You gotta throw up, get out, d'ya hear? Do it in the snow."

"Yessir," Meg said.

"I had the dispatch call your mother and tell her to come and pick you up," Jamison added. "We'll hafta get Pete out here with his tow truck to pull your pickup outta that ditch. It's in there pretty good. Axle's hung up."

"Yessir," Meg said again and stumbled past McQuaid.

Jamison yanked his cap down. "I want you outta the way, McQuaid," he said again, roughly. "But don't you leave. You and I are gonna have a talk. Unnerstand?"

McQuaid understood and nodded. "Might as well wait in my car," he said, and turned into the wind.

The usual things happened in the next hour, while he kept the Chevy's motor running and the heater going. Not much on the radio but some gospel music, and after a while McQuaid turned it off, wanting a cigarette. He'd stopped smoking years before, but the wish for it still plagued him, particularly when he was alone, with nothing to do. He thought it probably always would. After a few moments, though, he remembered the snacks and the beer in the backseat. He wasn't hungry, but a beer would go good about now. He located a can of Michelob, as cold as if it had been in the fridge. He popped the top, propped his boot up on the dash, and surveyed the scene.

It was like watching a movie he'd seen countless times before, where he already knew the plot and was familiar with all the actors. The EMS arrived first, parking on the far side of the red truck, bright emergency lights illuminating the scene, spilling black and blue shadows over the snow. McQuaid knew what would happen next. The medics were supposed to stand by until the police established the perimeters and took photographs. But in this case, five would get you ten that they wouldn't. They'd start digging out the dead woman hurriedly, as if there was a chance of saving her, which there clearly wasn't, and in the process they would destroy whatever evidence there might be.

Jamison should tell them to hold off, but he wouldn't do that, either. Not because he didn't know better, but because the victim's father was a big man in this county. He'd want his daughter out of her cold, snowy grave as quickly as possible. He wouldn't give a bloody damn about evidence until later, when he had time to think about it and wonder who had put her there. Then he'd take the police department to task for not being more professional, probably lecture the chief, who would in turn give Jamison a public reprimand and assign him to some training, but in private, tell him to forget it. McQuaid knew all this, because he'd been in Jamison's position, or something like, more times than he could remember. Case like this, you were damned if you did, damned if you didn't.

The medics were still scooping the snow away from the body when two more police cruisers arrived, one spilling out a pair of cops, the other a single. For a few minutes, the three of them and Jamison huddled together, while Jamison gave instructions. They broke, one of the cops going for a camera, a second to set up the perimeter tape, the third to watch the techs. Jamison went to his car, where he got on the radio again. Ten minutes later, a car pulled up and a woman got out. Meg got out of the cruiser and went toward it. There was a brief flurry of hugging, then the woman hustled her daughter into the car and backed up down the road to where she could turn around without getting stuck.

The car was barely out of sight when a pickup arrived and a burly man in a thick coat with a fur collar and a cap with earflaps jumped out. Arms flailing, he half-ran, half-stumbled through the snow to where the medics were lifting the body onto a gurney. Joyce Dillard's daddy, the town councilman. The one who had posted the forty-grand reward that the two girls would probably split. No doubt Meg and her mother were discussing the possibility of a newly enhanced college fund at this very moment, while back at Joe's, Annie was probably counting her money, and counting her lucky stars.

Well, what the hell. Somebody had to find the body and collect the reward. If it hadn't been for the girls spinning out and sliding into the ditch, Dillard might have laid there under the snow until spring thaw.

The car was getting warm, and McQuaid turned down the heater a notch, watching the scene, trying not to feel the worry rising in his gut, concentrating on the likely scenarios, the possible explanations for what had happened here. Joyce Dillard might have gone out for a winter evening's walk, stumbled into the ditch, bounced her head off a rock, and lay there until she froze to death. Hypothermia would come fast, this time of year. And even a light snow would have blanketed the body to the point where it wouldn't be noticed. He held his hands out to the stream of warm air pushed out by the heater. Things like that happened in Kansas in the winter. People went outdoors, got lost, got hurt, froze to death.

But there were other possibilities, criminal possibilities. Maybe she was walking along the road and was struck by a vehicle. Hit-and-run. That happened all the time, too. Icy roads, soccer mom in a hurry to pick up the kids, teenager blabbing on her cell phone, wino driving drunk. Driver hits pedestrian, driver panics, speeds away. Pedestrian pitches into the ditch, snow falls. The body isn't discovered for days, weeks. By that time the evidence is washed away by snowmelt, the driver gets his or her vehicle repaired in KC or Omaha, and that's the end of that. Case goes cold, gets shoved to the back of the file drawer, unsolved.

Or maybe—

Or maybe it didn't happen that way. China might argue for another scenario, if she were here. She'd say that maybe Joyce Dillard had named Jess Myers as the one who killed the Strahorns, and that he somehow got wind of this. He figured he'd better plug the leak before it got worse, before Joyce went to the cops. So he'd killed her and left her in the ditch, where he figured she wouldn't be found for a good long time.

McQuaid's head ached, and he cracked the window an inch, letting in some fresh air. He knew China all too well. Once she got her teeth into something like this, she was a bulldog. She wouldn't leave the story there. She would point out that if Myers killed Dillard because she had told Sally what she knew, maybe he wasn't finished. Maybe he couldn't afford to be. So he'd headed for Texas. He'd gone to Lake City, where he killed Leslie, on the chance that Sally had shared Joyce's information with her sister. And now (China would point out) he was in Pecan Springs. He was looking for Sally.

Speculation. All speculation. But it was possible, certainly. And McQuaid had learned a long time ago that when the ifs and maybes began organizing themselves into a pattern, it was time to get serious about the possibilities.

Four deaths. The Strahorns, then Joyce Dillard, then Leslie. There was a pattern. The next piece in the pattern was Sally.

Feeling suddenly cold, McQuaid plugged his beer can into the drink holder and reached for his cell phone. He glanced at his watch. It felt like midnight, but it was just past seven twenty. He was hoping that the Pecan Springs police had already picked Sally up. In custody, she'd be safe. But if the police hadn't detained her or had decided not to hold her, she would be with China this evening. Which would put China in jeopardy, as well. He'd better let her know that Joyce was dead, ASAP. She and Sally had to be careful. A lot more careful.

But China wasn't picking up. Sharply disappointed, he left a message—urgent, because that's how he felt.

"China, listen to me, and listen hard. I can't talk to Joyce Dillard, because she's dead in a roadside ditch, just outside Sanders. I'm at the scene. There's no word yet on the cause of death, but I'm beginning to think you might be right about Myers. I want you and Sally—if she's not in police custody—to hunker down at Ruby's and stay there. *You hear me?* Go to Ruby's and stay there. When the cops finish with Sally, she should stay there, too. Tomorrow, as well. I don't want her out on the streets. Call me as soon as you can. I may have an update on Dillard."

As an afterthought, he added, in a softer tone. "Love you, babe. I'm glad you got the kids out of the way. Be careful, please. I've decided that Charlie Lipman's Omaha job can wait. I'll change my flight and be home as quick as I can."

Be careful. Yeah, right, he thought, as he clicked off. Telling China Bayles to be careful was like adding sticks of dry wood to a fire. She had a bad habit of overlooking the risks when she was focused on something that totally captured her attention. Like the time, just a few months ago, when she was visiting a Shaker village in Kentucky and got mixed up in a murder investigation. But in this situation, he had to trust her and hope for the best. As far as he was concerned, best-case was Sally getting picked up by the Pecan Springs police and warehoused in an interrogation room, a cell, even. Anywhere Myers couldn't get at her.

Which led to another phone call, this time to the Pecan Springs police. After a three-minute wait, he got through to Sheila Dawson, who was still in the office.

"Mike McQuaid here, Sheila. Have you picked up Sally?"

"I wish," Sheila said crisply. "You've heard why we're looking for her?"

"China told me," McQuaid replied. "A person of interest in her sister's homicide." Leslie's image rose up in his mind, and he bit back the flash of pain that came with it. "Can you tell me anything more than that?"

"Not much," Sheila replied warily. "Haven't heard any of the details from Lake City yet."

McQuaid pictured her sitting behind the desk in her utilitarian, unfeminine office, no family photos or trinkets. Not even an artificial plant or a drape to soften the severe plastic blinds at the window. Just a very beautiful, very sexy, entirely self-contained woman, pretty much a renegade and an aloof loner who lived for her job. That the job was occasionally dangerous was only an added bonus for her. Or maybe danger was the bottom-line reason she did what she did. She and Blackie were uncomfortably paired where that was concerned. For Blackie, law enforcement had been his family's family business for three generations, and he was a family man. He had a couple of older boys by a previous marriage, but he'd like to have another family. He also liked to have the guys around, poker partners, fishing buddies—the more the merrier. Sheila wasn't keen on kids, and she wasn't the kind of woman who'd be waiting at the kitchen door, eager to fry up the big mess of catfish that her husband and his friends brought home. McQuaid had been glad to hear that she and Blackie were back together again, if that's what they both wanted. But he wouldn't lay a nickel on their long-term success.

Sheila cleared her throat. "I can tell you that we've got a stakeout on the car Sally was driving."

McQuaid shifted the phone from one ear to the other. "Brian's car?"

"Yes. It's parked in the far corner of the Congregational church lot, behind McMasters Office Supply. Ruby happened to notice it. We've had it covered since midafternoon, but there's been no sign of Sally. We're watching it for the rest of the night. In the morning, I'll consider other options. Just letting you know that the car may be out of commission for a while."

McQuaid felt a sharp stab of uneasiness. "Any indication of violence?"

"Nothing we can see through the windows, although we haven't gotten into the vehicle yet. Looks like Sally simply parked it, locked it, and took the keys. The bus station is within walking distance. They've got an automated ticket machine for short-haul riders, though, and bus traffic is heavy right now, with students going home for the holidays. No way to tell whether she got on a bus, and if she did, which way she went." Sheila paused. "I don't suppose you have any idea where she might go."

McQuaid leaned forward against the steering wheel. The car, abandoned. No sign of Sally. What if China was right, and this guy Myers was a serious threat? What if he had already caught up with her? Grabbed her, forced her to leave Brian's car in the lot, took her off somewhere. What if—

"Sheila, listen to me. This guy who's stalking her. The one China told you about. He isn't your ordinary garden-variety stalker."

"No such thing," she countered caustically. "Not in my experience."

McQuaid ignored that. "His name is Myers, Jess Myers."

"China told me. An ex-boyfriend."

"Maybe. But more than that, he was a suspect in her parents' killings. They were murdered. Shot to death, in Sanders, Kansas, ten years ago."

A taut silence. He knew he'd gotten her attention. Sheila was a professional, adept at putting pieces together. She'd make the connection. "Was a suspect," she repeated. "The police couldn't come up with a case against him?"

"I talked to the lead investigator this evening. The shooter took the gun and quite a bit of cash. Myers had done some remodeling work in the Strahorns' house—I'm guessing his prints were around the place. But no. They couldn't make a case. Or at least they didn't."

Be fair. Tell her that Sally was a suspect, too, nudged the voice in the back of his head. But that was irrelevant. It would only muddy the waters.

"Listen, Sheila," he said forcefully. "There's more."

"Yeah? I'm listening."

"Okay. I'm in Sanders right now. I came here to talk to a woman named Joyce Dillard. Dillard recently told Sally that she knew who killed the Strahorns. She gave Sally a name. Sally wouldn't tell me who it was, but she claimed that Joyce knew the location of the murder weapon—a Luger that belonged to Sally's father. I came here to interview Dillard and try to persuade her to tell me what she told Sally. I hoped to get what she knew about the gun, as well. But she's dead. I'm looking at the scene right now. A couple of girls found her in a ditch, buried in the snow."

Sheila put it together quickly. "And now the sister—Leslie—is dead, too," she said in a considering tone. "Did the sister know Myers?"

"They all lived in the same small town. The Strahorns, Myers, Sally, Leslie, Joyce Dillard." He swallowed. "Look, Sheila. I don't want Sally out where he can get his hands on her. When you find her, keep her in custody for as long as you can."

"You bet," Sheila said. "Anything else?"

He wanted to say, *You could lock China up, too, while you're at it,* but he didn't. Now wasn't the time for bad jokes. "Just find her," he said emphatically. "And don't let her go."

"We'll do our best. Thanks, McQuaid." Sheila broke the connection.

McQuaid clicked off the call, leaned back, and picked up his beer can. He was making a mental list of things he needed to do—call Charlie

Lipman, call the man he was supposed to interview tomorrow, call the airline to get an early morning flight out of Kansas City—when Jamison rapped on the passenger-side window, opened the door and slid in, bringing with him a rush of damp cold and the smell of snow, wet wool, and Joe's onions.

"How's it going out there?" McQuaid asked.

"About like you'd think." Not looking at him, Jamison yanked off his leather gloves, finger by finger, and held his hands to the heater, rubbing them. "Ugly, isn't it?"

"Never gets any prettier," McQuaid agreed. They didn't have to say that it was the scene that was ugly, and not the weather. They watched as the medics hoisted the gurney into the ambulance and closed the doors. The father trudged to his car, and both vehicles drove off. The medics didn't run the ambulance emergency lights. No emergency now. Joyce Dillard had already confronted the greatest emergency of her life, and there had been no one around to rescue her. The two men contemplated this truth in silence.

A moment later, the other patrol cars pulled away, as well. All that was left in the blowing, moon-shadowed night was Jamison's cruiser, the red pickup truck, and the yellow tape squaring off a patch of frozen ditch.

McQuaid reached over and turned the heater up a notch. "You on duty?"

"Nope. Quit at five. Council doesn't pay overtime. We'll be back tomorrow morning. Maybe we'll find something else in that ditch. Likely not, though," he added without inflection.

McQuaid agreed, although there was a chance. A piece of broken mirror or headlight, a strip of chrome. If it was a vehicular homicide, which maybe it wasn't. There was still the possibility that Dillard had been out for a walk and fallen accidentally.

He leaned over the seat and pulled up another beer. "You've gotta be thirsty." He handed the can to Jamison, who took it, popped the top, and drank briefly.

"Thanks," Jamison said, turning to McQuaid. His eyes were cop's eyes, eyes that had seen more than anybody wanted to see, ought to see, in a human lifetime. But there was no anger there, only weariness and a measuring appraisal that was neither opinion nor judgment. McQuaid recognized the look. He had seen it in the eyes of other law enforcement officers, especially those who had been on the force for a couple dozen years. He had seen it in his own eyes, in his mirror. Sally had seen it, too. Cold eyes, she'd said. Fish eyes. A cold, dead fish.

"You said your ex-wife wanted you to talk to Ms. Dillard," Jamison said. "Why?"

Time to come clean, McQuaid thought. Nothing to be gained by holding back now. Maybe something to lose if he didn't.

"I told you some of it," he said, "but there's more. Sally came back to Sanders recently with the idea of writing a book about her parents' murders. That's when you saw her."

Jamison swiveled to look at him. "You gotta be shittin' me," he said incredulously. "A *book*?"

McQuaid liked him for that. "Yeah, I know. But hear me out. She was working at the KC *Star* and decided to try for a story, or maybe a book, so she came to town to talk to people about the case."

"She didn't talk to me. Didn't talk to any of our guys, so far as I know."

McQuaid chuckled. "Yeah. Well, maybe you were at the bottom of her list. Anyway, when she got here, she ran into Joyce Dillard. Joyce told her that she had an idea who killed the Strahorns and what happened to the gun. She named a name, but Sally wouldn't tell me who it was. She wanted me to talk to Joyce and see what I could get out of her." He paused. "That's it, Jamison. That's why I'm here. I don't have a name to give you, and I don't know where the gun is."

"Yeah." Jamison grunted. "But I got this feeling, McQuaid. You wouldn't have driven down here from Omaha in a blizzard just on the chance of a chat. What else you got?"

McQuaid drained the last of his beer. "Myers," he said. He crumpled the empty can and tossed it over his shoulder. It landed with a chink in the open bag with the rest of the beer on the backseat. "Jess Myers. Suspect in the Strahorn shootings. You seen him around in the past day or two?"

"Myers." Jamison's voice held an odd tone. He closed his eyes and rubbed his forehead wearily. "Can't say that I have. How come?"

"Because Sally showed up in Texas day before yesterday, in the town where I live. She was looking for a place to stay. Myers showed up shortly afterward, looking for her. My wife talked to him on the phone, twice, once late last night. She said he sounded threatening. And Sally was scared."

"Scared, was she? Why am I not surprised?" Jamison pushed his lips in and out. "She say why?"

"No, and my wife didn't push it—although she was concerned enough to ask the county sheriff, a friend of ours, to detour a deputy past our place in the night. Then this afternoon, she learned that Sally's sister, Leslie, is dead. Lake City, Texas, where she lived. Homicide, last couple of days, maybe even more recent."

No need to tell Jamison the rest of it, that Sally was a person of interest. And anyway, the more he thought about this, the more he thought it had no relevance, except as an inconvenience to Sally (from Sally's point of view) or from his point of view, as a way to get her into police custody, where she would be safe. She wasn't the one the Lake City police wanted. They ought to be talking to Myers, find out what he knew about Leslie's death.

Jamison reacted more strongly than he had expected. "Leslie? Little Leslie Strahorn, used to work at Joe's?" He squeezed his eyes shut, opened them, shook his head. "Aw, hell."

"Yeah," McQuaid said, and was almost surprised at the pain he felt.

"Leslie." Jamison was gruff. "Pretty thing, bouncy. Always a good word. Saw the bright side."

"Yeah," McQuaid said again and looked out at the dark.

There was a silence.

Jamison cleared his throat. "Puts a different light on things, don't it?" he asked. "So how're you reading it, McQuaid? What's your take?"

McQuaid gave it to him—China's argument. The argument she would make if she were sitting in the backseat, looking over their shoulders at that snowy ditch where Joyce Dillard's body had been found. It didn't take long.

Jamison rested the beer can on the dash. "So you're pointing the finger at Jess Myers. You think he killed the Strahorns. Dillard, too. And Leslie. And you figure your ex-wife's next?"

"It's a possibility," McQuaid said. "Make sense? You tagged Myers as a suspect in the Strahorn murders. You must have felt he was capable of doing the job."

"We also tagged your ex," Jamison said flatly. A muscle in his jaw was working. "Try this on for size, McQuaid. Sally Strahorn is going through a divorce—from you. She's a little crazy and a lot desperate for money. She knows her folks have it but they won't fork it over and she's got to have

203

it. She sweet-talks Jess Myers into robbing her folks. She unlocks her family's gun cabinet. He gets the loaded Luger, waits for the Strahorns to come home from Wednesday night prayer meeting. There's a ruckus, the Strahorns end up dead. Sally and Jess are in it together, whether it was meant to be murder or not. They split the cash that's in the house. And when she finally collects her share of the insurance, she gives him a payoff."

The voice in the back of McQuaid's head said, *I told you so, didn't I? Could've happened that way. Except that it wasn't Sally. It was the other one. The crazy one. Juanita.*

The car was getting warm. McQuaid turned down the heater to low. "I thought you said Myers didn't show any extra cash."

"He didn't. But that's not to say he didn't have it. He's a close-hold kinda guy, secretive, keeps to himself. Could've stashed his share under his mattress for his retirement. Or put it into the stock market, or blown it in Vegas." He grunted gloomily. "All kinds of places where a man can put money these days without anybody knowin' about it."

McQuaid wasn't surprised that Jamison had this all worked out. He was a good cop. He hadn't closed out any options. And Sally had been on the suspect list, too, which made for a natural pairing with Myers and took care of the problem of the unlocked gun cabinet. He could see the logic.

Well, good, snapped the voice. *Maybe now you'll toughen up, McQuaid. Get smart. See what's real. Sally isn't what you think, never has been.*

Aloud, he said, "Don't suppose you've got any evidence to support your theory," knowing that if he had anything he could use to make a case, Myers and Sally wouldn't be suspects. They would have been charged and tried. Convicted, most likely, since the Strahorns were much loved and it would have been hard to find an impartial jury.

"Not enough, but some." Jamison gave him a grim half smile. "For starters, she was hanging out with him the week the Strahorns were killed. His neighbor thought she was sleepin' with him, which would've made her parents livid, if they knew. And as I said, she was bouncin' checks. Hittin' on her folks for a loan. And fightin' with them." He shook his head. "Enough bad family feeling to motivate the shootings, McQuaid. It's all in my notes from the original investigation."

Hanging out with Myers, the voice said. *Got that?* Sally had been in terrible shape while the divorce was going through. Sanders was a small town, and gossip was a major recreational sport. McQuaid hadn't supposed she'd come back home and start sleeping with one of her old flames, but he reckoned anything was possible, especially if Juanita was in the picture.

"You were chief then?" he asked.

"Yeah," Jamison said shortly. "Couldn't clear the Strahorn case, got replaced." He gave an ironic chuckle. "It was Joyce Dillard's daddy led the pack. I guess Patterson—he's chief now, took over from the guy who took over from me—will find out how it works. Clear the case or take a demotion. Or, since it's Dillard's daughter who's dead, maybe Patterson will get to walk the plank instead of just getting demoted."

McQuaid understood, and knew what else was going through Jamison's mind. If he could break the Dillard homicide—assuming that's what it was—maybe he would get his old job back. If breaking the Dillard case also resolved the Strahorn murders, maybe he'd run for county sheriff. He'd get a lot of coverage in the local paper. He'd be a shoo-in. And from that position, he could thumb his nose at the Sanders town council.

"So how do you think Joyce Dillard figures in this?" McQuaid asked.

Jamison gave him a hard look. "Come on, McQuaid. That's easy. She finds out who did the Strahorns and wants her cut of the take. Or maybe she's a good citizen and threatens to blow the whistle on Bonnie and Clyde. Either way, that's it for Joyce. Last act. Curtains."

"You're sure Dillard's a homicide?"

"The back side of her head was smashed in, I could see that much. The body will go to the state lab. We'll get the particulars back next week."

"So maybe Sally was sleeping with Myers and hitting her folks up for money. That's circumstantial." McQuaid frowned. "You got anything else? Anything that a clever defense attorney can't tear apart?"

Jamison's jaw set stubbornly. "What else is I see her and Myers together when she was back in town last time. She stayed at that motel you asked me about. Sycamore Court. Day after, I see her with Joyce Dillard." He paused for emphasis. "Then Joyce disappears." He turned down the corners of his mouth. "This ain't rocket science, McQuaid."

"But it's still circumstantial." McQuaid tapped his fingers on the steering wheel. "You say you saw Sally with Myers?"

Jamison nodded. "Walking. In the park. They didn't exactly look friendly. When she saw me, she did a fast fade. Beat it out of there. Didn't want to talk to me."

"Could've been a perfectly innocent connection," McQuaid said. "She knew Myers from a bad time—also knew that he was a suspect in her parents' deaths. He found out she was back in town and wanted to see her again. She wasn't thrilled at the idea. Which was why she wasn't friendly." He gave Jamison a crooked grin. "And she faded when she saw you because she knew you'd harass her."

"Yeah, it could've been like that," Jamison allowed with a shrug. His voice hardened. "Could also have been a pair of coconspirators who'd had a falling-out over money or something else and were no longer on friendly terms. But they had a job to do—taking care of Joyce—and they had to figure out how to get it done. Which meant that they had to get together."

"Yeah," McQuaid said grimly. "I suppose it could." He didn't like it, but he could see it both ways.

Good, the voice said. *Now you're using your head. Being realistic.*

Jamison tapped the rim of his can against the car window. "Word around town is that your ex has a serious psychological problem," he said. "Multiple personality, way I heard it. What do you know about this?"

Don't lie, the voice cautioned. *Don't protect her. If Sally—no, if Juanita had something to do with this—with any of it—she'll have to pay the price. Whatever it is.*

"Dissociative identity disorder is what it's called," he replied slowly. "I saw some evidence of it while we were married, but I was just a young, dumb kid. What did I know? Didn't even hear about the diagnosis until a year or so ago. We got the word from Leslie, who keeps—kept—us in the loop." He sighed. "Sally mostly stays away from us. She hasn't exactly been forthcoming about her problems, either, unless she wants to borrow money."

Or wants to hide out, the voice said. *Which is why she's in Pecan Springs right now. She just didn't count on Myers coming after her, that's all. Probably thought she was clear of him.*

Jamison eyed him. "The borrowing probably ended when the insurance came through, though. Two million was what I heard. After she and Leslie split it, she would've been livin' high on the hog. Right?"

"For a while. It didn't take her long to run through the money. There were always plenty of guys who were willing to help her invest it, spend it, give it away." He knew this would add fuel to Jamison's fire. The Strahorn murders were a cold case, but there had been a dead woman in that ditch, and Leslie was dead in Lake City. Three of these killings were on Jamison's turf. The man deserved his cooperation.

The Chevy was rocked by a gust of wind. The snow was starting again, or maybe it was sleet, icy pellets flung against the car. In the distance, a pair of bright lights topped by a revolving red light came down the road toward them.

"Pete's tow truck," Jamison said, and began pulling on a glove. "He's usually quicker'n this. Guess he had somebody else in the ditch and figured this one could wait." He looked over at McQuaid. "You know Leslie Strahorn well?"

"Yeah, pretty well," McQuaid acknowledged. He thought of that kiss and just as quickly pushed it out of his mind. There'd be time to think about that later. Time to feel more of the pain.

"What's your take?" Jamison made a noise in his throat. "You think there's a connection to what happened here?"

"I don't think Sally is capable of killing her sister, if that's what you're suggesting," McQuaid said flatly.

Maybe not, the voice put in. *But you have no idea what Juanita is capable of. Maybe she did it. Or she and Jess Myers—or he did it for her.*

"Not suggesting anything, yet." Jamison pulled on the other glove. "I hope for your sake that your ex isn't involved, McQuaid. But I'm going to give this my best shot. Lake City, Texas. That right?"

McQuaid nodded, knowing that—overtime or no overtime—Jamison would be on the line to Lake City and have all the details in front of him inside an hour. He'd also know that Lake City was looking for Sally as a person of interest.

"Yeah, right," he said. "Lake City." He fished for his wallet, retrieved a card, and handed it to Jamison. "Look. I don't have easy access to the Lake City police, but you do. I'm going to go down the road and check in at the Sycamore Court. If you find out how Leslie was killed, would you give me a call at the motel and let me know?"

"Depends," Jamison said. "But yeah, I will if I can."

McQuaid nodded. "Good enough. I'm planning to fly out of KC tomorrow, earliest flight I can get. Should be back in Texas by mid-afternoon. You come to any resolution on the Dillard case, you'll let me know that, too?" He didn't think there was a chance of that happening, barring a confession from somebody—Myers? Sally? A hit-and-run driver? But he said it anyway.

"Right," Jamison said, and got out of the car. He was closing the door when he paused and put his head back in. "Thanks, McQuaid. I appreciate it."

"Yeah," McQuaid said. "Same here."

The door slammed. Jamison trudged off into the dark. McQuaid sat, considering.

Could she do it? Kill or conspire to kill her parents, her sister?

No, he thought, with that half-angry, half-guilty twinge he often felt when he thought seriously about Sally. Hell, no.

Yes. The voice was crisp, cool. *Yes, she could. Not to say she did. But she could.*

He had to leave it at that. But as he put the Chevy in gear, a call came in on his cell. He flicked it open. It was China.

Chapter Twelve

In *A Christmas Carol*, Charles Dickens puts these sarcastic words into the mouth of the holiday-hating, penny-pinching Ebenezer Scrooge: "If I could work my will . . . every idiot who goes about with 'Merry Christmas' on his lips, should be boiled with his own pudding, and buried with a stake of holly through his heart. He should!"

"Buried with a stake of holly through his heart"? What's that about? Dickens is referring to the medieval idea that driving a stake made of holly (wood that was thought to protect against witches and other evil creatures) through the heart of a murderer might pin him down and keep his unsanctified spirit from rising up and terrorizing the neighbors.

China Bayles, "Hollies for Your Garden,"
Pecan Springs Enterprise

December days are short, and the evening sun was setting in a puddle of blood-red clouds by the time Big Red Mama got us through Austin, where the usual evening rush hour jam-ups slowed everyone down until the heavy outbound traffic shook itself out and began to move, thinning to a fast-moving stream as vehicles peeled off at the Round Rock and Georgetown interchanges, heading home to their sprawling subdivisions.

I can remember when Round Rock lay at the far northern perimeter of the Austin-area sprawl, with open land stretching to the horizon on either side of the north-south interstate. Ranches occupied the rocky, arid, grassland-and-juniper uplands of western Williamson County. Productive farms lay green across the eastern flatlands, where fertile soil and higher rainfall make it possible to grow good crops.

But no more. Fed by low-interest construction loans and subprime mortgages, Round Rock and Georgetown have merged and metastasized into an ugly octopus of supersized, overpriced McMansions and bloated retail shopping centers, with eager arterial tentacles stretching back into Austin, east to Texas Toll 130 and beyond, and west across the Hill Country to Cedar Park. Unless the current economic downturn and the rising price of gasoline slows development (which it might), the octopus will soon gobble up the entire countryside. The ranches and farms will be replaced by "luxury move-up homes" in gated "communities," exclusive enclaves that are the antithesis of real neighborhoods, boasting vast lawns and golf courses paved with thirsty Bermuda grass and tasteful "installations" of expensive landscaping in place of mesquite trees, native grasses, and wildflowers.

The wild creatures will adapt, naturally. The coyotes are already learning to live out of trash cans. The deer will happily substitute rosebushes and well-watered garden vegetables for their native forage. And the hawks and buzzards will enjoy more roadkill feasts, since there will be more cars, trucks, hapless dogs, and unwary cats. But the Texas wilderness will be gone forever, and more's the pity.

Lake City lies halfway between Georgetown and Temple, a few miles to the east of I-35, on the Little Blue River. As we turned off the freeway, I remembered, sadly, the happier times that McQuaid and I had driven in this direction, taking Brian to visit his favorite aunt or picking him up after he'd spent several weeks with her. Leslie had been a cheerful, energetic young woman with a great affection for her sister's son. She loved playing games with him, loved taking him to fish at Blue Lake, where he always caught a stringer of bass, loved camping in the wilderness area at the eastern edge of the state park, which was far enough away from civilization to be imagined as a wilderness, at least by a ten- or eleven-year-old boy.

Brian had been thrilled by these adventures, especially when he turned over a chunk of limestone one day and found a lizard with saw-toothed scales and blue patches along both sides of its belly. Leslie had taken Brian and his lizard to a biologist friend who showed him how to identify it as a spiny lizard that went by the Latin name of *Sceloporus olivaceus*. Renamed Spike, the lizard came home to live with Brian. It was the beginning of his interest in how scientists think and the start of a passionate love affair with lizards, snakes, and other creepy-crawling creatures that persists to this day. The boy would be devastated when he learned that Leslie was dead. I was going to leave it to his father to tell him when McQuaid got back from Omaha.

"Why not Sally?" Ruby asked, when I told her this. "Isn't she the logical one to tell him? She's his mother. Leslie was her sister."

The question had taken me momentarily aback. Why hadn't I thought of Sally? Was it because—

Ruby put it into words. "It's because you think she had something to do with Leslie's death." She gave me a sidewise look. "You don't want to think it. You're trying hard *not* to think it. But you know it's possible. It could have been one of those Juanita moments. Now, couldn't it?"

A Jaunita moment. Sometimes Ruby has an uncanny ability to hit the nail on the head.

I didn't answer for a moment. Then I said, "I'm trying hard to be analytical about this, Ruby. I know Sally has problems—big ones. She has

a long history of erratic behavior, and she doesn't always know the difference between what's true and what she's made up. This Juanita stuff only
complicates things. But I've been with her for the past couple of days. I've
watched her with the kids, especially with Caitlin. I don't think she could
have killed her sister and still act like a normal person."

Ruby laughed shortly. "Sally acting like a normal person is Sally acting abnormally, China. You know that. I know that."

I swung out to pass a slower car, discovered that I was moving into a
curve, and swung back into the lane again. "You're right," I said. "And yes,
I know it. And if you don't mind, I'd rather try to find out some facts before I start to speculate. In the meantime, why don't you phone the Pecan
Springs police and ask if Sally's been picked up yet? I'll feel better if I
know she's safe, even if it means that she's locked up for a little while."

A couple of minutes later, Ruby had our answer: no. The police still
had Brian's blue Ford staked out in the church parking lot, and there was
a bulletin out on Sally, but she hadn't been seen. And by now, I was seriously worried.

There were too many reasons for not being able to find her, all of
them bad, some of them a whole lot worse. Sally had said the night before that she would leave Pecan Springs. Maybe that's what she'd done. She
parked Brian's car, hopped a bus, and was off to another crazy adventure,
with five grand in her pocket. That would be just like Sally, wouldn't it?

But there were other, darker possibilities. Ruby was right: she could
have been involved with Leslie's death, either alone or with Myers. Maybe
she'd gone off with him, either voluntarily or—I shuddered—involuntarily.
For all I knew, he had grabbed her, killed her, and dropped her into a
ditch somewhere, a worry that had begun to take ominous shape in my
mind since I'd learned about Leslie—and since the idea had come to me,
in the phone conversation with McQuaid, that Myers could be the person

Joyce Dillard believed was involved with the Strahorn murders. The person Dillard had named to Sally, whom Sally had refused to name to McQuaid. "That's a reach," McQuaid had said, and he was right. But the more I thought about it, the more chillingly plausible it seemed.

Thinking of McQuaid, I took out the phone to call him and find out what was happening at his end. When I clicked it on, I saw that there was a message from him. "Just got to Sanders. Bitch of a drive. Hope to hell this is worth it, China. You and Ruby be good tonight. Keep Sally out of trouble. Call me when you get a chance."

I made a face. Keep Sally out of trouble. Oh, right. As if I could. I clicked the phone off. I'd wait to call him back until I had something definite to tell him about Leslie—and until he couldn't tell me not to go to Lake City.

"McQuaid's in Sanders," I reported. "No news, otherwise."

Ruby nodded. "So what are we going to do when we get to Leslie's?"

I raised my eyebrows. "You mean, you don't have a plan, Sherlock? I thought a sleuth like you would have everything all mapped out."

"I might, if I knew where we were going, exactly," Ruby said. "What do you think we should do, Watson?"

"How about if we split up?" I didn't want to hurt Ruby's feelings, but I wasn't crazy about the idea of going door-to-door with Big Bird. "You go in one direction, I'll go in the other. Somebody's bound to be able to tell us something."

Ruby settled back into the seat and stretched out her long yellow legs. "Sounds like a plan to me," she said.

FORMERLY a stop on the old Overland Stage and Pony Express route from Dallas to Austin and San Antonio, Lake City has managed to keep much of its historic character. It is nestled in an elbow of the Little Blue River, about ten miles east of I-35 and a mile or so below the point where the Army Corps of Engineers built a flood-control dam back in the fifties. That was when Lyndon Johnson was securely settled in the Senate, looking out for his friends and supporters back in Texas, making sure that they had all the pork they needed.

But truth be told, pork isn't always pork. The town—it was called Blue back then—was flooded every time the river rampaged, which happened at least once, sometimes twice a decade. The Little Blue's watershed takes in a lot of territory. When the western Hill Country was deluged with what is locally known as a frog-choker, the downstream settlements were inevitably flooded. Bridges were destroyed, buildings were inundated, people and livestock drowned by the hundreds. Back in the thirties, Blue's town fathers and mothers began lobbying for a dam, but most of the New Deal money that came to Texas went into the construction of dams along the Lower Colorado, forming the Highland Lakes. Blue had to wait for Lyndon to get elected in 1948, but by 1958, the town (much drier and a lot safer) had its dam and its very own lake—a recreational lake some ten miles long and six miles wide. It proudly renamed itself Lake City, reinvented itself as an art colony and tourist destination, and declared itself ready for an exciting new beginning. As time has gone on, the town—scarcely larger than a village—has gained a reputation as a center for fine Texas arts and crafts but has kept its zoning regulations strict, refusing to yield to the temptations of sprawl.

Dark had fallen when we drove into town, and the holiday lights were a welcoming sight. On this chilly evening, Lake City was all decked out for Christmas in festive garlands of green plastic fir and holly, studded with red berries, tied with huge red waterproof bows, and lit with thousands of fairy lights. The banner across Main Street declared that the town was celebrating a Festival of Lights from now until Christmas. There was a large, gaily decorated Christmas tree in front of a building that dated back to the stagecoach days. St. Mary's Catholic Church, another historic structure, featured a softly lit nativity scene, and the juniper shrubs around the elementary school were draped in colored lights. A little snow might've been nice, but although a nippy north wind tossed the trees, the temperature was about fifteen degrees too warm for snow—and about ten degrees too chilly for comfort.

"I hope you know where you're going," Big Bird said to me. Ruby had pulled on her yellow hat as we drove through town, to complete what she considered her "cover story." I had to admit that she was right about one thing. No self-respecting detective would be caught dead in such a costume. The cops would never suspect her of anything other than sheer lunacy.

"Yes, I know where I'm going." I made a right turn at the second corner past the library. I was swept by sadness, thinking of where we were headed. One block south and two blocks west and we'd be there.

Ruby looked around with some excitement. "I know this street!" she said. "I used to visit Shannon, when she was teaching here. She only lived a couple of blocks away." She looked out the window at the lighted street. "I remember several really cute little shops. One of them sells miniatures, down the street on the left. If I remember right, there's a doll shop and a quilting shop. Oh, and a terrific little bakery that makes fabulous fruitcakes. They ship them all over Texas."

She paused, and her voice changed. "Odd. I feel . . ." She paused, wrinkling her forehead. I glanced at her. She was wearing her intent, listening look—another hunch, I supposed. Then she waved her hand, as if waving the feeling away. "I'm glad we came, China," she said in a lighter tone. "I think we'll find what we're looking for."

217

Leslie's street, just a block behind the town's main shopping district, was a mixed-use residential and retail neighborhood, an interesting potpourri of older homes and houses that had been turned into small shops—craft shops, collectibles, artists' studios, boutiques—designed to appeal to tourists. The shop lights were on, and there were cars on the street. The shops were decorated, too, so that the whole block wore a festive air. The Festival of Lights, I supposed, and was pleased. The more people we could talk to, the more likely it was that we could find out something the Whiz could use.

Leslie's house—a modest gray frame cottage with blue shutters, a big yard, and a large oak tree in the front—was seven doors down on the right. Her car, a Prius, was parked in front of the garage at the back of the lot, and the front of the house was decorated with strings of icicle lights and lighted red and white candy-cane poles. It looked like a gingerbread cottage.

I pulled up at the curb and turned off the ignition. "We're here."

Ruby tilted her head to one side and studied the small house. "I thought you told me once that Leslie got a lot of money from her parents' insurance. Why was she living here? I would have thought she'd get something . . . well, bigger."

"She did get a lot of money," I replied. "She and Sally split a couple of million dollars."

"Really?" Ruby whistled. "That much?"

"Yes. That much." Sally's share was long gone, of course—spent by Juanita, I supposed, or ripped off by the boyfriend who had "invested" it in the market for her, in some sort of Ponzi scheme being run by one of his friends. "Leslie liked the house and the neighborhood," I added. "It's within walking distance of her school, and several of her friends had shops on the street. She did some remodeling—put in a new kitchen and bath and refinished the wood floors—and stashed the rest of the insurance money into savings. She thought she might retire early from teaching and open a shop of her own." I sighed. There would be no retirement now.

Ruby held up her tote. "Do you want to wear your Cookie Monster hat?"

"I think I'll skip it. Thanks all the same."

"Well, it's here if you need it." She put her hand on the door handle. "Are we ready?"

"As ready as we'll ever be," I said, reaching into the back of the van to get the two boxes of Cass' Thymely Gourmet dinners to go. We got out together and went up the walk, between the candy-cane lights, to the porch.

I had expected to see yellow crime-scene tape draped across the front of the house, but it wasn't there, which suggested to me that—however Leslie Strahorn had died—it had happened somewhere else. The only thing out of the ordinary was a big black bow fastened to a large green holly wreath hung on the front door.

I went up to the wreath and looked at the bow. There was a long white tag hanging from it. It read, "In Memory of our favorite teacher, Miss Strahorn. We miss you! Love forever." Beneath this, in their most careful cursive, were thirty-some children's names. What a terrible thing to happen, just at Christmastime. If Leslie had been as generous with her love to her students as she had to Brian, losing her would be very hard for them.

I spoke past the lump in my throat. "I'll take one of the boxes and go to the right, Ruby. You take the other box, and go to the left."

Mesmerized, staring wide-eyed at the wreath, Big Bird didn't answer.

"Ruby," I said, and nudged her. "Wake up, Ruby. If we're going to learn anything, we have to get started."

Ruby started and came to life. "Sorry. I was . . ." She gulped and shook her head. "What are you going to tell people?"

"What you suggested seems like a good idea to me. We were asked by one of Leslie's friends to deliver these dinners as a gift. But there's nobody home, and there's this black bow on the door, so we're not sure what we should do. We're trying to find out what happened so we can tell her friend, who will be anxious to know." It was as good an explanation as any and better than some. I was actually glad that Ruby had thought it up.

So Big Bird hopped off in one direction; I went in the other. The house on the near right was dark, the front blinds were pulled, and there was a sign in the window: For Lease. I could skip that one, I decided. Too bad. Leslie's next-door neighbors were the likeliest people to know what had happened.

The next house was clearly a residence, with well-tended perennial beds in the front, filled with salvias, artemisias, and even some parsley and sage. I raised the brass knocker on the red-painted door and rapped several times, but the occupants weren't at home. I gave it up, went back down the walk, and on to the next. This house was also dark, but there was a small light illuminating the sign beside the door. Law Offices. Below that, the hours were posted: 10–3, Monday through Thursday. Lawyers' hours. I didn't bother to knock. Lawyers probably wouldn't see any advantage to staying open for the Festival of Lights, unless they thought that somebody might slip on a banana peel and break a leg, in which event they would be on the case immediately.

The next place didn't look very promising, either. It was an old-fashioned ice cream parlor that was having a special on hot chocolate garnished with scoops of marshmallow ice cream. The shop was really busy. I doubted if anybody behind the counter would have a minute to talk, or that the customers—tourists, probably—would know anything.

But then I struck pay dirt. The next place turned out to be Quilters Rule, the quilt shop Ruby had remembered. The front door opened into a large, brightly lit room—once the living room of the house, I guessed. Head-high wooden shelves along two walls were filled with bolts of cotton quilt material, neatly arranged by colors: browns, reds, and oranges, yellow, green, blue, an orderly rainbow of fabrics. Above the fabric shelves were displayed a half-dozen bright, beautifully patterned quilts of different sizes and shapes. There was even a round one in reds and greens—a quilted Christmas tree skirt. On another wall hung quilting hoops, rulers, squares, supplies, and racks of quilting books and patterns—enough tools and gadgets to supply any quilter's addiction. Along the back of the room, there was a cutting counter and a cash register. And in the center of the room stood a quilting frame with a quilt stretched across it, and four women, two sitting on each side of the frame, needles in hand, heads bent over their work.

As I opened the door and came in, all four raised their heads and glanced up at me. They were in their forties and fifties, I judged. Two of them, the gray-haired ladies on the far side of the frame—looked to be identical twins. One woman, dark-haired and petite, wearing an apron that proclaimed Quilters Rule! got up from her chair and came toward me.

"Hello," she said cordially. "May I help you find something?"

"I just stopped in to—oh, what a gorgeous quilt!" I exclaimed with genuine pleasure. I'm not a quilter. That's Ruby's department. But I've always admired beautiful quilts. I went to the frame and bent over it. "Such tiny stitches! Oh, I wish I could do that."

"I'm sure you can, my dear," said one of the twins. She was round, plump, and pink-cheeked, with a pair of gold-framed glasses on the tip of her nose. She was wearing a green bib apron over her dress, with a pocket in the bib and threaded needles stuck through it. "All it takes is a little—"

"Practice," put in the other twin in an authoritative tone. She was equally round and plump, but her glasses were tortoiseshell and she wore a blue bib apron. She brandished her needle. "Of course, it helps to have a good teacher."

"That's where Molly comes in," said the first twin, her very blue eyes twinkling over her gold-rimmed glasses. "She'll be glad to give you—"

"Lessons," said the other twin, who had the same blue eyes. "And Molly is the best teacher in the entire state of Texas." She raised her voice a notch. "Molly, tell this lady about your classes."

"Now, girls. Don't gang up on the poor thing," said the third woman with a chuckle. "Maybe she's not ready for lessons yet. Maybe she just wants to see how it's done." She motioned to Molly's chair. "I'm Ruth. That pushy pair over there are Ella and Emma. Ella's on the right, in the gold glasses. Emma's the other one. Sit down, dear. Let us give you a quilting demonstration."

"Oh, but I don't want to take anybody's place," I protested—but not too hard. I was thinking that a quartet of gossipy quilters might know something about what had happened to Leslie. I put the Thymely Gourmet box on the floor beside me, sat down, and took off my coat.

"It's perfectly all right, really." The woman in the apron—Molly, I assumed, who must be the owner of the shop—unfolded another chair from a stack in the corner and sat down beside me. "The more needles, the faster the quilting, that's our motto. Anyway, there are usually five of us." She sighed heavily. "We're missing one of our favorite quilters."

"Poor Leslie," said Ella. "That's her chair you're sitting in, dear," she added to me, with a mournful look. "We're going to miss her very—"

"Very, very much," Emma put in. "She was our neighbor."

"Oh," I said, understanding. "Do you live in the house with the red door? I knocked there, but you weren't home."

"Exactly," Ella said. "We weren't home because we're here. We couldn't have asked for a better neighbor, you know. Leslie was always so helpful and thoughtful. An utterly delightful person. She had such a—"

"—*vivid* personality," Ella finished. "Those poor children at school. I don't know how they're going to deal with it. And the choir at church— however will we get along without her? She was a—"

"—sublime soprano," put in Emma. "So inspirational. I don't see how we're going to sing the Hallelujah Chorus without her. She kept Mrs. Brasenwood from going flat."

I had chosen far better than I had any right to expect. "I don't understand," I said. "Are you trying to tell me that something has—"

But Emma and Ella weren't listening. "Give her one of your threaded needles, Ella," Emma said, nudging her sister. "Let her try her hand at quilting." To me, she said, "Do you recognize the pattern?" Without waiting for me to answer, she said, "Every Texan ought to know this one. It's a Texas Star. We're making it for the school library. They'll use the money to buy a new computer for the children." She sighed heavily. "It was Leslie's idea."

"Leslie was always full of good ideas." Ella echoed the sigh and plucked a needle out of the bib of her green apron. She handed it across the frame to me. "Here, my dear. Molly will show you where to start."

I took the needle, although I wasn't exactly sure what to do with it. I'm comfortable in the garden, but when it comes to—

"Right there," Molly said and pointed to a place where the star, made out of several precisely-joined yellow and orange pieces, was set into the white material. "Just poke it in at a shallow angle and make the smallest stitches you can. Like this." Expertly, she ran her sharp-pointed needle into the fabric, gathered it on the needle, repeated this two or three times, and pushed the needle through.

"She'll need a thimble," Ella said. "Emma, give her your spare."

Emma fished in her bib pocket, pulled out a thimble, and handed it to me. I put it on my finger, and tentatively managed a few wobbly, uneven stitches.

"Bravo!" Ruth cried, leaning forward to inspect my work. "Why, you're a natural! It's just as if you've been doing this forever. You'll be an expert quilter in no time . . ." She paused, raising a curious eyebrow. "I'm sorry—what did you say your name was?"

"China," I said. "China Bayles. Actually, I stopped in to ask about Leslie Strahorn." I put my needle down and improvised on the story I'd planned, although as I spoke, I realized that it was true, for the most part. "I've known Leslie for years. I've stopped in to deliver a Christmas present to her—a gourmet dinner prepared by a friend. But I'm afraid that something is terribly wrong. There's a black bow on Leslie's door, and you said—" I bit my lip and looked around the group. "Has something terrible happened to Leslie? She's . . . She's okay, isn't she?"

The four women exchanged horrified glances, and all put their needles down at once. Ruth lifted her hand to her mouth, her eyes wide. "You mean, you don't know? You haven't heard?"

"Oh, dear," Molly mourned. "Oh, dear!"

Emma and Ella sighed, and then Emma said, in a stricken voice, "We're so sorry to have to tell you this—"

"But our dear Leslie is dead." Ella finished the sentence.

"Dead!" I exclaimed. "Oh, my goodness. I'm so sorry to hear that. But how—? When? It must have been very sudden. If she was ill, she didn't say anything about it." I looked from one to the other, hoping they knew the details. "An accident, maybe?"

"A horrible, horrible accident." Emma's blue eyes were brimming with tears. Ella handed her a tissue. "It was day before yesterday," she said. "Early in the morning. She was—"

"Struck by a car out on Wildwood Road," Ella said. "She was jogging—although why she was way out there, God only knows. She usually just jogged around the block five or six times, then changed and headed for school."

"Hit-and-run," Ruth said, wiping her eyes with her sleeve. "I don't understand how someone could do that. Hit a pedestrian and then drive away. How can they live with themselves afterward?" She took the tissue Ella handed her and blew her nose. "I just hope the police catch the person who did this awful thing—and soon. We can't have people like that in our community. Joggers and bicyclists won't be safe, not to mention the children walking to school."

"Hit-and-run?" I echoed dumbly. Sheila had said it was a homicide, and I had assumed that Leslie had been shot or stabbed. But her death was a *vehicular* homicide. Which suggested that—

No. I stopped myself. There was no point in guessing. It suggested several things, any one of which might be true. I needed more information. Much more.

"Hit-and-run," Molly repeated. "And it wasn't as if Leslie couldn't be seen. She was wearing a bright pink jogging suit—the same one she always wore."

I leaned forward. "Did anybody see it happen? Have the police identified the vehicle?"

"That's the bad thing," Emma replied. "It was early in the morning, and that road isn't very heavily traveled. The spot where she was killed was a couple of miles outside of town." She frowned. "Really—I just don't know why she was jogging out there. It's not like Leslie at all."

"The children were just devastated, of course," Ella said. "Leslie's class was putting on a Christmas program for the parents, and she—"

"—was in charge of the show," Emma said. "She promised she'd bring popcorn balls, too." She wiped her eyes again. "That was so like Leslie, of course. Always there for everyone, always going the extra mile and never asking for anything in return." She sighed. "I wonder if the driver was talking on a cell phone. They really ought to outlaw them in cars. Our niece's little girl, Sandy, was hit by somebody who drove around her school bus, talking on one of those blasted things. It took Sandy a long time to recover."

"So no one saw it happen," I said. "And the police don't have any leads?" Actually, I knew the answer to that. They had at least one lead, a "person of interest" named Sally Strahorn.

"Nobody actually saw it happen," Ruth replied. "But Mrs. Dunning, the woman who keeps the books at Jansen Plumbing, lives out that way. She was driving along the road on her way to work just a little before nine and happened to see Leslie lying beside the road. She was already dead, of course," she added. "The police say the impact killed her. She died instantly of a fractured skull. She didn't suffer."

"Which was a blessing," Molly said fervently. "I don't think I could bear to think of that sweet, dear girl lying out there, all alone, suffering."

"But if no one saw it, how do they know it was a hit-and-run?" I asked. "She might have been hit with anything." A stick of firewood, a golf club, a rock—the typical blunt instrument.

They were all looking at me, horrified. "But . . . But that would be murder!" Emma exclaimed. "That wouldn't be an accident at all. Whatever makes you think—"

"Nothing," I said hastily. "I was just asking, that's all."

"Anyway," Ella put in, "there were other injuries. I read in the paper that she suffered multiple fractures, but the cause of death was a fractured skull. And as for the police having leads—well, the chief said they might be able to identify the vehicle. There was something about paint. And a phone call to the police. A tip."

A phone call. Was it a legitimate tip, or something else?

"But they're not releasing any information until the lab reports are back," Emma said. She frowned at me. "Really, China. You must have been reading too many murder mysteries. To think that somebody might want to deliberately kill dear Leslie! Why, it's ridiculous, that's what it is."

"Ladies." Molly stood up. "I think it's time for refreshments. We could all use a cup of hot spiced punch and some cookies before we go home, don't you think?" She went toward the counter at the back of the store, and I noticed a Crock-Pot there, with a plate of cookies beside it. She began ladling punch into plastic cups.

"Did she say 'hot spiked punch'?" Ella asked hopefully.

"No, dear," Ruth replied. "That is, not unless you've brought your own hooch to spike it with. Now, move your chairs, and we'll set up the table."

We pulled our chairs back as Ruth spread a protective plastic covering over the quilt, then brought a piece of plywood, laid it across the quilt frame, and spread a flowered table cover over it.

Emma took off her apron, folded it neatly, and tucked it into a tote bag. "You must not be from this area," she said to me, "or you would have read the news about Leslie in this morning's paper. It was the—"

"—lead story," Ella interrupted, taking off her apron, too. "I'm sure that everybody in town knows about it by now." She moved her chair back to the table.

"I drove up from Pecan Springs," I said, as Ruth put the plate of cookies on the table. I leaned forward. "I'm also acquainted with Leslie's sister, Sally. I wonder—"

"Oh, Sally," Emma said, rolling her eyes. "Oh, yes. She was here last week. In fact, she—"

"—came here to quilt with Leslie," Ella said. She pursed her lips. "Those two are so different. It's amazing. You would hardly know they were sisters. Isn't that right, Emma?"

"Too true," Emma said. "It's a pity they couldn't get along better. Of course, I'm not one to speak ill of someone behind her back, but—"

"Then don't," Ruth said, putting her elbows on the table. "Really, Emma, your tongue is going to get you into trouble someday."

"I don't see how," Emma said, pouting, "as long as I tell the truth." Molly set down a tray with five cups of hot punch, and Emma took one. She nodded at the cookies. "Aren't those Leslie's gingerbread cookies?"

"Yes," Molly said. "She gave me her recipe last year at Christmastime. And this is her punch recipe, too. I thought it would be nice to make some for tonight—to remember her." She lifted her cup. "Here's to Leslie. We'll miss her!"

"To Leslie," we all echoed sadly and drank. Molly picked up the cookie plate and passed it around. The cookies were cut in the shape of gingerbread people and decorated with icing and colored candies. "Have a cookie, everyone," she added. "Leslie wouldn't want us to be sad. Oh, and I have copies of the recipe, if you'd like to have it."

I wanted to get back to the subject of Sally. "Is Leslie's sister staying at her house?" I bent over and picked up the Thymely Gourmet box. "This is the gift I brought—a gourmet meal. If she's there, perhaps I could leave it for her. At a time like this, she might appreciate it."

The women exchanged looks. There was a lengthy silence. Not even Emma or Ella seemed eager to say anything. Finally, Ruth cleared her throat.

"We don't know where Leslie's sister is," she said. "Yes, she was staying there. I think she arrived three or four days before the accident. Maybe a week. They don't . . . They didn't get along very well, you see. In fact, they were arguing the night Leslie brought her here, to our regular quilting evening."

Another silence.

"Arguing?" I prompted.

"Before they got here," Emma said. She lowered her voice confidentially. "They stood outside, but the door was open, and I could hear them. It was about money. Sally was trying to borrow some from her sister."

"Leslie came into a big inheritance, you see," Ella added helpfully. She sipped her punch. "Molly, this is delicious. I'd love to have the recipe."

"Insurance, dear," Emma corrected. "Insurance, not an inheritance. She could have moved to a larger house, but she liked it here. Leslie was a thrifty sort of person, always careful with money. Not like—"

"—her sister." Ella put her cup down and wrinkled her nose. "Sally was exactly the opposite. Always buying things. Clothes, jewelry, shoes—silly things, very flashy. I know Leslie didn't like it, but she didn't criticize. That wasn't her way. But she didn't want to loan Sally the money. I couldn't hear how much they were talking about, but it was a lot. She suggested that Sally might sell that yellow convertible of hers and buy something more serviceable. Get the money she needed that way." She shrugged. "Seemed like a pretty sensible idea to me."

"Sally's car was here?" I asked.

"Yes," Ruth said. "I live on the street behind Leslie, just across the alley. There's a graveled parking space back there, behind the garage. That's where it was." She chuckled ironically. "You couldn't miss it, really. It was such a gaudy color. Bright yellow. And cute. It's a really cute little car. But it's not there now. It's been gone for a couple of days, actually. I haven't seen Sally, either."

"Do you know when it disappeared?" I asked.

"When?" Ruth shook her head slowly. "Not exactly. Before the accident, I think. The evening before, maybe? I can't remember. I drove up to Waco to see my mother, and it wasn't there when I got back. I know, because that was when I heard the news about Leslie, and I went to the window to look. Haven't seen it since, either." A frown furrowed her brow. "Why are you so interested in all this, China?"

Emma was staring at me. "You don't think . . ." Whatever she was going to say, she bit it off. Above her tortoiseshell glasses, her blue eyes were sharp.

"No, no, no. Of course she doesn't," Ella said in scoffing tone. "Don't be a silly goose, Emma. Nobody could think *that*. It's totally ridiculous. Now be quiet."

"Think what?" Molly wanted to know. Bewildered, she looked around the group. "What in the world are you girls talking about?"

"China suspects that Sally might have been driving the car that killed her sister," Ruth said. Her frown deepened. She was studying me intently. "Isn't that it, China?"

"Well, I—" I stopped, not wanting to tell them what I thought, because I wanted to hear what they had to say. Emma obliged me. She wasn't going to let Ella have the last word.

"If that sister of hers was the one who did it," she said sharply, "it had to've been done deliberately." Her round, pink face became stern. "Which would make it murder, wouldn't it?" She narrowed her eyes. "Murder! Is that what you think, China?"

Ruth's mouth tightened. "And Sally couldn't leave the car there because somebody might spot the damage and report it. So she drove it away. That's why the car is gone. And that's why Sally hasn't been around since her sister's death. That's what you're thinking—isn't it, China?"

Ella snapped her fingers. "I'll bet she did it for money," she said emphatically. "I know for a fact that Leslie left her sister a lot of money in her will."

"Not everything, of course," Emma said. "She left some of it to her nephew. And I'm sure there must have been insurance as well. Her sister will probably get it."

Her nephew? That had to be Brian. I shivered. I hadn't thought of that possibility. It hadn't even entered my mind.

"And just how do you two know so much about Leslie's will?" Ruth inquired archly. "Have you been snooping again?"

The twins exchanged half-guilty looks. "We have not been snooping," Emma replied huffily. "Our niece, Janie, is a paralegal in the lawyer's office next door to us. That's where Leslie made her will."

"Janie told us," Ella confirmed. "She knew we'd be interested."

Normally, I might have made some cutting remark about attorney-client privilege, but at the moment, I was too busy being grateful for small-town gossip.

But Ruth had put down her cup and was looking at me suspiciously. "I'm really curious," she said, "about why *you're* so curious about all this. What's your interest in it?" She narrowed her eyes. "You're not a cop, are you?"

I was saved from answering by the tinkle of the bell over the door. A pair of customers came in, and Molly got up to greet them. It was my chance to get out. I picked up my box and stood, too.

"It was nice to meet you all," I said hurriedly. "Thanks so much for the quilting lesson, and for the cookies and punch. Oh, and the conversation, too. I need to be on my way. Good night, now."

"Wait!" Emma protested, pushing herself out of her chair. "You can't leave! We want to know what you—"

But I was pulling on my coat and heading for the door. I didn't think they could tell me any more than they already had—and they'd already told me a very great deal. I didn't want to be entangled in an argument where I might say more than I intended. I'd probably already done that, anyway.

Out on the street, I reached for my cell phone. I'd wait to call Justine until I found out whether Ruby, aka Big Bird, had picked up any information. But I could call McQuaid and tell him about Leslie. He'd want to know. When I clicked on the phone, though, I found a message from him, an urgent one, placed just a few minutes before, at seven twenty-three. What he had to say rocked me.

Joyce Dillard was dead. Her body had been found in a ditch beside the road.

I listened to the message again, holding my breath. *Beside the road.* The similarities between the way Joyce Dillard and Leslie Strahorn had died were chillingly clear. Two women, both victims—most likely—of vehicular homicide. Two women, connected through their acquaintance with Sally Strahorn. The implication of that connection would be all too obvious, at least to the police.

From the end of the block, I could hear the *clang-clang-clang* of a Salvation Army bell. A couple of women walked past me with a curious look, and I stepped back against the storefront, moving out of the traffic. I replayed the message a third time. It ended with "Call me as soon as you can. I may have an update on Dillard." I hit the talk button.

"You're *where*?" McQuaid demanded angrily, when I told him. "What the hell are you doing in Lake City, China? I thought you were with Ruby."

"I am with Ruby," I said, although I wasn't, at the moment. I didn't think it was a good idea to mention Big Bird. "Justine is willing to take Sally's case, if it comes to that, and she asked me to dig up whatever facts I could. Lake City seemed like the place to dig. Ruby came along."

"Now, look, China—" he began, but I stopped him.

"Let's not fight about this, McQuaid. Just listen, okay? It's important. I got your message about Joyce Dillard. And I've found out how Leslie died. Listen to this."

I sketched out what I had learned at the quilt shop, ending with, "One of the women I talked to says that Sally's car was parked behind Leslie's garage for several days. It disappeared about the time Sally headed for Pecan Springs. About the same time Leslie was struck. The cops don't have a lead on the hit-and-run vehicle. Yet. Or if they do, they're not making it public."

There was a silence. "Sally told you she came on the bus. Right?"

"Correct. But we don't have any way of knowing whether that's true. Maybe she drove her car to Pecan Springs and parked it, and Jess Myers picked it up. All I know is that when he phoned the shop, he told me to tell her he had it—the car, I mean. When I gave her that news, it scared her. Oh, and Hazel Cowan saw him driving it," I added. "In Pecan Springs, yesterday evening, around six."

"What else?"

"Only that Sally tried repeatedly to phone her sister yesterday evening. But that was after the hit-and-run. She wouldn't have tried calling if she had known Leslie was dead."

"You think?" McQuaid asked wryly. "Don't sell her short, China. Maybe she was just trying to establish her innocence. Maybe she lied. Maybe she wasn't phoning Leslie. Could've been Myers she was trying to reach."

"Damn," I muttered, feeling sick. He was right. All I had was Sally's say-so about trying to call her sister. And what was that worth? She was an accomplished liar. I could testify to that.

"The cop here—Jamison—is pretty well convinced that Sally did it," McQuaid went on. "Killed her folks, or at least set them up for Myers. Killed Joyce Dillard, too. Jamison is a good cop. Smart. He was the police chief when the Strahorns were killed, so he's got a good handle on the evidence—what little there was. He got demoted when he didn't clear the case."

"What does he think about Myers?"

I could hear the shrug in his voice. "Not so much."

"In spite of the fact that he was on the Strahorn suspect list?" I demanded. "And that he's in Pecan Springs right now, stalking Sally?"

"I'm just telling you what he thinks. And doesn't. And you don't know for a fact that Myers is *stalking* Sally. For all you know, maybe he's just trying to connect with her. Maybe the two of them are involved in a joint venture."

I felt even sicker. "What do *you* think?"

"What do I think?" He sighed. "I don't know what the hell to think, China. Myers could have done it. Sally could have done it. They could have done it together." He paused. Behind me, the Quilters Rule door opened, and the two women customers came out, clutching shopping bags and chattering happily. Molly had obviously made a sale.

"I guess," McQuaid said finally, "I'm leaning toward together. I somehow can't bring myself to buy the notion that Sally pulled the trigger on her parents, but I'm willing to entertain the possibility that she might have hired Myers—or seduced him into doing it. Jamison said she was sleeping with him before her parents were killed. I also think she might have spotted Joyce Dillard walking along the road and run her down—impulsively, maybe, without prior intent. Having done that once, she might have done it again—in Lake City. Or she might have gotten Myers to do it. Or she and Myers might have done it together."

"Wait a minute," I objected. "Wasn't Sally the one who insisted on your going to Sanders? Why would she do that if she knew that Dillard was dead?"

"Maybe she was trying to cover her tracks. Play innocent."

I tried again. "I can't believe that Sally could have sat at our table with the kids and acted like nothing was wrong if she'd just killed her sister— not to mention this woman in Sanders *and* her parents? Do you?"

"Do I? I don't know." He sounded tired. "Yeah, I guess maybe I do. Sally isn't always Sally, you know. Sometimes she's this other person, Juanita. When she's Juanita, all bets are off. And maybe there's a third character, somebody like Bonnie, of Bonnie and Clyde. I'm sorry, but that's a fact, and we have to face it."

I ran quickly through the rebuttal arguments and didn't find one that seemed persuasive, even to me. McQuaid was right, of course. Sally's dissociative disorder made anything possible, even the murder of her sister and her parents. But we were looking for an answer to a question that neither of us wanted to put into words.

"You're staying in Sanders tonight?" I asked.

"Yeah. There's a motel down the road. The Sycamore Court. The KC airport isn't that far away. With luck, I'll be able to rebook my flight from there. Should be home by midday. You're going back to Pecan Springs tonight?"

"As soon as I can connect with Ruby. That is, unless she's dug up another lead we ought to follow. We have to get something to eat, too." As I said that, I realized that I was hungry.

He grunted. "I don't suppose there's been any word from Sheila or the Pecan Springs cops. They haven't picked Sally up?"

"They hadn't when Ruby checked, an hour or so ago." I shivered. "You have no idea where Sally might have gone?"

"Are you kidding? I don't pretend to know what goes through that woman's mind. She could be in El Paso by now. Or Juarez." He sounded disgusted. "Call me when you get back to Pecan Springs. I don't want you to go home, remember. If this Myers is a threat, he might show up there."

"I am going to Ruby's," I gritted.

"Good girl." He paused, and his voice dropped. "Be careful, China. Joyce Dillard is dead. Leslie is dead. Sally is missing. This isn't a game."

Damn. I understood his intention, but "good girl" irritates me. I bit back a terse response and said only, "Yes, I know. I'll be careful. I promise."

"Good," he said. "Love you." He clicked off.

Chapter Thirteen

McQuaid: The Sycamore Court Motel

The Sycamore Court may have changed hands, but it still looked as seedy as it always had: a long, low, L-shaped brick-veneer building, with the office at the long end of the L. The roadside sign was still lit, with a red-neon Vacancy declaration beneath it. Optimistically, someone had used an ATV with a blade to scrape the snow from the parking lot, but if it was an effort to attract business, it hadn't been very successful, for there was only one car, parked beside the office. The desk clerk, maybe. Or the owner. When the Clarks owned the place, they had lived in the two units next to the office. On call twenty-four/seven, and never took a vacation. McQuaid shuddered. He couldn't think of a more restricted life.

The office was too warm. When he opened the door, the heat hit him like a blast from a tropical wind, heavily scented with perfumed air freshener. A woman was sitting behind the desk, reading a book. She was dark-haired, painfully thin, with a lined face, bright red lips, and sad, dark eyes rimmed in black pencil. Her heavy red sweater sported a green plastic holly leaf and a little gold bell pinned to it, over her name badge. Darnella, it read. *A sweater?* McQuaid thought in disbelief. The place was stifling.

Darnella put down her book, a paperback romance with a cover featuring a muscular man, half-naked, with long blond hair, entwined with a top-heavy raven-haired beauty wearing the barest minimum.

"Help ya?" she asked, in a tone that suggested that she would really rather go back to her book.

"Single, one night," McQuaid said and took his drivers' license and credit card out of his wallet.

"Smokin'?"

His cell phone rang. He shook his head at Darnella, flipped his phone open, and saw that it was Sally. "Where the hell are you?" he snapped into the phone, angrily disguising the thankfulness he felt. "People are looking for you."

"What did Joyce tell you?" Her voice was thin, anxious.

"Pets?" Darnella asked.

He shook his head again. "Sally, I need to know where you are. Tell me."

"I don't have much time. What did you find out from Joyce?"

"Turns out you got a dog or a cat in your car, we'll know, and you'll get a bill." Darnella slid a card across the counter. "Name, Address. Make, model, license. Sign at the X."

"Hold on a sec," he said to Darnella, and turned away, walking to a corner of the office, facing the wall. "I couldn't talk to Joyce, Sally."

He couldn't read anything into her pause. "Why not?" she asked.

"Because she's dead."

"No!" A small cry, a sudden intake of breath. "How? When?"

"How do you think?" he countered.

"How should *I* know?" she replied plaintively. "I'm not there, am I? How did she die, Mike? For God's sake, tell me!"

There was something in her voice that made McQuaid want to give her the benefit of the doubt, but he couldn't. Not yet. He'd already given her too much, maybe. And there was Juanita, always Juanita. "I don't know, Sally. She's . . . dead, that's all."

"You're lying," she said harshly. "She can't be dead. It's not possible. She can't . . ." She took several deep, hard breaths, as if she was trying to steady herself. "Tell me what you know, Mike." Her voice rose. "*Tell* me."

And then he didn't have a choice. He'd been a cop for too long. He'd spent way too much time interrogating people. He could taste a lie, and Sally wasn't lying, at least about this. She didn't know that Dillard was dead—although (he reminded himself) Juanita might know, or Sally might be involved with the situation in some other way. But still—

"She was found dead in a ditch by the side of the road," he said without inflection. "No word on whether it was hit-and-run or something else." He listened for a reaction, anything that would suggest that Sally was making a connection to Leslie's death. There was only silence. He went on. "Jamison is handling the investigation. Remember Jamison?"

"I don't . . ." She gulped. "The police chief?"

"Used to be. He got demoted when he couldn't clear your parents' murders." He toughened his voice, used what China called his cop voice. "Where the hell are you, Sally?" He didn't want to tell her that Leslie was dead and that the police were looking for her. He didn't think she knew, but part of him was still a cop, on the cops' side. He was playing fair. He settled for something else. "You know that Jess Myers is looking for you, don't you? Have you hooked up with him?"

She didn't answer. "Sally?" he said. "Sally? Damn it, Sally—" But it wasn't any use. She was gone. Maybe she was in a moving vehicle and had driven out of signal range. Or maybe she was with Myers and— He didn't want to complete the thought.

"Look, mister," Darnella said in a complaining voice, "if you're gonna check in, I wish you'd hurry up and do it. I've just got to the good part in this book. I wanna get back to it."

McQuaid pocketed his phone, finished the check-in, and was given the key to his room, with the disconcerting instruction to turn up the electric heater to high to warm up the room, but be sure to turn it down before he went to bed, or else it might cause a fire. "Old wiring," Darnella said and picked up her book again. "Shorts out sometimes."

"What time's breakfast?" McQuaid asked.

"Breakfast?" Darnella laughed sarcastically. "That'd be down the road toward town, place on your left. Open about seven, dependin' on whether ol' man Perkins gets his truck started. This morning, he didn't open up 'til after nine. Last week, it was noon."

The room was cold as the inside of a meat locker, and McQuaid could see his breath. He turned the heater up to high and flicked on the television. There were three network channels and that was it. No CNN, no Weather Channel, no NatGeo, and the reception wasn't all that great. He turned off the set and, still wearing his coat, sat down on the bed and looked around. The standard 1950s cheap motel room: a too-firm, unwelcoming bed; dresser, mirror, chair; dinky bathroom. Green-painted walls, water-stained tile ceiling, dark green carpet, not recently cleaned.

He opened his carry-on bag, got out his plane ticket, and spent the next twenty minutes on the phone, rebooking his flight out of Kansas City and arranging for the return of the rental car there, rather than Omaha. He called Charlie Lipman's office answering machine to let him know that he was coming home early because of a family emergency, then called

Peter Kennard to tell him that they'd have to wrap up the interview another time.

The room was finally beginning to warm up, and he took off his coat, glancing at his watch. Eight forty-five. One more call. He punched in Sheila's number. She picked up after five rings, sounding tired.

"McQuaid," he said. "Sorry if I've caught you at a bad time."

"You've caught me in the bathtub," Sheila said. "We haven't found her yet, if that's what you're asking. Sally, I mean."

"I know," he said. "I just talked to her. She wouldn't tell me where she was or whether she's with Myers."

He heard the sound of water sloshing and pictured Sheila sitting up straight in the tub. He smiled a little. Beautiful woman. Naked woman. Blackie was a lucky guy.

"Is she in Pecan Springs?" she demanded.

"No idea," he said. "She wouldn't tell me where she was, and the call was broken off. I don't know whether she was on the road and moved out of range, or—" He let that drop. He didn't want to think of the alternatives. "You might try putting a trace on her cell."

This would be easier in a few years, when cell phone carriers were finally required to have the capability of tracing the location of cell phone calls. But for now, it required expensive hardware and software and trained personnel. He wasn't surprised when Sheila said, "That's Lake City's responsibility, not mine. If they want her bad enough, they'll do it."

"Right." He paused. "Have the police up there told you how Leslie died?"

"Haven't checked in with them," Sheila said. Her voice was wry. "We've had a little situation here this afternoon. Domestic violence. Two dead, the shooter and his wife. Murder, suicide. Shooter had enough of an arsenal to take out the Dallas starting line and start on the coaching staff."

McQuaid sighed regretfully. Pecan Springs was still a small town. But that didn't mean that they were immune from big-city violence. They didn't have the drive-by or gang stuff, but there were guns. Too many of them.

"Understand," he said. "Well, maybe I can fill you in. It seems that my wife has taken it on herself—aided and abetted by Ruby Wilcox—to drive up to Lake City to find out what happened with Leslie Strahorn."

"Really?" Sheila laughed without amusement. "If I'd known they were going, I would've called the Lake City police and told them to duck."

McQuaid chuckled. "Here's what they've come up with—so far, anyway." He relayed what China had told him about Leslie's death.

Sheila made the connection without being prompted. "Uh-oh," she said softly. "*Two* vehicular homicides, huh?"

"Both women were found dead beside the road," McQuaid corrected her. "There's been no ruling on a cause of death for either. I learned about Leslie after I left Jamison, the investigating officer here in Sanders. He's probably on the phone to Lake City right now, getting the news."

"What's his take on the case?"

"He's leaning toward Bonnie and Clyde," McQuaid replied ruefully. "But talking to Sally, I'm of the opinion that she knew nothing about Dillard's death. She seemed shocked, disbelieving."

"An emotion easily portrayed," Sheila reminded him. "And from what China tells me, your ex has a split personality thing. She *is* your ex, remember? You might hate to admit it, Mike, but you aren't exactly unbiased."

He sighed. "Yeah, there's that, too, damn it."

He put the phone down with deep misgivings.

Chapter Fourteen

In Norse mythology, the sun god Baldur had become invulnerable because of the magical spells of his powerful mother, the goddess Frigga. But the mischievous prankster Loki discovered that Frigga had neglected to protect her son from the mistletoe. He crafted a dart from the wood and gave it to the blind god Heder to use in a game. Heder threw the dart and Baldur was killed, sending the world into winter-dark. After the other gods restored Baldur to life, Frigga pronounced the mistletoe sacred, ordering that from thenceforth, it would bring peace and love into the world, not strife and death, and that all enemies should come together once a year to exchange a kiss of peace.

Thus began the tradition of kissing under the mistletoe.

Norse myth

I finished talking to McQuaid and tucked my cell phone in my purse. It was time to find Ruby and hear what she had been able to learn, if anything. Then, as if I had conjured her up, I saw her coming toward me on the sidewalk, a six-foot-plus Big Bird, carrying her tote bag.

"Don't you think you can take off that hat now?" I asked mildly. "You've probably already established your cover."

She yanked off her yellow bird-billed hat and tucked it under her arm. "You'll never guess what I've learned," she whispered, in an excited I've-got-a-secret voice.

"That Leslie's body was found out on Wildwood Road?"

"Oh, you heard it, too?" She made a disappointed face. "It happened two mornings ago. She was jogging, apparently, before school. The book-keeper for Jansen Plumbing found her. She hadn't been dead very long. Hit-and-run."

"Well, maybe. I don't know if that's official yet." I looked around. "Listen, Ruby, I'm starving. Let's find a place where we can eat."

She nodded across the street, toward a sandwich shop with its window encircled in colored Christmas lights that blinked on and off. "There's Sandy's Wiches. Shannon and I ate there a couple of times. They have really good soups." She hefted her tote. "Or we could sit in Big Red Mama and eat Cass' sandwiches. I'll bet they're better than Sandy's."

A young woman walked past us with a miniature white poodle wearing a red and green crocheted sweater and a ruff of holly leaves. Ruby turned, looking at it. "Isn't that a cute sweater? Maybe I should get myself a poodle for Christmas. Oh, and I have something to tell you," she added. "About Sally and Leslie. I'm still waiting to get more of the details, but while we're eating, I can fill you in on what I already know."

At that moment, something occurred to me that I might not have considered under other circumstances. At heart, I am a law-abiding person who resists getting seriously crosswise of the authorities, except in exceptional circumstances. This qualified as an exceptional circumstance. We were here to dig up all the facts we could find for Justine. There was one more place we ought to check out—if it was accessible. And from what I knew, it just might be.

"I have another idea, Ruby," I said quickly, before my better angel could order me to get into Big Red Mama and head for Pecan Springs.

244

"Come on. Let's check it out." I started off, and Ruby fell into step beside me. "What is it that you have to tell me about Sally and Leslie?"

"Well, as I said, I'm still waiting for the details. I went into this really cute toy shop—you should see it, China! Lots of great educational toys." She plunged into her tote bag and pulled out a shaggy blue doll. "I bought this cuddly Cookie Monster for Baby Grace. Which gave me a chance to start talking to the owner."

"A Cookie Monster." I grinned. "Sounds like Big Bird found the right place."

"Oh, you bet." Ruby skipped and flapped her wings. "Erin Staples— she owns the shop—and I hit it off right away. When I told her we were trying to find out what happened to Leslie, she started telling me all kinds of stuff."

I wasn't surprised. The Big Bird costume was no doubt an appropriate entrée into a toy store, but I was sure it went beyond that. Ruby has a way of getting strangers to tell her things they'd never reveal to their closest friends. I don't know how she does it—empathy, I guess. Ruby is one of the most empathetic people I know.

"Anyway," Ruby went on, "when I asked about Sally, I really got an earful. Erin and Leslie have been friends for a long time, so she knows all the down-and-dirty. Apparently, Sally and Leslie have been having some really serious arguments. When Leslie found out that Sally was coming to stay for a while, she told Erin that she dreaded the thought of it." She sighed and shook her head. "That is totally too bad, isn't it?"

"Family disputes can be hellacious," I said. "Did Erin tell you what they fought over?"

"Money, mostly. Leslie was careful with hers, and Sally—well, 'Sally is Sally,' as Erin put it." Ruby hung air quotes around the words. "No matter how much she had, it was never enough. She was always hitting Leslie up for more. Recently, too." She frowned. "Erin said that Sally needed money 'to get away.' She was asking Leslie for five thousand dollars." She gave me a meaningful look. "Which is the amount of the check Sally cashed at the bank."

A pair of holiday shoppers went past us, the man loaded down with bags and wearing a long-suffering look on his face, the woman chattering gaily about what a wonderful shopping trip they were having together and wasn't this fun?

"Get away?" I repeated. "Get away from what?" But I could hazard a guess. Sally was either trying to get away from Jess Myers or from what happened to Joyce Dillard—or both. And that five thousand dollars. Was it Sally's getaway money or a payoff of some kind? If it was a payoff, who was the payee? I could hazard a guess on that one, too.

"Erin had the impression that Sally was involved with something ugly and dangerous," Ruby said. "She thought it was probably drugs. She saw Sally a few days ago and said she seemed really strung out."

Drugs. A good guess, except that in this case, the ugly, dangerous something was a lot worse. It was murder. "What did Erin know about Leslie's death?" I asked.

"Nothing but what she read in the paper. That's where she found out about it. She felt really awful about that—learning about it in the paper, I mean." Ruby reached into her tote bag and held up a folded newspaper. "I got this from one of the other shops."

She handed me the paper, and I stood still, reading. The headline read, "Teacher Killed While Jogging." There was a photograph of Leslie, pretty, perky, smiling. It hurt. I scanned the story and handed the paper back quickly.

"Unfortunately," Ruby said, "there aren't any details in the paper. Nobody saw it happen." She put the newspaper back into her tote bag. "But

I did learn something else from Erin, China. As it turns out, her sister-in-law Christina drove Sally to the bus station on Tuesday morning. Sally was leaving her car with Leslie, because Leslie's Prius needed some work. Christina was going to the station to catch a bus to Fort Worth and offered to take Sally."

"What time?" I asked quickly. This was crucial, and the reason for asking was obvious. "Before Leslie was killed, or after?" The question couldn't be answered, though, since the time of Leslie's death had not yet been established, at least as far as we knew. At best, the coroner would only be able to give a two-hour range.

Ruby shook her head. "Dunno. I wanted to talk to Christina, but she's with her daughter in Fort Worth right now, helping take care of her new grandson. He's just two weeks old. Erin is going to call her—Christina, that is—and give her my phone number so we can talk directly." We started walking again, and she turned to look at me, frowning slightly. "Is something wrong, China?"

"Yes. Very. Leslie Strahorn isn't the only woman who's been found dead by the side of the road." It took only a moment to relate what McQuaid had told me on the phone about finding Joyce Dillard's body. Ruby was stunned.

"*Two* women?" she asked, wide-eyed. "This can't be a coincidence, China."

"Not likely," I said, and relayed the rest of McQuaid's report: that Joyce Dillard either knew or guessed the identity of the Strahorns' murderer, and that she had told Sally who it was.

By the time I finished, Ruby was shaking her head. "It's so hard to believe," she whispered. "Joyce Dillard was killed—maybe—because she was a threat to the Strahorns' killer. But Leslie? Why Leslie? She didn't know who shot her parents—did she?"

I was saved from trying to answer that because we had reached Leslie's driveway. I turned toward the house, with its icicle lights and gaily lighted red and white candy poles—on an automatic timer, I guessed, since nobody was at home to turn them on and off.

"Act like we're supposed to be here," I said. "Act natural. We're just a couple of friends looking for Leslie."

The thing was, of course, that the police had not strung crime scene tape around the house. Which stood to reason, if they were investigating Leslie's death as a more or less straightforward hit-and-run, an accident that befell a jogger, the crime being the driver's failure to stop and render aid. Aside from the rather odd fact of her jogging so far out of town on a school morning, they had no reason to suspect otherwise—right?

I frowned. If that were the case, why had they named Sally as a person of interest? It didn't make any sense to me—unless they had some sort of evidence. The car, maybe? The tip Ella had mentioned?

Beside me, Big Bird was dancing a little jig. "We're going to break and enter?" she asked eagerly. She cast a glance to her right. "What about the neighbors? Won't they see us and call the police?"

"That place is empty right now. There's a For Lease sign on the front. What about the house on the other side? Did you check it out?"

"It's not a house, it's an accountant's office, and it's closed this evening." Ruby looked at me expectantly, her gingery eyebrows raised so high they disappeared under her unruly bangs. "Does this mean—"

"No, Ruby. We are not breaking and entering. We're just entering—I hope."

I had my fingers crossed. I was going way out on a limb here, and a fairly thin limb at that. I am not inclined to trade my bar privilege (even though I haven't used it for years) for a charge of criminal trespass (Sec-tion 30.05 of the Texas Penal Code, "Offenses Against Property"), which is a Class A misdemeanor, carrying a fine of up to four thousand dollars and a jail term of up to a year, or both.

There was also the question of whether what we'd get would justify the questionable means we used to get it. In theory, I usually came down on the side that this is never the case, while in practice . . . Well, real life is something else again, and I am a pragmatic person. The information that is only available by questionable means is sometimes so unquestionably useful that I have been known to ignore certain rules and regulations.

But more importantly, there was the question of whether anything we might find in Leslie's house would be admissible in court, if it came to that. That's the trouble with trespass as a method of discovery. If I happened to uncover something important to Sally's case, Justine would have to find another way to introduce it, because she couldn't put me on the stand and ask me to tell the court how I chanced to come across it. Believe me. Finding a legitimate way to introduce an illegitimately obtained piece of evidence is not as easy as it sounds.

But that question was moot, at the moment, anyway. I could postpone answering it, since I didn't know yet whether (1) there was a case; or (2) whether there was anything of interest in the house. If anybody asked (I hoped they wouldn't), Big Bird and I were just two of Leslie's gal pals from out of town, stopping by for an evening's girl talk, at her invitation. And since we hadn't come in the front way and noticed that telltale black bow on the holly wreath, we had no idea that Leslie was dead. We had simply let ourselves in and made ourselves at home while we waited for her.

That is, if we could get in, which was the next question I had to answer.

We had reached the back of the house. There was enough light from the utility lights on the street to see the Prius, parked in front of the garage. A turn to the left, a short walk on a flagstone path past a small flowerbed, a couple of steps up, and we were on Leslie's back porch. The kitchen door looked to be slightly ajar. I pushed it with my finger, and it opened at my touch.

Ruby was looking over her shoulder uneasily. "China," she said in a low voice, "I have the feeling that we're being watched."

I glanced around. The backyard was screened on three sides by a six-foot privacy fence. There was a gate beside the garage—to the alley, I thought, and remembered that Ruth had said that Sally's yellow convertible had been parked back there.

"I don't think anybody's watching," I said. "Unless they're peeking through a hole in the fence."

"Seriously, China," Ruby said. She shivered. "I'm feeling . . . spooky. There's something weird here. Something totally wrong."

"Well, yes," I said. "Something *is* wrong. Leslie's dead. No wonder you're feeling spooked." What's more, I knew that Ruby didn't want to face a charge of criminal trespass any more than I did. The thought of being hauled into municipal court was extremely spooky. I didn't want to think it.

The door opened into a narrow hallway, as I remembered, which led into the kitchen. "Let's put our food on the table," I said, as I took a step into the darkened hall. "That way, if we get interrupted, we can always say that we were so hungry that we decided to go ahead and eat while we waited for Leslie." I felt for the light switch just inside the kitchen door. "Burglars don't usually have a sandwich before they start burgling." Burglars don't turn the lights on, either.

Ruby was sticking close behind me, her hand on my shoulder. "I used to be hungry," she said in a low voice, "oh, maybe three minutes ago. Right now, I'm just scared. This is beyond creepy, China. Maybe we'd better . . . maybe we'd better go away and come back another time."

"Uh-uh," I said. "We're here. And it's okay, Ruby. Really it is."

But it wasn't. I flipped the switch and glanced around. The kitchen of the small house had been remodeled, with new wood cabinets, a new granite countertop, new appliances, and a new floor, although it still looked pretty much as I remembered it, cheerful and bright with teacup-print wallpaper and fresh paint. Leslie was a tidy housekeeper, and the last time I had seen this room, it was neat as a proverbial pin. Nothing out of place, except perhaps for a dish or two in the sink.

But not today. One of the red-painted wooden chairs at the small kitchen table had been tipped over, and one leg was broken. A box of Cheerios lay on its side, the contents scattered across the table, a half-gallon jug of milk beside it, and Leslie's cell phone. A cup of coffee had been knocked onto the floor, the china cup shattered, the coffee in a brown puddle. Beside it was a paper grocery sack, spilling popcorn balls into the coffee puddle, and an overturned basket of mistletoe. A woman's handbag lay on the counter, its contents—lipstick, coin purse, pen, keys, checkbook—scattered around, as if somebody had rummaged through it. A wallet was open on the floor, the driver's license showing through the plastic pocket. It was Leslie's, and I could see—without touching it—that there was money in it, bills, and several credit cards.

But most tellingly, a woman's pink Nike running shoe. It lay on the floor just inside the door.

Ruby dropped her tote, and her hands flew to her mouth. "Oh, my god!" she cried, aghast. "What happened here, China? Robbery?"

I pointed to the wallet. "If it was robbery," I said grimly, "the thief was pretty inept. Looks to me like an abduction." I bent over to examine the ring of keys on the counter. The key to Leslie's Prius was there, and several other keys—the house, maybe, and the school. "She must've been sitting down to eat her breakfast when somebody came in the back door and grabbed her. She struggled, and lost her shoe in the process."

Or kicked it off, to show us that she hadn't gone willingly. The police were probably theorizing that her missing shoe—the one that lay here by the door—had been knocked off when she was struck by the car. They could search the roadside for a week and not find it.

Ruby's eyes were wide. She looked from the table to the chair to the door. "And then he dragged her off and stuffed her into his car, which was probably parked in the driveway."

I straightened up. I wasn't going to quibble over the pronoun "he." Sally was smaller and lighter than her sister. There was no way she could have overpowered Leslie—and no reason for it, either. Leslie might have had reservations about going off with Sally, but there would have been no struggle. The person who came into this kitchen and abducted Leslie had to have been a male. And my money was on the man who seemed to spend a lot of time lurking in the shadows these days. Jess Myers, of Sanders, Kansas.

But there was something else. "He didn't put Leslie into his car," I said, thinking rapidly, putting two and two together. "He put her into *Sally's* car. It was parked behind the garage."

Yes. It was the only thing that made sense. Sally had left her car with Leslie, because Leslie's car needed work. Myers must have rummaged through Leslie's purse, hunting for the keys. That's why the contents were scattered. And taking her through the backyard to the car would seriously reduce the chances that somebody might see them, especially if he gagged her so she couldn't yell.

"Sally's car." Ruby sucked in her breath. "Yes, that's right! And then he drove her out on Wildwood Road and dropped her off—"

"And then hit her," I said. "Probably drove off, turned around, revved it up, and came at her from behind. The police said she died instantly." Which was the same way Joyce Dillard died, I was guessing. I closed my eyes, thinking about Sally's yellow convertible, the impact smashing Leslie, lifting her up, hurling her into space, letting myself feel the splintering, fracturing pain.

"But why?" Ruby asked, bewildered. "What possible motive could he have?"

I opened my eyes. Something clicked, and without even having to think about it, I knew the answer. "Myers somehow found out that Joyce Dillard told Sally that he was the one who killed her parents. He silenced Joyce. Then he followed Sally here to Lake City, perhaps not realizing that she was coming to visit her sister. When he understood that, he knew that Sally would have told Leslie what he had done. So he had to kill Leslie, too."

"Which means that Sally's next on his list!" Ruby exclaimed. Her eyes widened. "When he finds her, he'll kill her, too!"

"Unless he already has," I said grimly. There were things that had to be done, and fast. "Where's that Cookie Monster hat?"

"It's in my tote." Ruby blinked. "Why?"

"Because this is bigger than both of us, Big Bird. I'm going to call the Lake City police. And I want to have my cover story handy when they get here." I paused. "Don't touch anything. The cops are going to have enough to do. There's no point in muddying up the scene with our fingerprints."

But before I put in the call, I spent a quick five minutes looking through the rest of the house. Nothing was disturbed, but it seemed eerily, poignantly empty. The dining room table sported a centerpiece of red poinsettias. In the living room, Leslie's shapely Christmas tree presided over a number of wrapped presents, and her piano displayed a dozen family photos. There were pictures of her—her college graduation photo, in cap and gown—and several of her parents and of her and Sally when they were girls. There was also one of Brian, McQuaid, and me, taken during one of Brian's visits, and a photo of Brian proudly displaying Spike, the spiny lizard. On a table in the front hallway, I found a stack of Christmas cards, stamped and ready to mail. As chance would have it, ours— addressed to "The McQuaids"—lay on top. I took it. Why not? I doubted that anybody would get around to mailing them, and certainly not before Christmas.

Then there was Leslie's bedroom and the guest bedroom where Brian always slept when he visited. I found nothing out of order, except that the bed in the guest bedroom hadn't been made for some time, from the look of it. Sally wasn't the housekeeper her sister was, and it was a good bet that she'd been sleeping there. I checked the closet. It was crammed with clothes—Sally's, I guessed, glancing through the hanging garments, a few of which looked as though they might be Juanita's. The guess was confirmed when I found a Gucci handbag bearing the gold-colored initials *SS*. Which suggested that Sally had planned to return here after . . . After what? When?

I found the answer to that question in the kitchen, on the calendar on the kitchen wall, beside the refrigerator. It contained several penciled notes. On December 10 was written the word "Sally." On December 16, there were two notations, "Sally to PS" and "Prius to shop." There were several other events—the school Christmas program on December 19, the choir program on December 21, caroling at the nursing home on December 23, and the church party on December 24. On December 27,

I saw "Pick up Sally in PS." The next two days were bracketed, and the words "San An" were written across them.

All this was no more cryptic than my calendar at home, and it cleared up some of the mystery. Sally had been staying with Leslie since December 10. She left for Pecan Springs on the sixteenth, the day before yesterday. She expected to stay with us until the twenty-seventh, when Leslie would pick her up at our house and the sisters would drive down to San Antonio for a couple of days—something they probably wouldn't do together unless they had patched up their differences, more or less. Then they would drive back here, which was why Sally's clothes were still in the guest room closet. Only now, Leslie was dead. Sally would be coming back here alone. Maybe.

I still didn't quite understand why Leslie hadn't communicated with us, since she was clearly planning on coming to Pecan Springs to pick Sally up after Christmas. But that was a minor detail. There was one more important answer I needed, though. I found it in Leslie's checkbook, which lay on the kitchen floor. It was one of those handy checkbooks that allow you to keep a carbon copy of every check you write, so if you forget to enter the amount into the register, you have a backup record. I left it where it was but used a pencil to lift the pages until I got to the carbon of the last check written—on Monday, December 15, to Sally Strahorn, in the amount of five thousand dollars. I supposed that it might be possible for Sally to have written herself a check from her sister's checkbook, but I didn't think a forger would leave a carbon copy behind as witness to her criminal act. Leslie had written that check, although I had no idea why.

When I called, the police came promptly, a pair of male officers. One, Officer Swanson, was barely out of his teens and a lot more comfortable making traffic stops and checking drivers' licenses than investigating an apparent abduction. The other, Officer Parker, was pushing thirty, tall and dark-haired, and (I judged) harbored a burning desire to make detective. The investigator in Leslie's hit-and-run had gone to Houston for a family funeral, so she wasn't available. Her absence was giving Parker his chance to show his stuff, and he was out to make the most of it. He turned Ruby and me over to Officer Swanson while he did a preliminary investigation.

It didn't take much to convince Swanson that Ruby and I were just a pair of loony females who had come looking for a friend, stumbled onto a crime scene, and (by this time slightly hysterical) called the police. He took our statements, writing down our more-or-less truthful answers: We were friends of Leslie's and had expected to find her home this evening. The back door was unlatched, so we came in, and found—well, we found what they could see. We also discovered the wreath and the bow on the front door, and figured out that Leslie was dead. We were desperate to know what had happened to her, so Swanson—at Ruby's frantic begging—filled us in with the details.

And in the process, he told us something that a more experienced cop might have kept to himself. Early this morning, the police had received a telephone tip from an anonymous male caller who told them that the hit-and-run vehicle they were looking for was a yellow Mini Cooper convertible with a broken left front headlight. He had happened to see it leaving the scene, driven by a woman he recognized. Her name was Sally Strahorn. She was the victim's sister, and from what he understood from someone who knew them both, the two didn't get along. He thought Sally might have gone to Pecan Springs.

This important bit of information cleared up a major mystery, at least for me: why the cops were looking for Sally, and why they had named her a person of interest. I didn't have to be Sherlock Holmes to guess who might have placed that phone call.

Then, while Ruby kept Swanson busy, I made a pass at Officer Parker.

Well, not a pass, exactly. I gave him an admiring smile and let him know that I was impressed with the professional way he was going about his investigation. I mentioned (in passing, of course) that I was married to an ex-homicide investigator, which elicited a mild interest: that is, he glanced up from the broken chair and tilted his head, as though he might be listening.

Then I wondered out loud whether—since Leslie's death had first been investigated as an accidental hit-and-run—the victim's hands had been bagged. Probably not, I thought. If the coroner was still holding the body (privately, I thought this was likely, since Sally was the nearest kin and she wasn't pressing for its release), might it not be a good idea to ask for a fingernail scrape? Since the scene in the kitchen suggested a serious struggle, it was possible—wasn't it? Maybe?—that there would be some telltale DNA that would cinch the case against the driver of the murder vehicle? My husband had solved an important case in just that way. Wasn't that how they did it on *CSI*?

As I talked, I could see the scenario taking shape in Parker's mind, like a Hollywood movie, with himself in the starring role, maybe played by Tom Selleck, in the guise of Chief Jesse Stone, of the Paradise PD. He would order the nail scrape. The DNA would prove that Sally had forced her sister into that car and then run her down. And Officer Parker would be promoted to Detective Parker.

Well, he might indeed be promoted. But I was pretty sure that any DNA that might be found under Leslie's nails would not belong to Sally.

I was remembering something that Hazel Cowan had happened to mention when she told me about the man who had taken her parking space behind Thyme Cottage.

There were scratches on his face.

Chapter Fifteen

The ancient Italian opinion that mistletoe extinguishes fire appears
to be shared by Swedish peasants, who hang up bunches of oak-
mistletoe on the ceilings of their rooms as a protection against
harm in general and conflagration in particular.

Sir James George Frazer, *The Golden Bough*

I didn't think it was smart to tell Officer Parker what I knew
about Jess Myers. It would just lead to more questions I
couldn't answer. And anyway, I was sure that the man they wanted was
no longer in Lake City. He was in Pecan Springs, either looking for Sally
or with her, or—

I didn't want to think of the third possibility.

We left as soon as the police allowed us to go, taking our Thymely
Gourmet boxes with us. We finally got to eat Cass' sandwiches and salad
en route back to Pecan Springs, where we arrived shortly after ten.

It was late and we were tired, so we drove straight to my house, where
I packed my pajamas and toothbrush and clean undies and picked up an
accusatory Howard Cosell, who clearly feared that his entire family had
gone away and left him forever. But Howard isn't one to bear a grudge for
long, and when he found out that he was going for a ride, he galloped out
to Big Mama as fast as his stubby basset legs could carry him. We drove
back to town, to Ruby's house, where I fed Howard, took him out to

Ruby's backyard for his last-call chore, and bedded him down in the guest room where I was assigned to sleep. Then Ruby and I crashed.

But not before I made some phone calls. I reached McQuaid at the Sycamore Motel in Sanders, where he was just turning in for the night. He listened to my terse recap of what we had learned in Lake City, then agreed to call Jamison, the officer on the Joyce Dillard case, and ask him to run a make on all the vehicles that Jess Myers currently owned. One of them might have been the hit-and-run vehicle that killed Joyce Dillard. If I was right, Myers had driven it to Lake City, where he traded it for Sally's yellow convertible, which he used to run down Leslie Strahorn. Myers' vehicle could be parked somewhere in Lake City, not very far from Leslie's house.

"Oh, and when you talk to Jamison about Myers' vehicles," I added, "maybe you could ask him to phone the Lake City police and get them to look for it."

"Good idea," McQuaid said. "I'll do it. You're sure you're at Ruby's house?" he asked, although I had already told him where I was.

"I promise you, dear heart," I said in a reassuring tone, "that Howard Cosell and I are at Ruby's house. Howard is asleep on a folded quilt beside the bed, although I'm willing to bet that the minute I climb under the covers, he'll jump in beside me. Ruby is taking a bath."

"And the kids?" he persisted, clearly worried.

"They're fine, too. I called to check on them while we were driving back. Brian was playing a video game with a couple of friends, and Caitlin was having the time of her life reading *The Tale of Peter Rabbit* to Baby Grace. We're all safe from the bogeyman." I sobered. "All of us but Sally."

Sally. By this time, I was feeling terribly urgent about her. The longer we went without hearing, the more ominous the silence. And the hell of it was that we couldn't do a damn thing about it. We had no idea where to look for her—or *them*. But I knew with a certainty that if Myers had her, it wouldn't be for long. Sally was the one who had heard Joyce Dillard's accusations. Myers was obviously frightened beyond all rational thought. He had no reason to keep her alive and every reason to kill her—fast, before she could tell anyone else what she knew.

"Yeah, Sally," McQuaid replied grimly. "Well, I can tell you that she's still alive—or she was, an hour or so ago." He told me about Sally's phone call, and the fact that it was dropped. "Which might mean that she was in a moving car, trying to get away from Myers or—"

The unfinished sentence hung between us, but I could fill in the blanks. *Or Myers has caught up with her, and somebody will find her body beside a back road somewhere.*

I'd had another thought. If Myers had half a brain (which he might or might not) the smart thing to do would be to kill Sally and make it look like a suicide. That way, she could be blamed for Leslie's death and maybe Dillard's, too. All three cases could be closed, and maybe the Strahorn double murder, as well. Myers would be off the hook completely. It was a chilling thought that turned me cold to the bone. I didn't want to share it with McQuaid. He had enough on his plate already.

McQuaid let out his breath. "Look for me home by noon, China, if the snow quits and the planes are flying." His voice softened. "You know, I was really pissed when you and Ruby drove up to Lake City, but I'm glad you did. You've tied these cases together. Joyce Dillard and Leslie, I mean. We may not be any closer to winding things up, but we know a helluva lot more than we did."

"For whatever good that does," I said, but I was glad of his approval. We said our I-love-yous and our good-nights and hung up.

Next on my list of phone calls was Sheila. I caught her this time, not in Blackie's bed but watching television with him, at her house, at the end of a long day. I could hear the weariness in her voice as she filled me in on what little she knew.

No, nothing had been heard from Sally. Brian's car was still in the church parking lot, with a man watching it. Yes, Sheila had received an APB on Sally's yellow Mini Cooper convertible. No, it hadn't been spotted, either. And no, she still hadn't heard any of the details surrounding Leslie's death.

I gave her a brief rundown on what Ruby and I had uncovered in Lake City and waited for her to lecture me about investigating without a license, or obstructing justice, or trespassing on a crime scene, to all of which sins I had to plead guilty, more or less. But she only said, "Well, at least now we know why the Lake City police have named Sally as a person of interest. If we pick her up—or get a lead on her car or on Jess Myers—I'll give you a call, either on your cell or at the shop. Now, get some rest, China. You've earned it."

Coming from Sheila, that was praise, and it seemed like a very good idea. But I had one more phone call to make. I caught Justine just home from the office, cooking a late-night omelet in her apartment kitchen. The Whiz, whose life revolves around her work, lives in a very small condo (no pets, no maintenance, no grass to mow or flowers to water) that is as messy as any bachelor pad. I could picture her standing at the stove, a spatula in her hand, eggs, onions, mushrooms, and cheese in the skillet. She put me on the speakerphone so we could talk while she coped with her omelet, although before we were finished, it had turned into scrambled eggs. The Whiz never was much of a cook, but as she says, it all ends up in the same place anyway, so why bother?

I gave her the report I had given McQuaid and Sheila, with their contributions added in for good measure. Justine listened attentively, asked a couple of good questions, and summed it all up with "Good job,

China. I'll be glad to take you and Ruby on as investigators any time you're ready to sign up. You'll have to take the loyalty oath, of course."

"Loyalty?" I hooted. "Loyalty to who?"

"Whom," the Whiz corrected crisply. "Objective case. Object of the preposition 'to.' To *whom*." I heard the clank of a dish and the sound of a stool scraping across the floor. Justine was sitting down to eat.

"Whatever. Who should I be loyal to?"

She tsk-tsked. "'To whom' should I be loyal, China. Why, to the truth, of course. Who else?"

"That's assuming there is a truth," I said darkly, "and that we know what it is."

I am a skeptic where the truth is concerned. It's always much more complicated and nuanced than you might think. There is almost never just one truth, and often the so-called truths contradict each other. I was thinking of Sally and the lies she had told me. I thought I understood those lies a little more clearly now and knew that they were born of fear and denial and out of a desperate hope that she could hide from Myers. If she had come clean in the beginning, we might not be in this fix right now. Maybe. If Sally and Joyce Dillard had gone to the Sanders police with what they knew—or thought they knew—Myers might be in jail right now. More importantly, Joyce Dillard and Leslie Strahorn might still be alive. And Sally might—

"Let me know when Sally turns up," the Whiz said with her mouth full.

"*If* she turns up," I amended. I looked at my watch. It was nearly midnight. "She hasn't been seen for fourteen hours. It's possible that Myers has her."

"*When* she turns up," the Whiz replied. "Dead or alive. Sounds like it could be either. Sleep tight, China. Don't let the bedbugs bite."

"Tell that to Ruby," I said. "It's her bed I'll be sleeping in." I looked at the inviting blue and green patterned quilt—one of Ruby's own creations—spread on the double bed. "In about thirty seconds, as a matter of fact."

But before I turned in for the night, I did one more thing. I opened the Christmas card I had purloined from the stack on Leslie's hallway table. It was a lovely card, with a host of singing angels circled with a holly wreath, and it brought a lump to my throat. Under the printed message was written, in Leslie's neat elementary-teacher hand, "Merry Christmas to my favorite nephew, to Mike and China, and to Caitlin, from Aunt Leslie. See you soon!" Enclosed was a handwritten note, to me, dated December 9.

Dear China—

I just got a phone call from Sally, who is visiting in Sanders this week, where we used to live. She would like to come here to Lake City for a few days (says she's got something secret to tell me!). Then she wants to go down to Pecan Springs to see Brian. I've got stuff to do here over Christmas (choir program, school program, church party, etc., etc.) but if it's okay, I'll drive down on 12/27 and stay overnight. Sally wants to go to San Antonio and do some shopping, so we'll do that before we come back here. Hope you are all well. Bet Caitlin is looking forward to her first Christmas with you. I can't wait to meet her!

Lots of love, Leslie

The hot tears rushed to my eyes, and I held the note close to me for a moment. Leslie had been a very special person. We were all going to miss her terribly—Brian most of all. And then the sadness was swept aside by a fiercely corrosive anger at the person—the man, Jess Myers—who had killed her.

If it was the last thing I did, I was going to get him for it and for all that he had done.

I didn't fall asleep easily that night, partly because Howard clambered up into the bed to join me and partly because I couldn't stop thinking of Leslie. After I fell asleep, the troubled thoughts became ugly dreams. It was a long, restless night, and I was glad when the sky turned pale and the clock said six thirty. The bad dreams were still with me, though, like dark clouds boiling just above the horizon, and I felt deeply apprehensive as I got up, washed my face, and combed my hair. I pulled on clean undies and yesterday's jeans and shirt, and went quietly downstairs, leaving Howard Cosell sound asleep and snoring, tummy and personal parts exposed and all four basset paws in the air.

I had closed the shop early the day before, leaving several important chores undone. Dusting, for instance, which has to be done at least once a day, since dusty merchandise suggests that it's been on the shelf for a while. So I planned to go to the shop early this morning. I'd told Ruby she should sleep in for as long as she wanted, and I would open the Crystal Cave. When she did come in, she could leave Howard in her backyard, where he and Oodles the poodle could trade taunts through the fence. Howard would like that. There's nothing he likes better than barking at birds, squirrels, and dogs that are smaller than he is.

I was letting myself out the door when Ruby came down the stairs. "I just got a call from Christina Staples," she said excitedly. "You know—the woman who gave Sally a ride to the bus station the morning Leslie was killed."

"And?" I asked.

"And Leslie was still alive when Christina stopped to pick Sally up!" she exclaimed. "Christina spoke to her. And then she drove to the bus station and watched Sally get on the bus for Pecan Springs. So Sally wasn't even in Lake City when Leslie was run down. She's got an alibi."

"Good work, Ruby," I said. "Justine will be glad to know that. And Sally definitely owes you one." *When we find her,* I thought grimly. *If she's still alive.*

"Thank you," Ruby said. "You're leaving? Have you had any breakfast?"

"I didn't want to wake you up by clattering around in your kitchen," I said, opening the door. "I thought I'd get something at Lila's. See you later."

The sandwiches I'd eaten last night were ancient history, and I was anticipating a largish order of bacon, eggs, and hot biscuits with jelly. But Docia hadn't come in (Lila had no idea where she'd spent the night), and the kitchen wasn't up and running yet. Lila was pitching a hissy fit, but she stopped long enough to fix me up with two jelly doughnuts, one raspberry and the other lemon, and a big coffee to go. (I frequently remind myself that coffee is an herb, too. Couldn't get along without it.) That wasn't going to be enough to keep me going, but there was leftover quiche in the kitchen fridge at the shop—I'd seen it there late yesterday afternoon. I could warm it in the microwave and eat it with my jelly doughnut.

The morning was cold, in the upper thirties, with low fog and drizzle. The radio weather forecaster was predicting much colder weather for the weekend, and maybe even snow, the tail end of the same storm system that was bedeviling McQuaid in Kansas. He had called while I was at the diner to say that it looked like he'd be able to make his flight. With luck, he'd be in Austin by midmorning, home by noon, and would have the Christmas tree up before Brian and Caitie got home from school. We'd decorate it tonight and start getting ready for tomorrow evening's neighborhood party. Our guests were bringing potluck dishes, but after work this evening, I'd need to pick up the baked ham we'd ordered, and drinkables.

But while all this warm, comfortable family stuff was sloshing around in the back of my mind, my stomach was knotted up with a nervous anxiety. McQuaid had called the Pecan Springs police to check on the Sally situation, with no results. No news, which knotted me up even more. Where the hell *was* she? What had happened to her?

McQuaid could sense my apprehension and tried to soothe me. "You've done all you could, China. There's nothing more we can do but wait."

"I know," I said miserably. "But if we don't have news—good news—by the time Brian gets home from school, you'll have to tell him. And Caitlin, too, unless you'd like to let that wait until I get home." Caitie, sweet Caitie. She had already grown fond of Sally. Now, she'd have to cope with—

"We'll cross that bridge when we come to it," McQuaid said. "Just do what you have to do today. We'll deal with the kids tonight." He paused. "And when you see Ruby, tell her that she did a piece of good work, tracking down the woman who took Sally to the bus station. If the Lake City police suspect Sally of being involved, that should clear her."

It should—if Sally was still alive, I thought. But I didn't say so.

As I unlocked the shop door and went in, I was so preoccupied with my thoughts that I was barely conscious of where I was. It was a good hour before I had to open, so I stepped inside, turned on the overhead light, and locked the door behind me. I put my coffee and bag of jelly doughnuts on the counter and took off my jacket and cap and hung them in the broom closet. Khat was dozing in his usual spot: the rocking chair that sits next to the bookshelf. He leapt lightly down when he saw me and followed me into the kitchen, where I fed him some chopped liver from the fridge, warmed in the microwave. I put it down in front of him, watched him hunker down to address it with an eager passion, and felt somehow comforted. If you have a cat in your life, everything will be okay—right?

I went back to the fridge to get the quiche I'd been looking forward to and was startled to see that it was missing. What? It had been there yesterday, late, when Ruby and I closed up early and left for Lake City. I was sure of it. Had Cass come in for a late snack?

Well, no matter. I snagged a banana on my way through the tearoom into the shop, thinking that I would sit behind the counter and update my book orders while I drank my coffee and ate my jelly doughnuts. But when I went into the shop, what I saw made me drop the banana and give a stifled shriek.

A man was sitting on the stool behind the counter, finishing one of my doughnuts. He wore a bulky down-filled coat, maroon. He was dark-haired, with dark plastic-rimmed glasses. There was a mole under his right eye, and a long, fading scratch on his face.

Jess Myers.

He stood up. "Please," he said. "It's okay." His voice was soft, pleasant. But its very softness was frightening. "I'm not going to hurt you. I just want information, that's all."

I pressed my lips together, my heart pounding hard. "What—? Who—?"

I knew who he was. But maybe it was smart to play dumb.

"You're China Bayles?"

"That's right. I own this place. You're trespassing." I took a deep breath. I've been in ticklish situations before, and I know it pays to keep your head. Of course, keeping your head is a little easier when the man you're talking to is the mailman or your next-door neighbor—not a killer.

I took another breath. "And just who the bloody hell are you?" I demanded. "How'd you get in here?"

He grinned pleasantly. "Through the window in the shop next door." He nodded toward the open door that connected Ruby's shop and mine. "Piece of cake." He gave his head a cautionary shake, as if he were doing me a favor. "You really ought to pay more attention to security, Ms. Bayles. Next time, somebody may get in and vandalize the place. You wouldn't like that, I'm sure."

Ruby's window. We'd had a break-in before, a couple of years before. Same window. We were going to have to block it up or put bars over it.

"What do you want?" I asked, although I knew that, too. "Who *are* you?"

"I'm looking for Sally," he said. "Sally Strahorn." He got off the stool and stepped around the counter. "You're my only connection to her," he added, holding out his hands in an almost apologetic way. "I know she's been staying at your place. Tell me where she is. That's all I want. Just tell me, and I'll leave. I promise."

My first reaction was a kind of irrational glee. If he was still looking for Sally, he hadn't found her. If he hadn't found her, she must be still alive.

"You're wasting your time," I said, "and risking arrest for trespassing." I narrowed my eyes and looked pointedly at the telephone. "Give me one good reason why I shouldn't pick up that phone and call the police."

"If you did that," he said in a deferential tone, "I'm afraid I would have to hurt you. I have a gun, you see." He patted the side pocket of his jacket. "I really wouldn't like to do that, and I'm sure you wouldn't like it, either." He took several steps toward me. "Well? Where is she? Where are you hiding her?"

A gun. The thought was chilling, and so was his insistence that I knew where she was.

"I have no idea," I said. "She borrowed a car from me yesterday morning and split. I haven't seen her or the car since." True, although I knew where the car was. Since he didn't have her, it was more than likely that she'd boarded a bus and was safely on her way. For all I knew, she could be in Florida or Southern California by this time.

I was thinking as fast as I could, as coolly as I could, weighing all the options, but I couldn't think of anything that would give me even a fighting chance. Myers was five foot eight or nine, not tall, but stocky, sturdily built. I'm fit and fairly agile, but I'm no match for a man who outweighs me by fifty pounds. I don't keep a gun under the counter or anywhere in the store.

There'd be no help from the outside, either. Ruby wouldn't be in for a couple of hours. Cass would come in an hour after that. Laurel wouldn't be in at all today, and it was much too early for customers. I was here alone with a man I suspected of killing two women in the past week or so. And two other people ten years ago, if McQuaid had it right. It wasn't exactly a comfortable feeling. But there might be something, if only I could—

"I don't think I'm wasting my time," Myers said comfortably. He smiled. "I figure she'll show up here. I'll just wait." He came closer, stepping around the shelf of bulk herbs in the middle of the store. His smile was strange, oddly strained and crooked, and there was a too-bright glint in his eyes. Looking at him, I realized that this man must not be quite sane. If he were, he wouldn't come to a place of business where people might be expected to wander in and out.

When in doubt, talk and keep talking. "Aren't you the same guy who called here a couple of days ago?" I asked. I took a couple of steps to the right, along the shelves that cover much of the shop's back wall. "And didn't you call my house, as well?"

Myers nodded shortly, watching me, his face darkening, his shoulders tensing. He put his hand into his pocket. "What's your connection to Sally, anyway? You two friends or something?"

I could see what he was thinking. If I was a close friend, what were the chances that Sally had told me about him? Did I know what he had done, why she was afraid of him? I needed to deflect that, in a hurry.

"Friends?" I hooted. "Are you kidding? She's my husband's ex-wife." I laughed sarcastically. "We're not exactly on a huggy-face-kissy-poo basis. I put up with her when I have to, that's all."

He relaxed just slightly. I had reassured him.

"So what do you want with her?" I asked in a curious tone. I took another couple of steps. "When I told her what you said—that you had her car, I mean—she got all bent out of shape. Said you two used to date, a long time ago. What happened? Did you have a falling-out?"

Some of the tension left his shoulders. His hand came out of his pocket. "Used to date? Yes, you might say that, I guess. It was a while back."

I chuckled wryly. Just another step or two. "I'll bet you didn't put up with that woman for long. You look like you're too smart. If you ask me, Sally is certifiable."

"I would certainly agree to that. You can't believe a thing she says. She makes up the wildest stories." He looked around, looked up, and his face lightened. "Hey, mistletoe. You're standing under the mistletoe. Now, isn't that nice? Maybe I ought to claim a kiss, huh?"

There was that smile again, with a twist. Beyond creepy, Sally had said. She was right.

"But I'm married," I protested. It was a stupid thing to say, but it was

271

all I could think of. The last thing I wanted to do was kiss this guy, but I was backed up against the shelves, breathing hard, feeling panicked. I couldn't get away.

"So? Your husband wouldn't begrudge me a little kiss, now, would he? Hell, he wouldn't even miss it." His face hardened. "I'm in the habit of taking what I want, China. And after that kiss, you're going to tell me where Sally is. If you don't—"

"Hey, Jess," Sally said from the doorway to Ruby's shop. "Leave China alone. I'm the one you're looking for."

Jerking his gun out of his pocket, Myers whirled toward the sound of Sally's voice. And that was my chance, my one chance. I reached out quickly and grabbed something off the shelf, holding it in my hand, feeling with my forefinger for the teensy catch on the side.

"Wait, Jess," I said in my most seductive voice. I took a step toward him. "I thought you wanted a kiss."

He turned back to me just as my finger found the catch. I lifted the tiny canister, held it up within a foot of his face, and squirted him with pepper spray, catching him with his mouth wide open and his eyes staring, fixed on me.

I was the last thing he was going to see for quite some time. Those peppers are hot stuff.

THE police arrived at the shop within moments of Sally's 911 call. I handed over his gun and watched as they scooped Myers up off the floor, cuffed him, and placed him under arrest for—at least temporarily— attempted armed robbery. When they were pushing him out the door, I turned to Sally.

"Thanks," I said gratefully. "Did you know he had a gun?"

She nodded. "I think it's my . . . my father's gun," she said in a strangled voice. "Joyce Dillard told me he still had it. He's the man who killed my parents, China. That's why I wanted Mike to talk to her. I wanted her to tell him, because I knew he'd make her go to the police."

"But why didn't you and Joyce go to the police yourselves? If you'd done that, she might still be alive."

Her eyes swam with tears. "Because Jamison—the chief of police in Sanders—was convinced that I was involved in my parents' murders! He would never have believed me! He would've thought—" Her voice broke. "And now Joyce is dead. And it's my fault."

I put my arm around her and held her for a moment, then let her go. "You arrived at just the right moment," I said. "You distracted him long enough for me to get that spray to work. Where *were* you? Where have you been hiding?"

She dropped her head. "In your loft."

"The loft?" I stared at her. Of course. She had helped me hang herbs up there, so she knew where it was. She also knew that we wouldn't be going up there often during the holidays. It was a perfectly safe place.

Sally nodded. "I was really worried that if I went out on the street, Jess would find me. So I parked Brian's car where I thought it wouldn't be noticed for a while. Then I sneaked into Ruby's shop and went up the stairs, just before Ruby's mother came into the store yesterday afternoon." She smiled slightly. "She's not really all that crazy, you know. It was me she saw going up the stairs, not her daughter."

"I see," I said. "And I suppose it was you who raided the refrigerator and stole the quiche. I missed it when I went looking for breakfast."

"That was me, too," she confessed. "The loft was a great place to hide.

It's warm and cozy, and it smells really good, with all those herbs hanging to dry. It just didn't have any room service. I'm sorry. I was so hungry, and the fridge was full of food. I hoped you wouldn't mind."

"No, of course not," I said. "Sally, why didn't you tell me that you came here from Lake City, where you were staying with Leslie?"

She hung her head. "I should have," she said. "But I concocted that sob story about the flood on the spur of the moment, and then I was stuck with it. I'm sorry, China. I—"

The shop door opened, and Sheila came in. "Ms. Strahorn," she said, "I need to ask you to come with me. The Lake City police want to speak to you about—"

I put my hand on Sheila's arm, stopping her. "Let me tell her," I said quietly.

I had suddenly remembered that Sally didn't know that her sister was dead.

Chapter Sixteen

Sitting under the mistletoe
(Pale green, fairy mistletoe)
One last candle burning low,
All the sleepy dancers gone,
Just one candle burning on.
Someone came and kissed me there.

Walter De la Mare

McQuaid and I weren't in a mood to party. Brian wasn't, either, after his father had told him about Leslie's death. He took it hard, and the fact that it had come at Christmas only made things worse. But kids are resilient, and although it would be a while before he got over the loss, he would. He'd remember the loving moments, the warmth of their companionship, the fun they had together. Wherever he went in his life, whatever he did, he would never lose the important things she gave him.

In the mood or not, we went ahead with the party, and afterward, I was glad. As a family, trying to behave as we normally would forced a certain normality upon us. We managed to rise to the occasion, as most people do when they have to.

Sally didn't make it to the party. The police had impounded her yellow convertible, so she drove Brian's Ford to Lake City to tell the police what she knew, to be interviewed by Officer Jamison from the Sanders Police Department, and to begin making arrangements for Leslie's memorial service, which wouldn't be held until after the holidays. She said she hoped she could come back and spend Christmas day with us, and Caitie had to be content with that.

After Saturday night's party, there were a couple of family get-togethers, one with my mother and her husband, Sam, at their ranch near Kerrville, the other in Seguin, with McQuaid's family. One evening, we sang carols outside the library. Another, Caitlin and I went to Castle Oaks and helped the members of Pecan Springs' herb club, the Myra Merryweathers, distribute gifts—handmade herbal soap, cupcakes, pomanders, and some holiday candy—to the seniors.

On Christmas Eve day, McQuaid and I and the kids joined the PSPD Blue Santas to deliver presents to the homes of needy children, and that evening, we had our own private Christmas Eve family party. Santa came in the middle of the night, and when Caitie and Brian got up on Christmas morning, their gifts were under the tree. Sally didn't make it, but there was such a noisy crowd around the table for Christmas dinner—turkey, dressing, and all the holiday trimmings—that Brian and Caitlin didn't seem to miss her. For Brian, at least, his mother had been absent so often that he hadn't really believed she would be there. It was a wonderful day, and by nine o'clock that evening, the kids were ready to crash.

McQuaid and I had just settled down in front of the fire to share mugs of warm spiced tea and enjoy the sight of the Christmas tree, splendid in its lights and glittering tinsel, when Sheila stopped by on her way to Blackie's, to say Merry Christmas and update us on the situation in Lake City. She had given several of her officers the chance to spend the holiday with their families and had been on duty herself for most of the day, and as usual, things had been busy. A three-car pileup on I-35, a bicycle accident near the campus, a break-in at the pharmacy on the square—drug-related, of course. She hadn't taken time to change and was still wearing her uniform.

I poured a mug of tea for Sheila. She sat down wearily in McQuaid's recliner, and put her feet up. McQuaid and I sat close together on the sofa, my head on his shoulder, his arm around me, listening to what Sheila had to tell us.

Myers was in the Lake City jail, awaiting a bail hearing. He had been charged with vehicular homicide in Leslie's death, although before the hearing, it was likely that the charge would be upgraded to murder. Sally's convertible had been picked up a couple of blocks from Thyme and Seasons, with damage that clearly linked it to Leslie's death. The charge of vehicular manslaughter was pending in the case of Joyce Dillard. Myers' 1998 Dodge truck had been located in the Lake City hospital parking lot where he had left it. The final report wasn't in yet, but preliminary forensic evidence— damage to a fender, missing paint, a strand of hair—indicated that it was the vehicle that had struck Joyce. Myers' prints were all over both vehicles.

And then there was the gun Myers had dropped when I zapped him with the pepper spray. It was indeed Mr. Strahorn's Luger, the gun that had killed Sally's parents. It seemed likely that the Strahorn case would be reopened and charges filed against Myers.

"And what about Sally?" I asked. "What's her status?"

"The police seem to have satisfied themselves that she's innocent," Sheila said. "She has an alibi for the time of her sister's death, and Myers' cell phone records demonstrate that he phoned that tip to the Lake City police, implicating her. What's more, there's no evidence tying her to Myers. It's true that Jamison saw them together in Sanders before Dillard's death, but Sally claims that it was an accidental meeting. And even Jamison agrees that it isn't enough."

"I don't suppose there's any reason to hope that Myers will confess and clear all three cases?" McQuaid asked wryly.

"In your dreams," Sheila replied with a chuckle. "He's hired a defense attorney, some guy from Waco. And since there are two deaths involved—potentially four—in two different states, I wouldn't lay odds on a plea deal. This could drag on for years. And even when he's convicted, there'll be appeals."

McQuaid shook his head, disgusted. "Justice doesn't always win out, does it?" I knew he was thinking of the Strahorns and of Leslie, three people he had cared for deeply. He wanted to see their killer punished. But—

The phone broke the silence. I got up and went into the kitchen to answer it, so as not to interrupt the conversation. It was Hank Jamison, calling from Kansas. I listened for a moment, holding my breath, then wished him Merry Christmas, thanked him for calling, and went back into the living room, where McQuaid and Sheila were still seated, talking.

I put my hand on McQuaid's shoulder, and he broke off, looking up at me. "Yeah?" he asked. "Who was that?"

"Jamison," I said. "Hank Jamison. From Sanders."

"That's nice," McQuaid said, brightening. "Calling to wish us Merry Christmas, huh? I'll phone him tomorrow. He's a good man."

"No," I said. "Not Merry Christmas. Something else." I sat down and looked from him to Sheila. "He wanted me to tell you—both of you—that he had just heard from the Lake City police. Jess Myers is dead. He tore up a bedsheet, braided it into a rope, and hung himself from the bars of the window in his cell. He was pronounced dead an hour ago."

Sheila closed her eyes. "Ah, hell," she said softly.

For a long moment, McQuaid didn't say anything. At last, he let out a low, slow breath.

"Justice," he said. His voice was dark and heavy. "Finally. After all."

Justice. Not necessarily the kind of justice anybody wanted.

But justice, in the end.

SHEILA had gone, the fire was dying down, and still we sat, close together, watching the shimmer of the lights on the tree, the glittering tinsel. I was thinking of the children and how, in spite of everything, we had enjoyed a happy holiday. Things might be hard, the world might not be the way we wanted it, but we were together, and that was what counted.

On the sofa beside McQuaid, Howard Cosell shifted with a contented doggie sigh. McQuaid stirred, stretched, and got up, taking my hand.

"Only one more thing, and the day will be perfect," he said. He pulled me to the doorway, where the mistletoe hung.

"Perfect?" I asked, teasing. "Is anything ever perfect?"

"This is," he said, and took me in his arms.

Recipes, How-To, and
Ideas for Holiday Giving

Cass Wilde's Holiday Peppermint Cupcakes

½ cup butter or shortening, room temperature

1 cup sugar

1 large egg

2 large egg whites

1½ cups all-purpose flour

1 teaspoon baking powder

¼ teaspoon salt

½ cup whole milk

1 teaspoon vanilla extract

1 teaspoon peppermint extract

Cream butter until light and fluffy. Gradually add sugar and continue to beat until well combined. Add egg and egg whites, beating until blended. Set aside. In a bowl, sift together flour, baking powder, and salt. Add half the flour mixture to the creamed mixture; stir until blended. In a measuring cup, mix milk and extracts. Add to the batter; mix until blended. Add remaining flour mixture and mix very well. Divide batter evenly among 12 prepared muffin cups. Bake in a preheated 350° F oven until tops are just dry to the touch, 22 to 25 minutes. Remove cupcakes to a wire rack and let cool completely. Frost.

FROSTING

6 ounces white chocolate, coarsely chopped

4 ounces cream cheese, softened

4 tablespoons butter, softened

1 teaspoon peppermint extract

2–2½ cups confectioners' sugar, sifted, divided

6 peppermint candies, crushed

Place white chocolate in a small glass bowl in the microwave and cook on high for one minute. Alternatively, place in a double boiler and melt over boiling water. Stir until smooth and set aside to cool. In a large mixing bowl, combine cream cheese and butter. Using an electric mixer, beat until thoroughly mixed. Add cooled white chocolate; beat until mixed. Using the mixer's low speed, beat in peppermint extract and 2 cups confectioners' sugar. Using medium speed, beat until fluffy, adding up to ½ cup additional confectioners' sugar to make it spreadable. Frost cupcakes, and sprinkle with crushed peppermint candies.

China's Easy Slow-Cook Sausage–Corn Chowder

Made the easy way, with canned soup, canned corn, and cooked sausage.

1 pound ready-to-eat smoked sausage, cut in half lengthwise and into
½-inch slices

3 cups cubed potatoes

½ medium onion

2 medium carrots, coarsely chopped

¼ cup red bell pepper

1 bay leaf

1 15- or 16-ounce can cream-style corn

1 can mushroom soup

2 cups chicken broth

2 cups milk

1 teaspoon dried thyme

1 teaspoon dried savory
Sour cream
Snipped fresh chives or fresh parsley

Place sausage, potatoes, onion, carrots, bell pepper, and bay leaf in a slow cooker. Combine corn, soup, and broth, and add to the cooker. Cover and cook on low heat for 6 to 7 hours. Fifteen minutes before serving, remove bay leaf, stir chowder, and add milk and herbs. Cover and cook on high for 15 minutes. Ladle into bowls and top with dollops of sour cream and sprinkles of snipped chives or parsley.

Garden Quiche with Tomato, Basil, and Garlic

4 large eggs, lightly beaten
1½ cups sour cream
½ cup evaporated milk
½ cup freshly grated Parmesan cheese, divided
4 tablespoons minced green onion tops, divided
1 tablespoon fresh minced parsley
1 teaspoon dried thyme
¼ teaspoon salt
¼ teaspoon ground black pepper
1 unbaked 9-inch pie shell
3 tablespoons dry bread crumbs
1 tablespoon fresh minced basil or 1 teaspoon dried basil leaves, crushed
3 cloves garlic, minced
1¾ cups fresh or canned diced tomatoes, drained

Preheat oven to 350° F. In a medium bowl, mix eggs, sour cream, evaporated milk, ¼ cup Parmesan cheese, 2 tablespoons green onion, parsley, thyme, salt, and pepper. Pour into pie shell. Combine remaining cheese, bread crumbs, basil, and garlic in a small bowl; sprinkle over sour cream mixture. Top with tomatoes and 2 tablespoons green onions. Bake for 50 to 60 minutes or until knife inserted in center comes out clean. Cool on wire rack for 5 minutes before serving.

China's Hot Spiced Holiday Tea

This warm and cheering cranberry- and orange-flavored tea is a natural for the holidays. The recipe makes 12 cups.

> 12 whole allspice
> 3 small cinnamon sticks
> 2 teaspoons whole cloves
> 12 cups water
> 12 tea bags (an orange-spice tea is nice)
> 1 cup brown sugar, packed
> 1 cup cranberry juice
> ½ cup orange juice
> ¼ cup lemon juice

Combine allspice, cinnamon, and cloves with the water in a saucepan and bring to a rolling boil. Remove from heat and add tea bags. Cover and steep for about 5 minutes. Stir and strain. Strain a second time to clarify (a coffee filter is handy here). Add sugar and stir until dissolved. At serving time, stir in juices, pour into a glass or stainless steel pan, and reheat before serving.

Leslie Strahorn's Gingerbread Cookies

> 6 cups all-purpose flour
> 1 tablespoon baking powder

1 tablespoon ground ginger

1 teaspoon ground nutmeg

1 teaspoon ground cloves

1 teaspoon ground cinnamon

1 cup shortening, melted and cooled slightly

1 cup molasses

1 cup packed brown sugar

½ cup water

1 egg

1 teaspoon vanilla extract

In a large bowl, sift together the flour, baking powder, ginger, nutmeg, cloves, and cinnamon; set aside. In another large bowl, mix together the shortening, molasses, brown sugar, water, egg, and vanilla until smooth. Stir in the dry ingredients in two or three additions, mixing very well. Divide dough into 3 parts, flatten to about 1½-inch thickness, wrap in plastic wrap, and refrigerate for at least 3 hours.

To shape and bake: Preheat oven to 350° F. On a lightly floured surface, roll the dough out to ¼-inch thickness. Cut into shapes with cookie cutters. Place cookies 1 inch apart on an ungreased cookie sheet. Bake for 10 to 12 minutes in the preheated oven. Cookies will look dry but be soft to the touch. Remove from the baking sheet to cool on wire racks. Frost when cool.

Rosemary-Mint Soap for Holiday Gifts

HERE'S WHAT YOU'LL NEED:

Plastic candy molds (holiday shapes are nice) or small plastic
containers

Cooking spray or petroleum jelly

2 4-ounce bars of castile (olive-oil) soap

2 tablespoons water

1½ teaspoons rosemary essential oil

1½ teaspoons mint essential oil

2 tablespoons crushed rosemary leaves

HERE'S HOW TO MAKE IT:

Spray molds with cooking spray or grease with petroleum jelly. Grate castile soap into an enamel saucepan. Add water and essential oils and heat slowly, stirring. When the soap has melted and the mixture has the texture of whipped cream, add rosemary leaves. Quickly fill each mold, then rap the mold sharply on a hard surface to eliminate air bubbles. Allow to harden overnight in the molds. Turn soaps onto a wire rack and air-dry for a few days before wrapping. If any seem rough-edged, wet your hands and smooth the surfaces; dry thoroughly.

• Other fragrant floral possibilities: violet oil and violet petals; lilac oil and lilac florets; orange oil and calendula petals; lemon oil and dried chopped lemongrass and coarsely grated lemon zest; lavender oil and lavender buds with chopped rosemary leaves. Be creative!

• To make a gentle scrubbing soap, add 1 tablespoon chopped dried luffa, or ½ cup cornmeal or oatmeal (not flakes). Increase liquid slightly, if necessary.

Thyme & Seasons Christmas Simmer Gift Potpourri

1½ cups cinnamon sticks, broken into small pieces

½ cup whole cloves

½ cup allspice berries

½ cup whole rose hips

¼ cup dried bay leaves, broken

¼ cup dried rosemary leaves

¼ cup dried orange peel

¼ cup dried lemon peel

1 tablespoon cardamom seeds

1 tablespoon aniseseed

1 tablespoon ground nutmeg

Mix all the ingredients in a large bowl. Transfer to small lidded jars or plastic bags. Add a label with these instructions:

To use: Bring 2 cups of water to a boil in an old 1-quart saucepan. Add 2 tablespoons potpourri and reduce heat. You may also add 2–3 apple slices, if you wish. Simmer, adding water as needed. You may reuse the potpourri, but refrigerate between uses.

Two Pomanders for Holiday Gifting

An easy-for-kids-to-make artificial pomander starts with foam balls, oakmoss, a spice potpourri (made of whole allspice, cinnamon chips, sandalwood slivers, star anise, cloves), cinnamon oil, and white glue. Place the oakmoss on a plate. Cover the ball with glue, and roll it in the oakmoss until completely covered. Let dry, then glue pieces of spice potpourri onto the ball, starting with the largest pieces and filling in with the smaller ones. Dust with powdered cloves and dot with a few drops of cinnamon oil. Hang with a ribbon loop.

To make the real thing, you will need a small apple or orange, about a cup of whole cloves, and about 6 tablespoons of spice mixture (2 tablespoons each of cinnamon, cloves, and nutmeg) for each pomander you want to make. Poke holes in the fruit with a skewer or similar tool, so that when whole cloves are pushed into the holes, the tops are nearly touching. (You might want to try a few to see what distance you should leave between the holes.) When the fruit is completely covered with cloves, put it into a small plastic bag with 2 tablespoons of the spice mixture and shake gently, being careful not to dislodge any cloves. If there's an excess of spices, leave them in the bag. You have several alternatives for drying. 1) Put the pomander in your gas oven with the pilot light on; 2) use your electric oven turned to its lowest setting; 3) use your food dehydrator, set at 105–115 degrees. Dry overnight. For the next two or three days, repeat the spice treatment, returning the pomander to the heat source until the pomander is dry. (You will need less spice for subsequent treatments; make more as needed.) You may also wrap the pomander in toilet paper and put it in a dark, dry cupboard; it will dry in two to three weeks. Hang with ribbon or raffia.